Wolf Bride

(Wolf Brides Series, Book 1)

By T. S. Joyce

Wolf Bride
ISBN-13: 978-1503026827
ISBN-10: 1503026825
Copyright © 2014, T. S. Joyce
First electronic publication: October 2014

T. S. Joyce
www.tsjoycewrites.wordpress.com

NOTE FROM THE AUTHOR:
This book is a work of fiction. The names, characters, places, and incidents are products of the writer's imagination or have been used fictitiously and are not to be construed as real. Any resemblance to persons, living or dead, actual events, locale or organizations is entirely coincidental. The author does not have any control over and does not assume any responsibility for third-party websites or their content.

Published in the United States of America

First digital publication: October 2014
First print publication: November 2014

Other Books by T. S. Joyce

Wolf Brides
Red Snow Bride
Dawson Bride

Bear Valley Shifters
The Witness and the Bear
Devoted to the Bear
Return to the Bear
Betray the Bear
Redeem the Bear

Hells Canyon Shifters
Call of the Bear
Fealty of the Bear
Avenge the Bear

Chapter One
Kristina

The last day of the carriage ride to Colorado was just as exciting as the first day of our journey from Chicago. I grinned saucily at Ms. Birmingham who clutched tightly to her frilly, purple hat. The good Lord blessed that woman with the sourest disposition known to mankind, but in the days since our journey began, she hadn't once managed to dampen my mood.

Her cherished plum colored hat, which boasted gads of silk ribbon and an array of dark plumage numerous enough to shield the perpetual frown underneath, gave me distraction from the endless wrenching of the carriage wheels on rugged road. There was no way the bird whose feathers decorated that hat had survived. Poor thing.

Ms. Birmingham was growing fidgety under my smile. My happy demeanor did that to people—made them uncomfortable—but I couldn't help myself. At nineteen, the possibilities of my future stretched on and on, like the stars of a midnight sky.

Her disapproving gaze slipped to the immodest cut of my dress for the hundred and sixteenth time. I'd been counting. I wasn't well versed on the area, because I hadn't ever traveled outside of Chicago, far as I could remember, but I was pretty sure there were whores in Colorado Springs just the same as everywhere else. Why, far as I could tell, whores were the nation's first ladies to settle here to keep the men happy.

Tipping my chin up primly, I slid the foot and a half to the window.

Besides, I was mending my ways. I was going to be a proper lady with a husband and a house and everything.

With a sigh, I rested my elbows against the wooden window frame as another jolt in the road nearly made my tailbone jump through my throat. For the price of an entire week's wages, Jack Bronson found me an advertisement to get me out of Chicago. I could count, but reading was beyond me, and going out on a limb to hire that drunkard seemed like a sound enough investment at the time. He'd found me an advertisement in the paper about a man seeking a wife. It was a simple ad and I'd memorized it easily because I'd recited it in the months that finally led to my travels.

Man seeks wife. Good birthing hips, tidy, quiet. Will cook for three brothers.

Well, one out of four wasn't bad. My hips were sound. I'd never been accused of being a petite little old thing. I wasn't big, but my curves didn't belong on a waif either. My reply had been equally short, but he seemed to like it fine enough, because one month later he wrote to me directly and told me to make arrangements for my travels with the money he'd sent along. Escaping had been tricky, but I was a wily creature and one not easily caged.

I bet Jeremiah Dawson was waiting right at this very moment for me in town. He wouldn't be a handsome man, or why would he be putting out an advertisement for a wife? Probably had a pockmarked face and rotted teeth, but who was I to cast stones? I was an ex saloon girl after all. Even if we didn't get along, he was just one man to please. I'd worked lots of them, and if ever there was such thing as a professional man-handler, well I held a certificate in that.

Perking up, I shoved my chest half way out the window. "I can see it," I squealed to Ms. Birmingham, who'd apparently been dozing off because she jumped straight in the air and smushed the top of her hat onto the roof of the buggy.

Her mutterings were uncharitable, but I didn't give two figs what she had to say because we were finally there and I was finally going to meet him. Jeremiah.

His momma did right to give an ugly man a named that rolled off of the tongue like that.

Over the matching chestnut backs of the four horses that seemed to pull us even faster with the prospect of town and a bucket of oats, a small wooden bridge was all that stood between our carriage and the first buildings of Main Street. I assumed it was Main Street, because every tiny railroad town we'd driven through on our travels had one. I slurped myself back into the carriage and tried in vain to fix my hair. A pointless effort because curly hair like mine wasn't meant to be tamed. I gave up on the pins and finished braiding the length of it as we pulled to the front of a supply store. Animal hides hung from nails outside and the air smelled like a collision between man and forest.

"After you," I said gallantly to Ms. Birmingham, who was all but falling over herself to escape the cabin of our transportation.

She groaned as she sank into the near foot of mud that coated the road under the carriage step. Mud didn't bother me. In fact, I'd rolled in much filthier with a man for a coin. I hopped right down into the muck with a giggle. Ms. Birmingham squawked unattractively as little mud sprinkles flew out to grasp onto the hem of her slowly soaking dress. She tried to flee but her fine heeled shoe got caught in the glop, so I reached out to steady her. Even if she was obviously repulsed by my touch, she didn't have much choice. It was me, or fall face first into a smelly pile of a horse's meadow muffins.

"You have to slide your feet, ma'am," I said helpfully. "Hey mister?" I yelled to the carriage driver who was apparently too busy watching the show to lend a hand. "You mind?"

I swear he chuckled but still he scaled the carriage and half dragged Ms. Birmingham onto the wooden deck in front of a row of stores. And then he retrieved her mud filled shoe. Our hero.

Ms. Birmingham's family was waiting in front of the supply store and loaded her bags into a flat bottom buggy before they even touched the ground. The clunk of my one small luggage was drowned out by the noise of the busy town. Why the driver put my bag down in front of the saloon next door, I hadn't a guess but my inner compass pulled me to it like a bug to a candle jar.

No one was waiting for me.

Looking like a scantily dressed slug, with my mud trail following me, I pushed open the swinging doors to a raucous song the girls of the house were singing from atop the bar. I smiled privately. Say what you will about whores, but we sure knew how to have a good time.

The conversations were muffled around me but one perked me up right quick. "Them Dawson boys ain't right and you know it. Something's got to be done about that disappearin' livestock," a wiry older man with a handful of cards growled. Five other gentlemen around the table nodded in agreement under worn cowboy hats.

Huh? Was I marrying into a family of thieves? I shrugged. Still an ex whore. Still not casting stones.

"You here for a job, miss?" the dour-faced man behind the bar asked.

"Not at the moment. I'll try my hand at marriage and then we'll see," I said with a wink.

"What can I do you for?"

"Would you happen to know where I can find Jeremiah Dawson?"

The girl's song had ended and as they slid off the countertop, the conversations around me dipped into an uncomfortable silence.

"What do you want with Mr. Dawson?" the bartender asked.

"Why, to marry him."

His look went cold and the blue in his eyes turned a little frostier. He jerked his head once toward the window. A man sat reading a paper in a buggy across the muddy channel.

"Thank you, sir," I managed, unable to quite take my eyes away from the dark haired mountain that leaned comfortably into the wooden seat like it was a four poster feather bed.

I shuffled out of the saloon, trailing my slime behind me, and hoisted the bag to my hip. Fifteen sloshy strides later and I was standing by the buggy. The man graced me with a glance, then went back to reading, so I took the opportunity to ogle his beautiful face. He had short, dark brown hair that peeked out from beneath his cowboy hat, and a leather duster that protected him from the elements. His jaw was shaven clean and the planes of his face were sharp like glass.

He huffed an irritated sound. "Can I help you?" He slid a coffee colored glare in my direction and held me frozen fast.

"Jeremiah Dawson?"

He frowned. Well that was yes enough for me. I hobbled to the back of the wagon and hefted my bag into the back.

"Don't tell me you're the wife I advertised for."

"The one and only."

He hopped down from the buggy in one startlingly smooth movement and stood to his full height. This man didn't belong in a dusty cattle town. He belonged with his feet in the ground growing roots to hold him in place, and his snow dusted mountain shoulders holding the weather at bay. Somewhere in his lineage, a giant had crashed into his family tree.

"Mother of pearl," I breathed as I stretched my neck back to see his face. No doubt about it, I'd made the right choice in coming to Colorado Springs. This man could offer protection from all that was coming for me. He might even live through it. A tiny weight lifted.

He squinted down at me and cocked his head. "Can you really cook?"

"No."

"Clean?"

"I can learn I suppose."

8

"You a quiet woman?"

"Not particularly."

"Then why'd you answer the dadburned advertisement?" His deep voice was scary when he was mad.

"Would you have brought me here if I didn't say I was all those things?"

He dragged opaque eyes across every inch of my dress and took his time about it. I fidgeted until he sighed. "Are you a whore, ma'am?"

I gave my most charming smile. "Not anymore. Quit last Thursday."

He groaned and looked at the sky like that lone storm cloud would wash me into better wife material. "You ain't the woman for me Miss…"

"Yeaton. Kristina Yeaton, but you can call me Kris," I said, holding out my hand. I was undeterred. Any man worth his boots needed a little convincing with just about anything. It was a man's way.

He stared at me until I dropped my empty hand back to my side. "Look, I can't go back where I came from and you've already put up the money to get me here. Might as well try me out for a day," I said, waggling my eyebrows.

He didn't look amused. His frown did give way to a smirk, however, as he looked at something over my shoulder. "Like I said, you ain't for me, but my brother wouldn't have any qualms about marrying a saloon girl."

My shoulders sagged. "Your brother?" Here was where the other boot dropped. I thought I was getting this fine specimen of a man for my very own husband for a moment, and now what I was really getting was Quasimodo. Jeremiah Dawson, that brute of a man, had ruined everything. I'd been perfectly happy to marry an ogre until I saw him and got my hopes up clear to the sky. Damn him.

"Who's your brother?" I sounded ungrateful even to myself.

He pointed behind me, and I wanted to kick his smirk straight into his throat.

A man stood with his back to us, talking to a storekeeper. He wore a dark gray vest over a sky blue cotton shirt with the sleeves rolled up to reveal muscular forearms that rested comfortably on his waist. He wasn't quite as big as Jeremiah but he was still a head taller than the man he was talking to, and much taller still than me. His hair was longer and dark under his hat and had an appealing wave to it. The vest over cowhide pants cut a mean line with a trim waist and wide shoulders. Okay, so his face was likely atrocious. It had to be.

"Luke," Jeremiah said quietly from behind me.

Instantly, the man jerked his head to the side and I got my first view of his profile. Now if I'd had to service men this beautiful in Chicago, I'd have loved my job a lot more than I did. Dark stubble brushed his jaw and it matched animated eyebrows that probably betrayed every emotion he ever had. I couldn't tell the color of his eyes from where I stood, but they were stunning. That much, any woman with working lady parts could see. If I looked hard enough, which I was, the outline of his shoulder muscles could be seen beneath the thin fabric of his shirt. Tall, dark boots held his pants close to fit legs, and his spurs jangled attractively as he turned.

Green. His eyes were bright green.

"I'll pick them up when we come back through town," he told the storekeeper before hoisting a sack of flour off the porch like it was a yard of rolled fabric. He sauntered easily toward us.

My mouth was hanging open wide enough to catch flies, so I closed it. He had to be mine. I wanted him more than I'd ever wanted anything in my entire nineteen years. My favorite food was bacon, and I'd gladly give up pig for the rest of my life if I could have him.

"Best if I tell him," Jeremiah whispered in my ear.

"Tell me what?" Luke said from much too far away to be able to hear us over the street noise.

Strange.

"It's a surprise," Jeremiah said shortly. "Load up."

The towering men headed for the front seat of the buggy and I glanced around frantically. No help for it then. I scrambled into the back with my skirts flying nearly to my hips. I was pretty good at first impressions.

"What the hell?" Luke said, glaring at his brother. "You gonna help her or what?"

"Ain't my job," Jeremiah said with a grin. "Hup!" He slapped the backs of the two black horses in front with a snap of the reins.

Luke looked back at me once more with a slight frown, then shook his head like his brother had lost his mind.

My husband didn't know he was caught yet.

Chapter Two
Kristina

I white knuckle gripped onto the railing of the buggy for dear life. I'd been perfectly content to endure the endless jouncing carriage ride into Colorado Springs, but at this point in my journey, I'd say my tailbone was thoroughly bruised. And though the skirts of my royal blue and black lacy dress were full, the material was quite thin and of little use cushioning my battered bum. I needed a distraction. "Can I ask a question?"

"No," the men said in unison.

"Where is your other brother? The advertisement said three brothers."

No answer.

"How much farther?"

The sound of the creaking buggy and the locusts were the only noises.

I arched my eyebrow. "Why haven't you two found wives yet? From where I'm sitting, women would sell their teeth to be tethered by the pelvis to you boys, so what gives?"

"See, this is why I advertised for a quiet wife," Jeremiah muttered.

"Well it isn't as if I am incapable of being quiet, it just isn't in my nature, sir."

Luke slid a green-eyed glance back at me. "Our brother, Gable, was in the war. Hasn't made his way back home yet is all."

A shallow sadness washed over me. I'd seen it a hundred times.

Men came into the cathouse I worked, ripped up from the War Between the States and only ghosts of the people they once were. They would cry after I was with them and tell me horrible stories of things that had been done to them. Things they'd seen. Things they had done to others, like I was a priest and they were confessing their sins. Those kinds of admitted horrors weighed on my soul and visited my dreams from time to time.

"You sure he's coming back?" I asked before I could swallow the words back down.

Luke's back tensed. "Of course he's coming back."

Even if he did make it back home, it would only be part of him, but these boys probably already knew that. "Did the war reach this place?" I asked.

"The war reached every place in this neck of the world, but folks around here don't care so much about it. They have another war to worry over."

I twisted in my less than comfortable seat to stare at his back. "What kind of war?"

"One with the Indians."

I scanned the wild woods that edged the road and a chill crept across my skin. There weren't many Indians in Chicago but I'd heard stories, horrible tales of scalping and frontier families murdered in their sleep. My voice sounded very small when I asked, "You have much of a problem with Indians?"

Luke's voice harbored a smile when he spoke. "The natives don't mess with us much. You don't have to worry."

For some reason, his confidence settled me, so I slumped back into the discomfort of the splinter adorned wood.

The drive was an hour and a half from town to the edge of the Dawson homestead. Cattle milled about a clearing, and through the trees were the jerky movements of deer on the alert at the sound of our approach. Oak and pine grew in bunches and the meadows were filled with wheat so tall, it waved like laundry in the wind. A girl could get swallowed right up in the vastness of this fairy land.

"There's nothing like this place around Chicago," I breathed.

"Course there isn't," Jeremiah snorted. "It's a city. Cities kill places like this."

I turned to find Luke's glorious eyes resting on my bouncing bosoms. The dress really did leave little to the imagination up top. Clenching my hands, I stifled the instinct to cover my chest with my arms. Generally, I didn't mind men looking. It was part of the job after all, but with Luke, a tiny piece of me, one I thought long buried, wanted to be a lady for him. I wanted him to see me differently than the howling, spitting men at the bawdyhouse did.

His eyes met mine for the briefest moment, and confusion swam in them before he turned away. From where I sat, I could've sworn Jeremiah was smiling, but I couldn't be sure.

Dark was falling as the homestead became visible against the backdrop of the setting sun. It was a sizeable house, surprisingly so, and I made a conscious effort to close my mouth as I stared. It was raised on stilts and had a large front porch. The home was made of dark, aged wood, with some kind of white sealant plastered between each board to keep the bugs and weather at bay. The different colored wood in back said the house had been added onto over the years and a large barn nearby stood stark against the waning light. A horse nickered a welcome, followed by a second from the corral beside the barn.

Luke hopped out and lit a candle that sat in a fruit preserve jar hanging by the front door frame.

Jeremiah turned. "We have to put the team up and I'll talk to him then. Make yourself at home inside."

I tried to struggle my floral carpet bag out of the back but he waved me off. "Leave it. We'll get it on the way in."

I waited for the punch line.

"Go on," he said impatiently.

Okay, so a man was really going to get my bag and without me asking him. That may have been a first in my entire life. I hesitated only a second more and slid out of the back like a noodle. My body was officially unimpressed with travelling. Stumbling to the front porch, I smiled shyly at Luke as he passed. He tipped his hat and muttered, "Ma'am," before walking to the barn after the receding buggy.

What had this man done to me? I'd bedded dozens of johns and none of them gave me the queer jittering feeling this man did. I could talk every one of them under the table and never spare a blush. If I was good at anything, it was talking to a man, and here I was going all weak in the knees for some person who spared a cordial word for me. That had to change. Right after I stopped ogling his backside as he disappeared through the barn doors.

The heavy front door intimidated me off of actually going inside. Jeremiah had said to make myself comfortable, but I'd rather have the grand tour before claiming a room. So instead, I sat in a rickety old rocking chair on the porch and watched the bugs swirl lazily around the candle jar.

It was quite peaceful until the yelling broke out. The sound of the brother's fighting filled the barn right up until it overflowed and drifted to me on the breeze. I only caught bits and pieces of the furious conversation, but it was enough. It seemed Luke wasn't keen on settling down.

Now I prided myself on my happy disposition, but that isn't to say I'm not affected by rejection, and this was the second one for the day. Jeremiah then Luke, and how could I blame those fine men for not wanting a plain ex-working girl for a wife. Even if they were country, those Dawson boys were well-bred. Anyone with eyes in their head could see that. I was definitely diluting the breeding stock.

Jeremiah emerged from the barn, slapping his hat against his thigh in a motion that seemed more agitation than habit. "He'll come around," he said gruffly before disappearing into the house with my bag.

My chest was so tight I couldn't breathe. I was stuck in the wilderness, in Indian country no less, with two men I didn't know—neither of whom wanted to bed me, much less marry me. The predicament I'd managed to carve out for myself was impressive.

Oh, stop it! I'd been in much worse situations than this, and moping and moaning never saved anyone. No one was going to rescue me. It wasn't the way of the world. I had to help myself.

****

Luke

I'd never been so tricked and betrayed in all my life.

Ordering some woman like you were shopping in a catalog for window glass? That was Jeremiah's thing. He'd had a woman of his own before and lost her, now he wanted to feel again. Good for him. Not good for me. I'd watched the animal in him rip Jeremiah up from the inside out after he lost Anna. I'd be damned if I'd let a woman affect me in such a way. They were fragile, weak, helpless creatures who died much too easily. Catch your finger on a nail out in this territory and you could perish of blood poisoning before you ever found a doctor sober enough to tend your wound.

The woman's footsteps were ridiculously loud and highlighted how inept she was for living in the wilderness.

"No!" I yelled before she even opened the barn door. "I need time."

She threw it open anyway and looked around the barn with a fierceness that bordered on desperation. She wouldn't find me down there. I was up in the rafters with my leg dangling down, and it was too dark for her to see that far in this kind of light. I, on the other hand, could see her just fine.

She wasn't a bad looking woman. Healthy enough for a saloon liaison, and she didn't smell of sickness or even sadness the way most of them did. She wasn't pin thin, but I'd never been attracted to fragile looking women. A small waist gave her a figure like one of the hourglasses for sale in the general store. Her hair was wild and curly, and the color of beach sand I'd once seen. Her face was still to be determined. I couldn't get a feel for her with all that blasted rouge and powder she wore.

She punched tiny, angry fists to her hip bones and yelled, "Where are you?"

Feisty little woman. I lifted my chin. "Up here."

Her mouth opened and shut again like a floundering catfish as she lifted her face in my general direction. "How the devil did you get way up there?"

"What do you want?" I countered.

"I'm hungry."

This wasn't where I thought the conversation would be going. "There'll be food in the house. Ask Jeremiah to show you where."

"I don't want to ask Jeremiah because he isn't the one who's supposed to be showing me around. You are. So if you're quite done throwing your temper tantrum, show me around your house so I don't have to ask where everything is."

Thank the heavens she couldn't see in the dark because a smile burst out of my face before I could stop it. She was a sassy little thing.

I cocked my head to the side. I had a perfect view of those perky breasts she'd probably been famous for wherever she came from. They heaved attractively when she was angry.

"Look, this isn't what I signed up for either," she said. "I thought I was marrying Jeremiah, but he doesn't want me. And I know you don't either, but I aim to stay here so one of you needs to man up. I might not be exactly what you boys were looking for in a wife—"

"I wasn't looking for a wife at all," I interrupted under the flare of another wave of searing anger. "And I don't aim to be pushed into something I don't want to do."

"Well I can't just live here in sin! A woman out here with two unmarried men? It isn't right!"

"But you're a whore. Living in sin obviously hasn't bothered you until this very moment."

The sound that screeched forth from her throat drew me up short. When an animal made that caliber of noise in the wild, a wise man didn't mess with it.

"I'm not a *whore* anymore." She made the word sound like a curse and it left a bitter taste on the end of my tongue. "I'm changing my life. I'm going to be a proper lady here. I left that grit behind and I don't want the town shunning me for keeping old habits."

She spun on her heel and bolted for the door. I was to her before she even left the barn and grabbed her elbow. Her terrified scream had me hunched in pain with my hands over my ears, and she fell onto her backside with a thud. A little dirt explosion filled the air and she coughed as she scrambled farther away from me.

"How'd you do that?" The whites of her eyes shone all around what looked to be cornflower blue colored irises.

I cursed softly. My intention hadn't been to frighten the danged woman. I just didn't know my own speed sometimes. "Stop running," I growled.

How could a woman so frustrating make me feel like a monster? I hadn't felt this way in years. As I grabbed her ankle, she sucked air to scream again. My ringing ears couldn't take another helping of terrified woman so I clamped a hand over her mouth and pressed my weight on top of her. She chugged breath through her delicately flared nostrils like a racehorse, and the animal in me liked the way her figure felt writhing against mine.

"Stop it," I said. "You keep wiggling around like that and it ain't gonna be good for either of us, okay? I'm not going to hurt you. I swear it."

She nodded slowly and I released her soft lips from my grip. And then she screamed again before I could cover the sound.

"What the hell are you doing to her?" Jeremiah asked from above us.

"I'm trying to get her to stop shrieking. She's killing my ears."

"Well, you heard her. She's a lady now, and ladies don't want no hanky panky before they're wedded, right?" he asked the woman.

She nodded frantically.

How did I become the bad guy in all of this? Had everyone lost their danged mind but me? No, I wasn't trying to force her, but what was the big deal with hanky panky before the wedding night? She wasn't exactly fit to wear white on her wedding day. Incredulously I said, "But she's a whore."

She slurred something behind my hand and I lifted it slightly. Her eyes burned with fury. "Lady," she argued.

"Whatever," I muttered and pushed off of her.

Whore, lady, or mongoose, that woman was trouble.

16

Chapter Three
Kristina

L uke offered me a hand but I refused it primly. I hadn't ever needed a man's help before now, except for the coins that lined their pockets, and I certainly wouldn't need one's help to stand. He gave a frustrated grunt and held his arms up like I was the one being unmanageable. I dusted my dress off as best I could and straightened my spine.

I didn't know what was wrong with him, but something was. He was an ornament in the barn rafters when I started my escape and then suddenly he was there behind me. It didn't take him but a second to cross all that space.

I tried to keep the quiver from my voice. "Are you evil, sir?"

The small light from the front porch gave enough of itself to flicker across his striking features. All of the beauty in the world meant nothing if his soul was ruined.

"What?" he asked. To his credit, he did look genuinely taken aback.

Slowly I asked, "Are you evil?" The answer mattered.

"I don't make all the right decisions and I ain't gonna be nominated for sainthood anytime soon, but no. I'm not evil, far as I know."

"And you swear not to hurt me? Both of you swear it!"

"We swear it," the Dawsons muttered in unison.

"Now, I don't know what's going on here, and right now, I don't

17

really care. I've been traveling for days, my backside feels like the south side of hell, I'm exhausted and I'm starving."

It was Jeremiah who braved the reprimand first. "I didn't cook today on account of being in town since this morning. We have some leftover bread from yesterday though."

My stomach growled at the mention but it wouldn't be enough. "Are there any eggs I can fry up?"

"I thought you couldn't cook," Jeremiah accused.

"Frying an egg isn't really cooking, now is it, Mr. Dawson?"

His eyes were shrouded in the night's darkness but if I had to guess, I'd say the look he was giving me wasn't a happy one. "Luke, show your fiancé where to get the eggs."

Something whirled inside of me at the word *fiancé* that was fit to rival a twister. I didn't know if it was good or bad, but it was one of them. Luke didn't even argue, but from the slump in his shoulders, I thought maybe it was because he was just tired of fighting.

"This way," Luke muttered as Jeremiah strode off in the direction of the house.

I'd never actually seen a chicken coop, but I hadn't in my wildest imaginings ever come up with what I found around the side of the barn. The chicken coop was more like a chicken prison, made with steel enforced bars and railroad ties. They didn't seem to mind though as they roosted happily on ledges and in nests, clucking absently in the quite rest of evening. Maybe they felt safer in their impenetrable chicken castle.

Luke opened a latch and swung the door wide. "Well, go get 'em," he said testily.

Never in my life had I touched a live chicken, so I didn't know what the protocol for stealing eggs out from under them was. Did one say please? Open sesame? Should I just reach under there and snatch one quickly? That sounded right. I picked a great white hen shining against the dark. Surely she warmed a thousand eggs under her plump bottom and wouldn't miss a few.

"Hello clucky," I crooned as I slid my hand across the rough hay of her nest box. She let out a loud *bagawk!* and pecked me right on the wrist bone.

"Ouch," I yelped in surprise and retreated. "She pecked me." My feelings were hurt. I'd been nice and polite and she'd hurt me.

"You're bleeding." Luke didn't ask. It was a statement.

As a matter of fact, there was a dark spot swelling up against the thin skin across the bone. My hurt expanded a little more.

Luke sighed loudly and scratched his forehead with the back of his thumb before entering the chicken coop. "Let me show you." He pushed the hen out of her nest, to her squawking surprise, and snatched the five eggs nestled inside.

"I was trying to be nice about it," I told him defensively.

"Being nice out here will make you bleed."

I glared at his receding back. Touché. By the time I latched the door behind me, Luke was half way to the house with his long deliberate strides. Hefting the hem of my dress, I jogged to catch up. I followed him up the steps and walked through the front door of the cabin for the first time.

The den was open with three oversized chairs placed near the stone fireplace. A bearskin rug smothered the smooth wooden floors beneath them. Four swaybacked chairs sat haphazardly around a knotty pine table. A wood burning stove stood in the corner of the room next to a set of shelves and a huge, potbellied sink full of dishes.

Luke paused to set the eggs on the table, then removed his hat and placed it over a peg on the wall. He shook out his dark hair and ran two hands through it to straighten it out of his face. A trill resonated through me with the realization that the hat had hidden some of his masculine allure. He unbuckled the leather belt that housed his pistol and hung it on the nearest chair.

Even still fully clothed, it was intimate to watch him get comfortable in his home. I was an invader watching a dance he'd done hundreds of times, unable to take my eyes away from the spectacle.

"Here," he said gruffly, snatching my arm.

My instincts screamed to flinch away, but for whatever reason, I was bear grease in his capable hands. He dragged my arm under one of the hanging oil lanterns and eyed the small dot of blood on my wrist.

"You'll live," he announced with a spark of humor in his green eyes.

He wiped the drop off swiftly with the sleeve of his shirt and released me, to my heart's annoying disappointment. Jeremiah, meanwhile, had been dutifully stoking the fire in the stove and shut it with a clang. He pulled an iron skillet from the sink and placed it on the hot surface.

Unsanitary.

"Let me just wash this," I said, stealing the crusty pan from the warmth of the stove top.

The brothers both looked downright amused, but I'd be hanged if I was getting stomach gripes from their questionable hygiene. Luke brought me a bucket of water that had been sitting by the door and I scrubbed the pan as best I could with a full sink. Once clean, I put it back in its rightful place on the stove and cracked the eggs into it. After they were all fried up a minute later, I handed a plate of the crunchy eggshell portion to Luke and told him, "Happy engagement."

His eyes tightened at the corners but he ate it without complaint. When he came to the shells, he simply spat them out and took another bite. Maybe cooking for them wouldn't be so hard after all.

The meal with the leftover bread was just what I needed to feel human again and sighing happily, I leaned back in the chair.

Luke was staring at my décolletage again.

"Do you mind?" I asked, placing a hand over my cleavage.

"I don't mind at all. If you're going to wear dresses that show off every square inch of skin on your top half, I'm going to look."

Unapologetic oaf.

"It's the only dress I have."

Jeremiah leaned back on two legs of the chair with a frown before he strode determinedly into a room down the hall. When he returned, he held a length of beautiful gray and red floral fabric and a thin booklet of dress patterns of the much more modest variety. "Can you sew?" he asked.

"Not really."

"Well, I suggest you learn. The dress you got on ain't gonna do you any favors out here."

I couldn't quite keep my traitorous fingers from touching the softness of the cloth. It really was quite beautiful. What in the world were two bachelors doing with such fine fabric within arm's reach? And dress patterns? The mysteries that surrounded the Dawson men were piling up by the wagon load.

"Are you sure?" Luke asked his brother.

Jeremiah shrugged. "She needs a new dress," he said, and with that, turned. His boots echoed off the hollow floor and he slammed the door to the bedroom behind him.

"Should I not take it?" I asked Luke. I couldn't bear to wear something that was a painful reminder to someone else. "I really don't know anything about patterns or sewing. What if I ruin this fabric?" Suddenly a new dress seemed like a very bad idea. Sure my dress was inappropriate for basically every occasion on the frontier, but it didn't matter if the lacy thing got dirty, or torn, or eaten by badgers. It didn't mean anything to anyone.

Luke rifled through the patterns and pointed to one with a gigantic buck knife he'd pulled out of thin air. Where'd he been hiding that?

"Here, try this one," he said. "It seems like it would be the easiest one. Write down your measurements and I'll cut them out for you tonight." He offered the knife hilt first. "Unless you'd like to make the cuts?"

I imagined a whole lot of ways I could maim my hands with a

glistening blade that big and shook my head.

"You can start on the dress tomorrow while Jeremiah and I are working. You'll need something to keep you occupied anyhow."

And just like that, Luke Dawson found me a hobby.

****

Luke

There'd be no sleeping tonight. The wildest parts of me hummed to be set loose and I thoroughly blamed the woman for bleeding in front of me. She made me feel like a monster and then pushed the beast out of me. I threw my hat at the barn wall. I was stalling like a coward.

Squatting down until the muscles of my thighs stretched, I scented the tiny droplet of blood on my sleeve for the tenth time. It smelled rich and full of iron. All blood smelled different, but hers smelled particularly good. My tongue scratched against the rough fabric of my shirt as I tasted it. I wasn't a man-eater, but I just wanted to feel that tiny part of her on the tip of my tongue.

Maybe I *was* a monster.

The house had gone quiet hours ago and I needed to give myself time before dawn. "Just get it over with," I grumbled as I unbuttoned my vest. As I undressed, my hands shook from fear of the first tingles of the animal stretching inside of me. Anticipation of the pain had my breath shaking like a leaf before I even slid out of my boots.

I pulled a worn leather strap into my mouth and swore, as I always did, I wouldn't scream this time.

Chapter Four
Kristina

I jolted awake. My breath was rushed like I'd been running from something, and a thin sheen of sweat covered my chest and forehead. Desperate to feel cool air against my burning skin, I struggled out from under the covers and stumbled toward the window. The nightmare remained stubbornly on the edge of my memory, but it must have been bad because it was a rare occurrence I woke in such a state.

The window was simple and easy to push open and the cool breeze against my face was ecstasy. The moon gave a pathetic amount of light away and the night was still dark and long removed from dawn. Outlines of trees that edged the clearing were the only things visible from the window of the room Luke had tossed my bag into earlier.

My bladder was downright uncomfortable. I hadn't emptied it before bed and was paying dearly for it now. Squirming, I considered my options. Find the outhouse or pee the bed. I wouldn't hold until morning. My nightdress was much too thin for mixed company, but the Dawson brothers would be fast asleep at this time of night, so I set out on my mission.

Creak. I froze and put my foot onto a different floor plank. *Creeeeeeeeeeeeak*, it went under my weight. Seriously? Was every single board in the house made to booby trap me? I listened but didn't hear any movement from the bedrooms down the hall. With a little luck, maybe the Dawson's were as sound a sleepers as I usually was. *Creakcreakcreak*, I ran for the front door.

I didn't remember an outhouse by the barn but I'd try there first. One of the oil lanterns stood invitingly on the table near the door and I lit it as quietly as I could before making my escape. The low light threw everything outside of a few feet into shadow. An eerie thing it was to have such limited vision in an unfamiliar place. The slow wind was chilly as it caressed my thin nightdress and the hairs on my arms raised like they knew something I didn't.

I imagined Indians watching me from the shadows just beyond the light and froze in fear. Ridiculous imagination. Turning back for the door, I weighed my options again. My desperation offered a new one. Wake up Luke and have him escort me to the outhouse, stand guard while I relieved myself, then bring me back to the safety of my room. I bit my lip until it hurt as punishment. I saw the way he looked at me when I got pecked by that ornery chicken. He thought I was pathetic. Waking him in the middle of the night to act as my pee-pee escort? Wasn't going to happen.

Be brave, be brave, be brave, I mouthed, and it seemed to help. The outhouse wasn't by the barn or corral. It wasn't in the clearing at all as far as I could tell, and just when I was about to pop a squat in the side yard, there it stood around the back of the house. The chills that found my skin when I stepped through the door and into the night hadn't eased up, but they were happily ignored in my private celebration of a pot. The outhouse had a few spiders and I was pretty sure there was some sort of snake trapped down in the deep latrine beneath it, but I'd been in much, much worse and the physical relief I felt was almost tangible. Closing the door behind me, I smiled as I made my way the distance back to the house.

It wasn't until I was about halfway to the back porch that the shivers in my spine went from a low warning to a scream. Instincts long buried by city life sprung into existence when a low snarl sounded behind me. Fear froze me into an immoveable being. I couldn't even breathe as I searched the edges of the lantern light. The noise tapered off to a bone chilling sound that tore at the edges of my frayed mind. Slowly as a stream in frozen winter, I turned.

A pair of glowing eyes danced just outside of the light, so I backed toward the house. I had no weapons, save the lantern, to fight whatever had found me. I turned the nob on the side of the lantern until the light was as bright as it would go, and the muzzle of a great gray and white wolf with gleaming bared teeth greeted me. I swallowed a scream and ran for the back door. It was right on my heels and the gnashing of its teeth sounded like cannon fire. I nearly fell on the porch steps but caught myself and flung my frame into the back door.

It didn't budge.

"Help!" I screamed, as my fists pounded against the thick wood that barred me from asylum. "Help me, please!"

Any moment, the wolf would be on me and I'd die a horrible death within inches of safety. Pounding harder, I fell into the opening door. I hit the ground hard and shoved the door closed with my bare foot. "Latch it. Latch the door!"

Jeremiah did as he was told and squatted in front of me. "What's happened? What were you doing out there at this time of night?" The anger in his tone made me want to scramble away from him.

Heartbeat thrashing against my ribs, I squeaked, "I had to use the outhouse."

He spared a glance for the door and then offered me a hand. "Tell me, were you bitten?"

Bitten? I replayed our small conversation but I definitely hadn't given away what had chased me.

"Bitten by what, sir?" I said carefully.

A frustrated noise escaped his throat and instead of answering, he lifted the hem of my nightdress and scoured my legs.

I snatched my dress and retreated. "I beg your pardon! What on earth are you doing?"

Unapologetically, his eyes searched the bare skin of my arms.

"I'm telling Luke of your atrocious handling of me."

"Be my guest," Jeremiah offered. "He's sleeping out in the barn, so have fun getting there."

He turned and disappeared into his room in the back of the house and I stood there, filled to the brim with fear and fury and with no outlet to release it. Rushing for the window, I pulled back the daffodil colored curtains far enough to glimpse the outline of the barn. A graceful movement loped across the area in between, and my blood went cold as winter. What if the wolf got in the barn and hurt Luke? And why was he sleeping in the barn when he had a perfectly good bed inside?

The curtains slid out of my fingertips. I knew why. Because he couldn't stand to sleep in the same house as me.

I creaky stomped loudly back to my room. How silly had I been to think when I answered that advertisement things would just come together? I'd imagined a hundred different ways my mail order marriage would work out, and none of those imaginings offered an involuntary husband or a wolf attack. And this was day one! I flung myself in a very star-like shape onto the lumpy bed and, for lack of either Dawson brother, glared at the ceiling instead until I tumbled into a fitful sleep.

****

My body had been dragged behind a horse. It had to have to feel like this. And all the soreness was just from sitting there, traveling. Any actual manual labor around the homestead would likely kill me. I was still staring at the ceiling in the same position I'd fallen asleep in by the time the rooster crowed for the sixteenth time. The long, cold slab of anger that tethered me down the night before still clung to me like a second skin.

I was a naturally happy person, but since I'd arrived in town exactly one day ago, I'd gone through waves of insecurity, despair, and fear. I wasn't myself. This wild place had me reeling and if I didn't get ahold of myself quickly, what would stop me from free falling for eternity?

I tried a smile. It did make me feel better so I showed some teeth. Smiles were the best medicine, Mother used to say.

A long strand of gray window light brushed a dusty chest in the corner of the room. Emboldened with the prospect of an interesting find, I flopped out of bed and padded to it. Kneeling in front of it, I blew a healthy layer of dust, which looked pretty in my mind, but really the dirty breeze hit the wall and blew back into my dumbly smiling face and lodged itself in my throat. When I was done coughing, I polished a metal plate on the chest that read, *G. Dawson.*

Lifting the latch, the door slid open easy enough and I waved the remaining dust cloud away. Folded cotton shirts sat in a neat pile and a worn pair of boots lay forlornly in the corner, abandoned by their owner. On a pair of stained chaps, a two letter bundle was tied neatly with rough twine. Fingering the yellowing envelopes, I read the return name aloud. "Gable Dawson of Colorado Springs." The room took on a new meaning. It belonged to Luke and Jeremiah's missing brother.

I shut the chest before any more ghosts could escape.

Did the room enjoy being occupied again? Or was I a disappointment after it had housed another for so long and then been left to undusted desolation? I stood and reached for the scandalously cut dress hanging from a corner chair. I'd take good care of the room until he returned, because I, like the other Dawsons, liked to think the one they waited for still existed in the world somewhere.

Shimmying into my blue, lacy dress was a challenge with sore muscles, but with the high of accomplishment, I headed for the smell of yeast that wafted from the kitchen. A plate of rolls warmed over embers, and a generous slab of soft butter sat invitingly on the table. A feast for a king where I came from. Jeremiah had one such roll dangling from his mouth as he pulled his duster on by the door.

Cheerfully, I said, "Morning."

He frowned suspiciously. "Mornin'," he said around the biscuit.

"Heading out?" I asked. Really I wanted to know where Luke was, but it would be rude to ask right away. Men needed to be buttered up like the soft rolls first.

His biscuit dropped into his waiting hand. "Lots of work to be done around a place like this. I left a basket of sewing stuff by the fireplace for you." His eyes dropped disapprovingly to the black lace on my bodice. "Try to finish the dress today so we don't have to see you flouncing around in that get up any longer."

"Got it. No flouncing. Do you happen to know where your brother is this morning?"

Obnoxious knowing grin! "He's already out with the cattle. He's alive and well, Miss Yeaton." The door creaked as he opened it wide. "See you tonight."

The closing of the door behind him made a terribly lonely sound.

****

Luke

The black horse under me was a skittish creature, but I liked that about him. There was always risk when riding him. A chance at a surprise ride at top speed was a possibility that could happen at any moment.

A skittish mount kept me on my toes.

The stirrups jangled as I dismounted and tied the horse off at a tree to check the damage. One cow wasn't bad and at least I'd had the good sense to hunt our own livestock last night. I stood over the remains and pulled a blue handkerchief over my sensitive nose. The wolf in me didn't mind the smell of rot, but the human in me sure enough did.

The flies had already found the deceased animal. I pulled on my gloves and gathered the back hooves before dragging the carcass off into the woods. Normally, I wouldn't worry about it because there was enough space on our property that the other cattle could escape the gore and predators and scavengers it would bring in. However, I'd taken this one much too close to the watering hole for comfort. Cattle needed to drink.

The sound of hoof beats in the distance motivated me to work a little faster. Jeremiah's horse wasn't even stopped yet before he jumped off.

I said, "Now look—"

His fist crashed into my jaw like a stone. I was quick too though, and tackled him at the waist before pummeling him to the ground.

"I didn't bite her!" I yelled through the flying fists.

The fight lasted longer than it should've, but my instincts said my brother needed this. He needed to let his pent up rage out on something or someone, and my face wasn't made of glass. After it was finished, we sat in knee high grass gasping and bleeding as the cattle watched us like the show had been acceptable.

Jeremiah broke the silence. "Ever since she showed up, you've been acting a crazy fool. You had her pinned in the dirt like a rutting animal last night and then your wolf chased her into the house. What were you thinking? You think the first night is the time to introduce her to what you are? Did that really play out well in your mind, Luke?"

"I explained about last night by the barn, and yes, I changed, and yes I chased her into the house but I did it for a reason. I don't know what she was doing out at that time of night, but she can't be wondering around outside. What happened to Anna can't happen again."

"Don't," Jeremiah said. "Don't use Anna as an excuse for your behavior."

"I have to! I can't let that happen to this lady. She *should* be scared of going outside at night. It ain't safe for her. If we don't learn from our mistakes with Anna, then our bloodline might as well fade into oblivion. If we can't protect them, we don't deserve wives, children, none of it. Now she knows not to leave the safety of the house at night. I saved her life and she don't even know it."

"Well, what did you expect her to do?"

"What do you mean?" I asked. Why did I already feel guilty?

"She had to use the outhouse, Luke."

My stomach slumped to the grass beneath me. I hadn't put enough thought into the reasons she was outside in the first place. Sure, the animal ruled when I changed, but I still had some human logic syphoning through. With a soft oath, I shook my head. "I didn't know."

"The point is, yes, you're right. She should know the dangers of going outside by herself at night. At the same time, situations like this are going to come up, just like they did with Anna. She needs to be taught to protect herself if ever there comes a time we aren't here to keep her safe."

I chewed slowly on a sweet stem of long wheat while I mulled that over. "What do you suggest?"

"She needs to be taught to shoot. She needs a backbone if she's going to make it out here."

"So who teaches her that stuff?" I asked.

Jeremiah pushed me over as he stood. "Her husband does, you dipshit."

Chapter Five
Kristina

I tried not to laugh at my workmanship, but if I didn't laugh I was going to burst into tears. After scouring the house, I'd discovered a full length pane of mirror glass attached to the back of Luke's bedroom door. Even in the fading light, the dress I'd tried to sew looked atrocious. Single-handedly, I'd ruined all that fine fabric. I was in a fit of hysterical laughter when Luke burst through his door with a look on his face that said he thought I'd been dying.

"What's wrong with you, woman?" he asked with wide eyes.

"Do you like my dress?" I asked through a giggle. I curtsied clumsily.

His stunning green eyes traveled the length of my tattered gown. Square corners of fabric stuck out here and there, and there were holes in the puff sleeves where my pieces hadn't quite matched up. The stitches were loose and the front and back didn't quite fit together. The corner of his lip twitched. Once. Twice, before he gave a chuckle that sent me into a fit of laughter all over again. I turned and admired my not-so-handiwork in the mirror once more. It was the least flattering, most ill-fitting dress I'd ever encountered.

"Did I cut the pieces wrong?" he asked, watching me through the mirror with a half stifled smile.

"Oh, I'm sure the pieces were cut fine, but you Dawson boys don't seem to be hearing me when I say I really can't sew." There it was; the sob I'd been trying to keep in. This cloth meant something to Jeremiah and I'd ruined it forever just like I knew I would. I slumped onto the edge of Luke's bed and cupped my cheeks with my hands.

Luke looked terrified, as most men did in the presence of a crying woman.

"I've ruined Jeremiah's fabric," I explained.

"Oh," he said quietly. He wiped the palms of his hands on his tanned hide pants and shut the door. "He'll understand," he said as the bed creaked beside me under his weight.

I wiped my eyes on the deformed puff sleeve and hoped he was right.

"You seem like you have a tender heart for a…" He didn't finish and cleared his throat instead.

"For a whore?" I was too defeated to be mad. "I was raised by a tender family and I was only a whore for a year before I came here. Not enough time to become bitter just yet."

"I don't really know anything about you and I'm going to marry you," he said, sounding surprised. "I don't even know your name."

I held out my hand for a shake. A manly gesture, but hang it. "Kristina Yeaton. My regulars called me Kris."

He smirked at my hand and shook it. "Luke Dawson, ma'am. Pleased to make your acquaintance."

I got a good look at his face for the first time since he'd barged in. "What in blue blazes happened to you?" I reached out and touched the open cut on the side of his cheekbone. The bruising was already making an appearance and his lip was split.

"I fell."

"Off a building?"

He hissed air through his teeth and jerked back when my prodding got too close. There really was no use fussing over a man who didn't care to be fussed over. I lay my hands gently in my lap and waited with an impatiently arched eyebrow. All right, if he kept staring at me like that, I was going to melt into a useless puddle and fall right through the cracks in the floor boards. "What?"

"Well, you look right pretty without all that powder on your face." He stroked the curve of my jawline with his fingertip and my insides went warm from the line fire he created. "Your cheeks are all pink from crying and your skin's fair." He trailed his thumb softly over the fullness of my lips.

"Are you saying you prefer me without my war paint?"

His chuckle was deep and reverberated off my waiting ears. "I do." Pulling away, he dug around in his pocket. "I'm sure you'll do well enough as a wife and I'm not too picky besides." He plucked a thin gold band from his vest pocket and slid it onto my finger. "Don't really

Wolf Bride | T. S. Joyce

know how to do this but, you want to get hitched? To me?"
It might not have sounded so, but sitting here in my ruined dress
with damp tear tracks still on my cheeks, a good looking man giving
me compliments about the way I looked, and an offered gold ring was
just about the most romantic thing I'd ever witnessed—and it was
happening to me.
There was no reining in my smile. "Okay. Yes."
I was staring at the new band on my finger that said I belonged to a
man when he spoke again. "I owe you an apology."
"What for?" I breathed, holding the ring up in the light.
"The wolf last night." The deep green of his eyes searched mine
for a long time, like he wanted to tell me everything that had ever been.
"I should've been there to keep you safe," he said.
"I didn't tell anyone about the wolf, so how did you know about
it?"
His gaze was tortured and the words sounded torn from his throat.
"They're a problem around here."
He stood to leave but hesitated at the door. "We'll take the dress
into town. There's a dressmaker there who can fix it. I'll take you
tomorrow, if that sits well with you."
I nodded, and he left me sitting on his bed with more questions
than when he'd entered.
The smell of frying chicken was enough to pull me out of the
comfort of Luke's room. The horrendous dress fell from me like it
couldn't wait to escape the woman who'd ruined it, and I avoided
looking at the sad pile of fabric while I wiggled back into my immodest
garments.
I'd skipped any kind of luncheon in my concentration on not
stabbing my fingers to death with a sewing needle and was nearly
ravenous. Jeremiah stood over the iron skillet feeding it flour covered
strips of poultry and humming softly. He wore a cotton shirt with the
sleeves rolled up to his elbows and tanned pants with suspenders
showing. His boots were lined up neatly by the door. Such an odd sight,
an imposing man cooking in the kitchen like a common woman. I
supposed they hadn't much choice through the years than to learn to
cook with no woman around to fill their bellies. I didn't know him from
Adam, but from what I did gather about Jeremiah, he would make a
fine brother-in-law.
With hands scrubbed clean in the sink, I turned and said, "Well,
show me how to fry chicken."
He was a patient teacher who let me do most of the work and by
the last of it, only two pieces were inedible. Triumph. Sitting across the
table from Jeremiah over two plates of steaming food was a test in self-

discipline. The man's face was torn up even worse than Luke's was. Oh, he fell all right. They both did. They fell all over each other's fists. Ridiculous, squabbling men.

"Go on and eat," he said, while I sat waiting with hands clasped in my lap. "Luke won't be hungry."

Jeremiah ate with single-minded tenacity, and slowly, I picked up my fork and ate with one eye on the door.

Luke didn't even spare a glance for us as he bustled into the house with a pail of milk. Without a word, he began to strain it through a layer of cheesecloth and into another bucket.

"A man your size should be eating much more if you're going to keep up your strength," I said.

Luke only grunted.

Maybe he just needed a little enticement. "I made it myself. Why don't you just try a small piece of fried chicken? I'll make you a plate."

His face went positively green. "Let it rest, woman."

"Are you unwell?" I knew all about the stomach gripes. The cook back at the bawdyhouse had been an unsanitary little beast and not overly worried about cooking the meat all the way through for me and the other girls.

"No, Kristina. I just ain't hungry is all."

Even angry, I liked the way he said my name with his deep, velveteen voice.

The evening stretched on and brought a darkening sky. With the setting of the sun came my unease. I'd been thinking about that wild wolf all day. My heart seemed determined to focus on its ferocious teeth and the sound of its snarl caressing the back of my bare ankles. No way was I replaying that little scene. I might not be a smart or educated woman, but I paid attention and didn't make mistakes twice. That trick kept people like me alive and kicking long after people expected me to. One hurried trip to the outhouse later with a sharpened stick and my heart skipped a beat with relief when I closed the back door behind me. I leaned my forehead against the cool wood of the door and puffed a sigh of relief.

"We have a soaking tub if you want to use it," Luke said from right behind me.

I jumped and stifled a screech, but he acted as if he didn't even notice he'd practically scared the living daylights out of me.

"I hear womenfolk like to take their time about cleaning, so I can bring it into your room if you want."

A soaking tub? Hmm. That actually sounded heavenly. As much as I'd appreciated sponging off in the bedroom last night, there was still a healthy layer of travel grit that would only come off with time in a tub and a thorough scrubbing with a horse bristle brush. I'd have said so, but I really was trying to be more ladylike.

"Yes, that would be lovely, thank you," I said instead when my heart had stopped trying to eject itself from my throat.

The soaking tub was small but I easily fit into it if I curled up my knees. It was tarred in the cracks to prevent leaks and we didn't bother warming the water up. Luke offered, bless that man, but I was too tired to wait the hour it would take. Tepid water would do just fine for me. I loosed my wild curls and washed them with lavender hair soap. After I was finished cleaning my tresses, I scrubbed and rubbed my sensitive skin until the water turned brown and my hide shone like an eggshell in the sun.

What was the point of putting my nightdress on? My bedroom door was closed, and not once during my stay had either Dawson brother so much as looked in my room. I cuddled into bed, all sparkling clean like I'd just been minted, and wearing nothing but the clothes I'd been born with. Almost before my head even hit the pillow, I fell asleep.

The slumber that followed was glorious, right up to the point where Luke shook my shoulder as I lay on my stomach floating around in dreamland somewhere.

"Kris, wake up," he said gently.

I was so deep into that sleep, I couldn't even remember where I was or who was staring at me with grinning green eyes. The soaking tub, still filled with my dirty water in the middle of the floor was an unpleasant reminder of my surroundings. My hair had dried overnight and likely resembled the mane of some wild animal and I jerked a glance to make sure my backside was covered up by the linens. It was, thank my lucky stars.

"Do you know you're sleeping with not a stitch of clothing on?" Luke asked through a grin.

"What are you doing in here?" I'd be more embarrassed if my previous occupation hadn't given me nary an ounce of modesty. And really, most of me was covered up except for my back and legs. It could've been much worse.

"I want to show you something," he said.

The stars still twinkled through the window pane and the rooster was still probably fast asleep among his hens.

I plopped my face back into the pillow and mumbled, "I don't know why you don't require sleep, Luke Dawson, but I do. I need it. I'll be terribly grumpy without it and lash out at you without warning. Are you sure you still want to drag me out of my warm bed right now?"

"I'll take my chances." Damn that smile in his voice.

I turned far enough to glare at him, but his interest seemed to be taken with the curve of my backside against the sheets.

"You mind if I at least get dressed before we go gallivanting off on whatever unwelcome adventure you have planned for us?"

He waved his fingers regally. "Be my guest."

Really? "Turn around at least!"

He did so easily enough, and it wasn't until I was dressed that I realized he was facing a small mirror that stood over the washbasin on the opposite wall, and could likely see everything from my hips up. I wacked him in the back of the head with my pillow but he only laughed and gallantly bowed as he opened the door for me.

As infuriating as the man was, he did offer his arm when I hesitated on the back porch.

"I won't let anything hurt you," he said.

His confidence was infectious and I took his offered arm gratefully. I still scanned the area the lantern touched, but the fealty of a big strapping man with a foot long hunting knife visibly sticking from his belt sure made me feel safer.

"You know," I said, "you really shouldn't see me in that state of undress until we're married."

He frowned slightly and looked at me like he couldn't tell if I was teasing. "I put a ring on your finger that says you're mine. Far as I'm concerned, we're good as married."

"When are we planning on making our little union official?"

"As soon as the circuit preacher comes through town again, which should be any day now. Jeremiah sent for him the day we picked you up in town. You should wear your hair like that more often. You look like some wild, fierce thing."

He could douse the lantern and my inner glow from that unexpected compliment could light the clearing. I'd always liked my hair fine, but never had anyone else said anything nice about it. "Well, it wouldn't be proper to wear it down and whipping around in town with all those high fallutin' ladies and their pearl hairpins, now would it?"

"No, I suppose not." He sidestepped so I wouldn't walk too close to the woodpile by the barn.

"Maybe I could wear it like this just for you though. When we're here. And when you're being particularly nice to me."

He pushed the barn door aside and brushed his fingers against my back as he guided me toward the horse stalls. "I'd like that."

A dark mare stood exhausted over a foal in the hay. Still wet, the baby was just starting to test pressure on his front legs.

I gasped and sank down to watch him through the wooden bars of the stall door. "Oh Luke! He's just the dandiest little thing!"

"I know you didn't want to get up, and you surely could've seen him tomorrow, but then he'd be running around and dry and well on his way to independence. There's something magic about seeing them when they're so new and haven't walked yet. Seeing them eat for the first time and buck around when they think they're big enough to run."

I was having legitimate trouble keeping the squeal of delight securely in my throat.

"There he goes," he said, squatting next to me and resting a hand comfortably across the stall door.

Indeed the little colt was wobbling upward in a grand effort at his first steps. The mare nudged and sniffed him as a reward for his attempts. After a few falls into the soft hay beneath, the tiny horse with the blaze of white down his nose stood and wobbled over to nurse from his mother. The remnants of an umbilical cord still hung from his underbelly and the mare licked his dark coat clean as he fed.

Luke was right. Tender moments like these were surely magical.

Chapter Six
Kristina

I was at a loss as to what to do, and it was utterly infuriating. The boys, who worked like a well-oiled flour mill to load the wagon, weren't the cause of my frustration. Instead, I was angry with myself for not somehow knowing how to help. Likely, these two cowboys had been working together long enough that they just knew how to get everything packed for town between the two of them without even saying a word. But there were three of us now, and one of us was expending a lot of energy flitting around and accomplishing absolutely nothing.

In my defense, I did manage to fry us up some crunchy eggs.

The sun was just peeking its sleepy head over the horizon, and the gray sky was streaked with the bright pinks and oranges that told of a clear day to come. Luke somehow wrangled two half wild and wholly enormous pigs and tossed them in the back of the buggy like he was in a daisy bouquet tossing contest. His strength was downright disturbing but would serve me well enough in the future.

Tied or not, those pigs were frightening and I'd walk all those miles to town rather than sit in the back with their hungry, beady little eyes on me. Thankfully, Jeremiah offered to sit in back this time. He didn't know it, but my bruised bum thanked him. My heart did too, because the seat up front wasn't very big and I had to sit hip to hip with Luke while he capably drove the two horse team.

His warmth seeped slowly through the thin fabric of my dress and I greedily accepted it. And every once in a while, when I was certain he wasn't paying attention, I would sniff him nonchalantly. He smelled of man and earth, hay and horse, and shaving cream he'd found the time to use on his face this morning. He was intoxicating.

Luke was a dashing man bearded, but shaven? I wanted to sleep in his left dimple.

"You did something different with your hair," he said, interrupting my silent swoon.

I had, in fact, and how very observant of the man to notice. Braids cupped both sides of my head and met in the back, where my curls were pinned neatly into place. "I saw a lady wear her hair like this once and I always wanted to try it."

He poked out his bottom lip and nodded as if he were impressed, and I graced him with a wicked grin. "You been with many saloon girls, Mr. Dawson?" I asked a little too innocently. "You seem to have a lot of misconceptions about how we should act and look."

When he talked, the corner of his mouth turned up. "Just trying to find out more about you, Ms. Yeaton."

"You didn't answer my question."

"A few," he admitted. "You been with many cowboys?"

I tipped my chin up and tried not to smile. "A few."

"Well, good. I expect you to have a trick or two up your sleeve then."

I had to swallow my laughter while Jeremiah lit into his brother for the inappropriateness with which he spoke to me. The grin on Luke's face said he didn't pay much mind to the lecture either. True, sometimes Luke was crass and too honest for his own good, but I realized at just that moment I liked that in a man. Jeremiah's instincts had been right to foist me off onto his brother. We would've made a terrible match.

By the time our wagon ambled onto Main Street, most of the town's residents were up and about, running their errands or talking comfortably in small groups in front of the various stores. I couldn't read a letter of the wooden signs that hung over the shops, but I could guess at most of them. A trio of men laughed in front of what was likely a cabinetry or wood working store. Two scantily dressed ladies draped themselves around one of the columns outside the swinging doors of the saloon and catcalled passersby. And two women sat on a bench outside the land office with their heads tipped toward each other, whispers hidden by delicately gloved hands.

Their smug glances my way had me trying my best to look anywhere else. It was foolish to let the gossip of others affect me. And besides, I didn't really know what they were saying so it could've even been something kind about me.

Cruel giggles drifted across the wind.

Or maybe not.

Luke pulled the wagon up to the general store and hopped out. He reached for my waist and pulled me easily over the mud and onto the stairs. The furred hides that hung from the door waved in the wind and the sweet smell of candy that wafted from the shop was a strange combination with animal and mud.

"I need to take these pigs to sell to the butcher first thing and I don't think it's the place for a woman."

My heart flip-flopped uncomfortably at the thought of being separated from him. "I'm sure I will handle a butcher shop just fine."

"That's the thing. It's not really a shop. He's a big German man, does most of his butchering out front. Bloody business, his job is."

I tried to keep the green out of my face. He handed me my dress, subtly wrapped in brown paper and tied with twine to hide it from Jeremiah. "My brother will make sure you get to the dressmaker's safely, and I'll meet you out front when you're done."

A slight nod and he was back in the wagon and off for the south side of town.

"Mind if I run an errand real quick?" Jeremiah asked, offering his arm. "It won't take but a second and we're right here."

"Sure." I slipped my hand into the curve of his elbow and he led me to the post office two shops down. My heeled, leather shoes made soft clomping sounds against the worn wood of the walkway and I nodded demurely to a couple of cowboys who tipped their hats to me. They burst out laughing as soon as we passed and for the first time in a long time, I wished I wasn't dressed like a saloon girl. It certainly wasn't making me any friends. A man whistled from across the street. Well, all right, it wasn't making me the right sort of friends.

Jeremiah opened the door to the post office and waited for me to enter before following behind. He leaned against the counter and pulled a linen paper envelope from his duster pocket. His hat was the same color of brown as the counter, and he set it down respectfully and rubbed a hand through his short hair. It must've been a family habit because Luke often did that too. No one came immediately to the front of the store, so Jeremiah pressed the bell on the end of the table.

"What're you mailing?" I asked.

"Another advertisement for a wife." He winked and said, "This time I was a bit more specific in my wants."

For reasons I couldn't myself explain, my gut went cold. It could've been the realization that I really hadn't been good enough for Jeremiah, or the worry over another woman coming into the fray out here in the wilderness, but likely it was the part of me that sang that Luke would like this new woman better. She'd be able to cook and sew and milk cows, and then he'd realize how completely useless I was to him.

Jeremiah's eyebrows turned down slightly and his coffee colored eyes searched my face. "I still want a wife, Kristina. You get along fine with Luke, don't you?"

"Oh, yes. And I know I'll grow to care for him in time. It's just..." How did one explain matters of the heart to a man? I didn't even understand my worry. "What if she's some highborn lady with good breeding and education and taste, and Luke realizes what he's missing out on?"

Jeremiah snorted. "Luke ain't one to fall for proper ladies, Ms. Yeaton. He calls them uppity. You're plenty safe if that's what you're really worried about."

I gripped onto the wrapped dress and the paper made a satisfying crinkling sound as his assurances washed over me. Jeremiah should put another ad out. Anyone with eyes could see he was wanting for a woman of his own. I couldn't let my insecurities ruin his chance at happiness.

"Well, I wish you the best of luck. Hopefully you don't get another saloon girl. Could you point me in the direction of the dressmaker's shop?"

"You take a left out the front door and it's on this side of the street. It says Marta's Dress Shop on the sign out in front of the store."

Hesitating, I opened my mouth and closed it again. "Okay," I said slowly. "What does the word *Marta's* look like?" The heat in my cheeks was growing more uncomfortable by the moment.

Jeremiah lowered his voice and leaned forward. "Do you not have any words?"

"No, sir. I didn't do much schooling in Chicago." The admission tied my stomach in knots. Not the sort sailors used on their boats, but the kind of knots lawmen tied hangman's nooses with.

He grabbed the package out of my hands and I stifled a yelp. He was going to see what I'd done to the dress and hate me for it and something deep inside of me wanted Jeremiah to accept me for Luke. He didn't open it though. Instead he pulled a pencil from a wooden cylinder on the other side of the counter and wrote a jumble of letters across the front of my package.

"It looks like that. Look for this letter first because there aren't any other stores that start with M."

Mortified, I took the package from his outstretched hand and shuffled out the front door just as the postman entered. Not knowing my letters and reading hadn't been as embarrassing in Chicago because the lot I hung around with weren't of the highly educated sort. Most of us couldn't read or write, but we didn't need to either. Those were the skills of the frivolous. But here, I found myself silently hoping Jeremiah wouldn't tell Luke of my shortcomings.

I couldn't see the signs well enough without standing in the street, so by the time I matched the first word to that of a shop, the bottom six inches of my dress hem were soaked and a wet, dingy brown. And my shoes? Well those hadn't even been cleaned after my first day fresh off the carriage, so now they boasted a second helping of muddy grit on them. I stomped my heels off as best I could on the wicker mat out front and trudged into the shop.

It was a small room but smelled of clean fabric, and the two small windows out front held pretty sunflower yellow curtains. I smiled at the beautiful readymade dresses that hung from the wood panel walls in all of the colors imaginable.

A gray haired woman with a bun that sat right atop her head looked over her spectacles with a frown of disdain. "Don't come in any further," she said in a voice that cracked with age. "You're tracking mud all through my store."

I'd lifted the hem of my dress to avoid it but my shoes had, in fact, made little spots where the soles still held the remnants of my dirt laden hike. "Oh, terribly sorry."

"What do you want?"

The malice in her voice made it hard to put my thoughts together and I stuttered. "I-I needed a dress mended. Redone, really, to better fit me."

"I don't make dresses for whores."

"It's not a working dress. I wanted a fine dress to wear to town. See, I'm not like that anymore." She stared at me blankly and I arched my eyebrow. "I don't whore anymore."

"You and your kind won't find any help here."

A slow boil rose from my toes and I fought the urge to give that grievous woman the tongue lashing of her life. My kind? What did that even mean? I had to do what I had to do to survive. I didn't have some frilly dress shop to be able to make a living, or a man to support me in Chicago. It was just me and if I didn't work, I didn't eat. And despite my occupation, I was still a person.

"You have a nice day," I gritted through clenched teeth as I made my way carefully back out the door.

I sat with a huff on a wooden backed bench outside. If the only dressmaker in town wouldn't help me, then how in tarnation was I going to ever get a proper dress? A traitorous tear slipped the corner of my eye and I wiped it with the back of my hand before it made a full trail down my cheek. I sniffed.

"Are you already done?" Luke said.

"Aaah!" I yelled in the most unfeminine sound that ever graced anyone's throat. Lovely.

Luke rubbed his ear and reached for the door handle to the dress shop.

Panicked, I asked, "What're you doing?"

He hesitated. "I'm going to pay the lady."

"No need. I've decided to go somewhere else."

"There is nowhere else," he said slowly as a suspicious frown commandeered his face.

"Then I'll try to fix it myself."

"What's going on?"

"I'm hungry."

His glorious emerald eyes tightened. "You know you play on my instincts when you tell me you need something like that. I think you do it to change the subject."

"I know nothing about that," I argued. It was mostly true. "I just know I'm hungry." And with that I stood and stomped toward the saloon.

"Ho!" he said, gripping my arm. "We aren't eating at the cathouse."

"Well, why the devil not?"

"Because I've been with half the girls in there and it ain't the place for us to have our first meal in public together. We'll eat at Cotton's instead."

I stopped and searched his face. "Will they serve a girl like me?"

His eyes softened. "Cotton's serves everyone. C'mon, it's across the street."

Fantastic. More mud. Except when I took the last step to plop my poor abused shoe into the filth, Luke bent over and lifted me easily into his arms. I was just as shocked as the choking gossipers in front of the land office. It did warm me up inside and the view of Luke's smooth jawline was quite lovely, so I wrapped my hands delicately around his neck and enjoyed the ride. Once across, he offered his arm gallantly and smiled when I fit my fingers into the crook of it.

Chapter Seven
Kristina

Cotton's was a boisterous eatery with long tables filled with town folks enjoying their meals. The smell of the place was a mixture of beef, gravy, and heaven. My stomach growled loudly, but I doubted anyone heard it over the noise. Luke pulled me over to a couple of empty seats on the far end of the room and we sat amongst a raucous group of arguing men, and a husband and wife with their six young children spread between them. I smiled at the woman but she was too preoccupied with her family of picky eaters to smile back. Or so I told myself.

A feminine voice with a thick southern accent sounded from behind me. "What can I do you for?"

The woman was young, around my own age, and thanks to the Emancipation, was a newly minted freedwoman. Her caramel colored skin was smooth and rich and her dark hair was pulled back out of her face. She might've very well been the prettiest lady I'd ever seen.

"What's the special," Luke asked.

"Trout's been selling like hot cakes today, Mr. Luke."

"Sold," he said with an easy smile.

"And for you?" she asked me.

I wasn't much of a fish eater. "I need something that'll stick to my ribs. What's your favorite?"

"My beef stew's so thick you can eat it with a fork."

"That sounds exactly right. I'll have that."

She hurried away and swished through the kitchen doors and that was when I noticed her dress. It was a fine looking garment with puff sleeves, and white eyelet lace accents. The fabric was floral and the fit looked lovely on her slim body. Moody Marta wouldn't likely be making the woman's dresses if she was opposed to working with a saloon girl, so where'd she get it?

"Are there a lot of freedmen around here?" I asked Luke.

"Trudy's the only one that I know of around these parts."

The gray-haired man sitting directly across from me spat on the floor. "And it's a good thing too. One of them's one too many around here, if you ask me."

"Well, nobody asked you," I gritted out.

Trudy returned and set metal plates overflowing with food in front of Luke and I, and the man sneered at her. "In fact, if I had my way, we'd be running this one out of town."

"Shut your gaping pie hole or you'll catch flies," I spat. "I *said* nobody asked for your rotten opinion, and I meant it, sir."

The man stood so fast his chair fell with a glorious crash behind him, and the room went deathly still. In his eyes burned the hellfire of hatred and it was aimed directly at me. A bone chilling sound I'd never heard in my entire nineteen years ripped from Luke as he stood in a motion so fast he blurred. And with a great shuddering thunk, he stabbed his hunting knife so deeply into the table, it could likely be seen from underneath. The gleaming blade landed just a hair away from the tender skin between the man's pointer and middle finger. The air around Luke grew thicker by the moment until it was hard to breathe.

My breath caught somewhere in my throat and the fine hairs on my arms rose as something just below the senses filled the room.

"Advance another centimeter on my woman, and I'll slit you from adam's apple to cock," Luke growled into the man's face.

The man's skin went pallid and the whites of his eyes shown all around the tired gray color of his irises. His pupils had all but disappeared and a fine sweat sprang up on his forehead. "My apologies," he whispered.

Luke's voice was as deep as it was quiet. "To her."

The man cleared his throat and nodded his head to me. "My apologies, ma'am."

At some point in the exchange, Trudy had placed her hand on my arm. "You two been disturbing everyone's dinner and now you're coming with me." She picked up our plates and swished back toward the kitchen. "The rest of ya'll get back to eating."

Desperate for an escape and a bite of that beef stew, I followed before Luke even pulled his knife from the table. Something about having him at my back put a chill up my neck though, so I scuttled sideways and waited for him to catch up.

"Leslie," Trudy said to a fair haired lady finishing up a plate of food. "I'm taking my break. You get on out there and let me know if they get too rowdy for you."

The girl smiled shyly at me as she passed to put her plate in a deep bellied sink before she headed out to handle the crowd. Another woman worked tirelessly over a couple of stoves on the other side of the room and Trudy set our plates on the table Leslie had been eating at.

Luke ate in earnest like he hadn't almost stabbed a man, and I put a bite in my mouth tentatively with one eye on him and one on Trudy.

"I know what you are, Mr. Luke. And if you keep carrying on the way you did in there, the whole town's going to know what you are too."

He looked up slowly from his meal and the expression on his face made my blood go cold.

"What do you mean?" I asked her.

Trudy's dark eyes studied my face for a long time before she sighed. "I just mean a man with a temper is all. You'd do best to not trifle with a temper like his. Wouldn't want to see you get hurt."

"I'd never hurt her," he said quietly.

"And I'd like to believe it, but I've been around and I've seen your kind say the same thing just before their poor girl goes missing."

Luke went back to eating. "That ain't me."

"I've said my piece and now I'll leave you alone. Thank you kindly for what you did in there, Ms.—"

"Kristina. You can just call me Kristina," I offered.

"Kristina. Now it was mighty sweet of you to defend me, but it's pointless. They'll say what they want and then come in here tomorrow and say it again. You can't change their stubborn minds about anything."

"Where'd you get your dress?" I blurted out. She was the first woman to talk to me civilly since I'd been here and I didn't want her to leave.

Her smile was a surprised one. "I made it myself. I was a house servant and did a lot of sewing and cooking. I picked up the same habits after the war, but the difference is now I get paid for the work."

"Will you make one for me? I tried to sew one yesterday but it turned out awful, and I can't just keep going around town in a whore's dress when I'm not one anymore and Ms. Marta…well—"

Trudy raised her hand and stopped my ramblings. "Enough said. I'll work on your dress and charge you less than that snooty old windbag would anyhow."

"No, we'll pay you the same," Luke said, tossing a napkin over his empty plate. "I insist."

"That's not what I usually charge," Trudy argued.

"Well," Luke said through a sly grin. "You ain't seen what she's done to that poor dress yet."

I slapped him on the arm but it only made his obnoxious grin bigger.

****

Luke

Trudy was lying. She didn't mean I was just a man with a temper. She knew the truth and it was written all over her face when she talked to me. I'd have to corner her and find out how she knew about me. She'd obviously rubbed elbows with wolves before and I was itching to see if I knew them or not. I knew most of the families from here to Texas, but that wasn't too hard. There were very few packs left. If what she said was true and a girl disappeared...the thought of man-eaters made my stomach lurch. I wouldn't ever hurt a hair on Kristina's head, no matter how hard she pissed me off. I wouldn't let myself, but no amount of convincing was going to comfort Trudy. Over time, I'd just have to prove I wasn't a danger.

Trudy's knowledge of our dark secret put us all at risk, and if she took a fancy to protecting Kristina from a threat she imagined, and decided to share that information with the town? Well, me and Jeremiah would be hanging by a noose with our boots on fire at dawn.

Trudy led us down the street to the tiny house she shared with her man. She needed Kristina's measurements before she went to work trying to save that tattered dress. A little shiver of excitement lit me up. You could tell a lot about the quality of a person by their reaction to unexpected situations, and so far Kristina had been entertaining to watch. She'd stood right up for Trudy in Cotton's, and even if it was none of our business, pride had filled me when she popped off to that jack-wagon, Ray Ellerby. He'd been asking for it for years, and it was tiny, pretty, spirited little Kristina who gave him the walloping he deserved. Maybe I'd gone too far with the knife, but the animal inside was happy with the way I'd defended my mate, so it was pretty hard to stay mad at myself.

Trudy opened the front door to her home and I watched Kristina's face as she introduced her man.

Elias Jones was tall, good-looking, easy smiling, and unquestionably white. Kristina's eyes went wide with surprise just before she burst out into a grin bright as the sun when he shook her hand. I swear, I was going to get more enjoyment out of watching her animated expressions than I'd ever know what to do with.

Kristina's hair was right pretty all done up in pins, and her face was clear and glowing without all that powder. Her lips were full and a shade of pink I'd only seen on wildflowers. A delicate nose and fine eyebrows just a shade darker than her sandy colored hair graced the feminine shape of her face. I wanted her and even the meanest, most stubborn bits of me had been taken with her and given up without a fight. I made a pathetic monster.

I had trouble paying attention to my conversation with Elias because Trudy was delicately wrapping Kristina's chest with a flimsy measuring tape. I wouldn't miss other men's eyes on her cleavage, but I'd miss the dress for my own pleasures. Maybe we'd better keep it for fun later on.

Fifteen minutes later, Kristina came out of the back room wearing a fine dress of pinstripe navy with cream details. It fit her everywhere but the chest and the women laughed as Trudy let the stitches out a bit to better fit her shape. I was proud to have her on my arm in her whore get-up, but now I'd be dragging her to town every chance I got.

Damn, she was a pretty woman.

"I'll charge you half price for this one, and then you'll have two to wear," Trudy said.

"Do you like it?" Kristina asked me with the most appealing look of hope in her eyes.

I'd like it better on the floor of my bedroom, but she probably wouldn't appreciate the compliment. Instead, I smiled easily and said, "That's a fine dress for you."

She lit up like the North Star.

Trudy bit one last knot and stood back to admire her handiwork. "I'll have the other one done in a couple of days if you want to stop by and pick it up."

"What do we owe you?" I asked.

"Does one-fifty for the dress I'm re-sewing and two dollars for the new one sound fair?"

I hadn't a guess on what women's fashion cost, but it likely would've been a pretty penny more at Marta's. I handed the money to Elias while the girls said their goodbyes.

Trudy wrapped up the old whoring dress and walked back as far as Cotton's to take her turn feeding the masses again. After she waved us off, Kristina put her delicate hand in the crook of my arm as she hummed a song I'd never heard before. Did she feel safe with me? The answer meant more than I ever thought it could.

Lifting her over the muddy street was something I didn't mind one bit. She was so light and her body so warm where her clothes touched mine. "We're going to have to get you a horse sooner than later," I said.

"And you'll need to learn to drive the wagon in case you ever need to get to town without me or Jeremiah."

Her arms wrapped slowly around the back of my neck as I walked. "Horses are terrifying."

"I don't imagine you're afraid of much, Ms. Yeaton. You'll do just fine on a horse. The mare you saw the other night would be the best one for you, but she's got a foal on her now and won't be ready to separate for a while." I lifted her into the seat of the wagon and leaned against it until it groaned against my weight. From this position, we were almost eye level. The blue of her eyes rivaled a clear summer sky.

A beautiful challenge swam in her expression and her elegant nostrils flared slightly. "I saw a polka dotted horse one time. When you find me a polka dotted horse, then I'll ride."

Dropping my gaze to her lips, I matched her smile. I liked a challenge too. "A polka dotted horse it'll be then. Wait here while I load up our order from last week. Do you need anything from the general store?"

She fidgeted. "I have enough money left from my travels to buy an apron if you get a cheap one."

I nodded slowly. "An apron would probably do you good. Save your dresses in the kitchen and keep you from burning your hands. You can keep your money if you want to though, Kristina. I don't mind getting you the things you need."

"I've always taken care of myself, and while I appreciate you buying the dresses, I truly do, I need to buy my apron."

Her hand stretched out with a small coin purse and it jangled softly as it hit mine. Our fingers touched for just a moment before she pulled away. Her hands were soft and smooth—a woman's tender skin—and I would've given anything I owned to feel her fingertips on me again.

Turning abruptly, I made my escape before I said something that would really scare her off. I looked back once and she was watching me with the most confounding expression. Worry and intrigue all wrapped into one.

Chapter Eight
Kristina

The apron was made of cotton and edged in ruffled eyelet lace. The softness of the material brushed my skin as I ran revering hands over the folded fabric in my lap. It would make a handsome contrast up against the dark blue of my new dress. The first chance I got, I would sneak into Luke's room and admire it in his full-length mirror.

Luke had been sending sideways glances in my direction the majority of the long buggy ride home, and a mixed feeling of pleasure and self-consciousness washed over me. Maybe he was looking because he liked what he saw, or maybe he liked me better in the other dress.

"Rains will be here tonight," he said to no one in particular.

Jeremiah lay in the bed of the wagon with his hat over his face. "Yep," he mumbled. "I feel it too."

They had to be playing with me. The sky was a beautiful deep blue without a cloud in sight. The air smelled of late summer flowers and earth, and my hair, which curled into a wild bird's nest at the first sign of moisture, was quiet and content under its pins. Luke's face was passive as he pulled the team around a pot hole as deep as a grave. If he was joking, I was missing the punch line somehow.

The entrance to the Dawson ranch already seemed familiar, even though I'd only seen it twice before, and a little piece of me I didn't know had tensed up relaxed when we turned for home. Funny how a place could feel so familiar this quickly. I'd worked a year at a brothel in Chicago with a tiny room of my own and everything, and not once did it ever settle in my gut as home. Maybe it had to do with my open door policy to strangers, or my discomfort with life there, but there had to be more to it than that. Something deep down and instinctual. Despite the wolf attack, which still gave me chills when I thought of it, and the threat of Indians, I hadn't felt this safe in as long as I could remember. Though my mind skittered away from thoughts on what was wrong with Luke, and I knew there was something very wrong, my heart didn't seem to care and pressed me to move farther inside his bubble of protection.

Not even a little piece of me doubted he would've made good on his promise to slit that man open on my account, but then he offered me his arm, and carried me across the mud so as not to get my shoes dirty. And he'd bought me lunch, and dresses and helped me out of the carriage. Admittedly, he frightened me, but he intrigued me much more. And besides, I'd seen real beasts of men in Chicago—horrible men with violent appetites. I'd lost friends to men who satisfied their needs by killing the women they bedded. It was a terrible way to go and more often than not, those monsters got away with murder.

I'd heard Trudy when she said to be careful, and I would. I'd be wary of his temper because I'd seen too much not to take heed to warnings like hers, but my heart sang that Luke had been telling the truth when he said he'd never hurt me.

"Whoa," Luke said as he pulled the horses to a stop. "Jeremiah?"

"Yep, I smell them too."

Luke's nostrils flared and he jerked his head to the west. "Stay here with her. I'm going to see what they want."

The wagon shifted and righted itself as he hopped off the side. A cold clenching feeling came over me. "What's happening?" I asked.

"Indians," Jeremiah said shortly as he jumped out of the back, rocking the buggy once again.

I held the apron tighter, like the fabric would protect me. I'd only seen a handful of Indians in my lifetime and they'd looked like terrifying warriors with fearsome face paint and animal claws hanging from necklaces.

Ten spine-chilling minutes later, Luke returned and three Indians melted out of the woods beside him. He talked to the one in front with a solemn look on his face, but he obviously felt comfortable enough to bend down and pluck a long stem of grass before putting it in mouth. The tan skinned men wore buckskin leathers and the one talking to Luke wore an elaborate head dress with a knot of animal tails trailing down the side. Various tendrils of beadwork snaked down his chest and his face was free of paint. His sun leathered skin was deeply wrinkled and his dark eyes seemed to miss nothing. The two men who followed silently behind wore similar clothing, but only wore a single feather in each of their braided hair.

"Kristina, this is Kicking Bull and his two sons. They are Ute and come down this way to trade from time to time. Kicking Bull, this is my woman, Kristina."

The old man smiled, the white of his teeth a stark contrast to his dark skin. "It would take a wily she-wolf to tame this one."

Luke cleared his throat and the slight shake of his head wasn't lost on me.

Kicking bull said something to his sons in Ute and they all laughed. One of them slapped Luke on the back and for all his reluctance, a grin still sprouted from his face.

"Kicking Bull says they followed a couple of men in. They came from the southwest, didn't use a road and ended up at our house. He said they went through our home but didn't take anything that he could see. The men left a few hours ago."

I tried to keep my voice from shaking but my mind had gone to the darkest place. "What did these men look like?"

"Kicking Bull said one had long hair down his back the color of corn, and the other was short with a scar across his eyebrow."

"Hells bells," I breathed. I had no doubt my past would eventually come back to haunt me, but I'd never in a million years thought she would find me so soon.

Luke and Jeremiah's eyes crashed onto me, and their looks of suspicion became eerily alike. "Thank you, Kicking Bull. Is there anything you lack?" Luke asked.

"Not now," the old man said. "This information is to maintain our alliance."

"Well, take these to your grandson's just the same," Luke said, pulling two peppermint sticks from a sack he'd retrieved from the general store. He tipped his hat before the men disappeared into the woods.

When Luke was seated again with reins in hand, he asked, "Mind telling us how much trouble we're in, Ms. Yeaton?"

The formality of my proper name on his lips stung. I clamped my mouth shut, unwilling to talk about it before I sorted through my racing thoughts. I thought I would've been long married before her lackeys showed up. Luke would've had a reason to protect me then. But now? My heart pounded in my ears like the roar of a steam engine.

I was as good as dead.

The silence that followed was filled with a slow fury. Luke didn't spare a glance for me the rest of the night. He was angry with my quiet refusal to tell him about my past, but every time I opened my mouth to confess the danger I'd put he and his brother in, the words got caught in my throat until I was drowning. The moment I told him would be the moment he told me to pack my bags, and the selfish, horrible little bits of me wanted to hang on to my home for every last second I could.

Dinner was a miserable affair filled with pushing my food around my plate and daring not even once to look into Luke's disappointed eyes. He and Jeremiah disappeared after dinner to button down the hatches in preparation for the imaginary storm and I retired to my room to tidy the things Matthew Streider and Ricky Burns tossed around. I was angry with the idea that those awful men touched my undergarments. The only man I wanted seeing or touching those was furiously working to avoid me. If I listened hard enough, I could hear an occasional distant murmur as he and his brother tossed orders back and forth.

Damn those beastly trackers for ruining everything.

Sleep came fitfully. The boys hadn't come in as far as I could hear and I was too cowardly to peek my head outside the door and check to make sure. I dreamt of horrible things—creatures with glowing eyes, and snarling fangs snapping at my ankles as I ran through the forests in search of safety. Just as I would feel I lost them, the creatures of the night would reappear in front of me and chase me back where I came from in a loop of endless circles. Though my legs never tired as was sometimes the case in the fog of dreams, I never got a break from the rampant fear that tore at me either. I woke with a start to the sound of my own screams, only to realize they weren't mine at all. They were the screams of the wind outside my window.

How had those Dawson boys known? The smooth wood of the window frame was cool under the palms of my hands and I searched in vain for the voices I could've sworn I heard through the howling of the storm. There. One short yell wafted to me on the whipping currents. My eyes were strained, yet I still failed to see anything past the sideways rain that pelted the house.

What if that was Luke yelling for help out there?

I flew into action. I didn't pay any mind to trivial things such as shoes or a shawl to cover the thin cotton of my nightdress. I only sought to get to him as soon as I could. Something had gone terribly wrong, and the very marrow in my bones sang with urgency. I fumbled in the darkness, but familiar enough with my surroundings, I searched the tables with the pads of my hands until they landed on an unlit lantern and a set of matches. My trembling fingers dropped the first but ignited the second and when it was lit, I shut the small hatch and turned the lantern up as bright as it would go. Bolting out the door, I didn't even bother to shut it behind me.

I froze on the porch, desperate to realize the direction the yelling was coming from but the wind carried the sound to and fro in a frenzied fashion. Maybe he was at the barn. I scrambled down the steps toward its general direction as the rain pelted the side of my face until it stung. Sliding and slipping on the muddy earth, my toes scrabbled for purchase and as a great lightning flash lit the sky, I gasped and slid to a stop.

A black horse bore down on me in the rain, running full speed with a terrified look in the whites of his eyes. He didn't turn his head from side to side as his hooves pounded the earth toward me, and I doubted he would be able to see me at all before he ran me over. Fear kept the scream lodged in my mouth and I backed up only a step as he thundered toward me. Another lightning flash lit his wet coat and he let out an animal scream as he rushed right for me.

A tremendous weight hit me from the side and the great animal passed so close the wind was blocked for just a moment from the proximity of his giant body. My lantern had been flung to the side and lay dark somewhere in the mud, but strong arms picked me up and an instantaneous relief flooded my veins. The stinging rain was relentless against my face and eyes, so I closed them tightly and held onto his neck. I'd made it farther from the house than I thought, and the journey back took a long time. So long, in fact, I frowned and tried to open one of my eyes against the rain. My feet hit the mud as realization dawned on me of my vital mistake.

Matthew Streider grabbed my hair in an iron grip as he covered my mouth with his giant hand. "Death by horse trampling is too gentle an end for you, girl," he growled through foul breath.

I bit his hand until the taste of blood was bitter and iron against my tongue, but before I could scream, he slapped me hard enough to stop any warning I meant to give. The darkness was consuming as a million stars shone through the haze of rain and blurred the corners of my vision.

"No, girl. Don't you pass out on me now. We've got a long way to go together."

He hoisted me over his shoulder, and though I beat my fists against his back and kicked wildly, he only gripped my legs tighter with fingers that seemed to dig to my bones. The wind screamed louder than I ever could and I fought until I was exhausted.

Ricky waited in the woods with two horses, and after I was firmly tied by the hands to the back of a big bay, they mounted up and set out at a quick clip. I struggled to keep up. My feet were bare, and though the mud was soft between my toes, the tree roots, rocks, stickers, and other such cutting items didn't care about my comfort. Desperate, I tried to step carefully and avoid a twisted ankle but it would be only a matter of time before I couldn't use them anymore and would be dragged to my death behind the horse. Trampling by the great black horse would've been a much easier end than the one I was headed for.

A sob tore from my throat. I would never see Luke again. I'd die knowing he was angry with me. I'd die before I ever got to tell him the truth about myself; before he ever saw the real me.

My thin nightdress was soaked through and the fabric clung to me like a second skin. It didn't hide a single inch of my body, but the men in front only had eyes for their escape with me as their captive.

We walked for hours in that awful storm before the first light of dawn hit the horizon. I'd never been so thankful for illuminating lightening as I was that night. It had prolonged my life, but as daylight drew closer, I wished I were dead already. My head and shoulders sagged with exhaustion and my maimed, bloody feet dragged. Every muscle in my body screamed against its treatment, and the ropes around my wrists were soaked in the watered down blood of my struggles. My cheek had its own pulse where Matthew slapped me and my eye didn't seem to want to open anymore. The rain slowed to a constant drizzle and fine water droplets fell from of the ends of my eyelashes.

Ricky pulled his horse up short and dismounted. "I have to take a piss. Grab some jerky out of your saddle bag so we can eat on the go."

Matthew's long blond hair was plastered to his back under a cowboy hat and he turned with a vicious grin. "You thought you was home free and now look at you." His eyes traveled the length of my exposed body as he fished around for their breakfast.

My tied hands lay conveniently in front of my thighs, but my breasts puckered against the wet material with nothing to hide them. I lifted my chin defiantly. Nothing else in my life had broken me, and I'd be damned if Matthew Streider would be the one to do it in my last few breaths.

Ricky stood in front of me and undid his belt buckle. The corner of his mouth turned up in the most evil smile I'd ever seen, and he pulled out his filthy cock and began relieving his bladder on my knees. I wouldn't give him the satisfaction of running. Instead I spat in his face.

The look of hellish fury made my insides turn to ice, but I kept my face carefully still. He wiped his face slowly and then lifted his fist. It would be my last blow and I started to close my eyes with the acceptance.

Luke came down like a ferocious hellion, moving so fast it defied what a man should be able to do. The flash of green in his eyes held only focus and unbridled savagery. He jumped on Ricky's back as I scrambled out of the way, then slit his throat neatly. I stared in wide-eyed bewilderment as my tormentor's neck split open and blood gurgled forth. Luke shoved his face in the dirt and swung his gaze to Matthew.

No time to mount a horse, he was already running through the trees. Luke flipped his long hunting knife dexterously and threw it with such strength, it had a sound to it. Over and over the knife flipped until it was lodged in Matthew's hand, which was thus pinned to a large tree. Ricky gulped at air like a drowning trout and Luke slowly stalked the other flailing tracker. Matthew grunted in pain and tried desperately to dislodge the bloodied knife. His movement became frantic as Luke approached.

"Please," he begged.

"Shut up," Luke growled. "You're so brave you steal a woman in the night and drag her behind a horse? The least you can do is die well." He put his foot against the tree and yanked the knife out.

Matthew hadn't a chance to run because Luke's hand was around his throat and dragging him, gasping, back to me. He unbuckled the man's gun belt and tossed it over the saddle of the horse I was tied to and threw him in the mud beneath me.

Something in the tone of Luke's voice raised the hair on the nape of my neck. "It's time for your first shooting lesson. This man is yours to kill. You can give retribution for your abuses or you can charge me with carrying it out. Either way, you'll hold a gun to his head and make the decision who pulls the trigger."

He dragged his knife across the leg of his pants, leaving two smears of crimson, then cut the ropes that bound my wrists in one confident motion without nicking my chafed skin. My arms sagged to my sides and I swallowed a sob at the relief.

Luke looked like an avenging angel in his damp duster and hat and as he moved his jacket aside, he pulled a dry pistol and handed it to me, grip first. He pointed to the hammer but I shook my head.

"This ain't my first shooting lesson."

His gaze collided with mine and surprise pooled in the emerald depths. He nodded and gave me some room. Pulling the hammer back was an effort because of my injured wrists but I kept my face straight and pointed the barrel down at Matthew's forehead.

"You thought you was home free, and now look at you," I said in a trembling voice, repeating his calloused words.

The sniveling man began to cry, and his words were no longer understandable. He reeked of urine and fear.

"She'll send more people," I said to Luke. "The woman who's

after me will keep sending them until I'm dead or back at the brothel."
Silence filled the woods. "You want to send her a warning?"
"I do."
Luke nodded once and I eased the hammer back down before lowering the Peace Maker. In a motion as fluid as stream water, he had my tormenter pinned against a tree while he choked the life from him. "Who sent you here?"
"She knows," Matthew rasped, pointing at me.
"What's her name?" Luke ground out.
"Evelynn French."
"You tell Evelynn French and all of her known associates what's happened here today. You tell her if she sends even one more person, I'll travel to Chicago and personally slit her throat. Repeat it."
Matthew floundered for air and gasped, "If she sends anyone else for the girl, you'll travel to Chicago and slit her throat."
"Now, run before my woman changes her mind." Luke dropped the man and waited until Matthew was fleeing on horseback before he returned to me.
My legs shook and twitched so badly, I was struggling to stay upright. He shed his duster and draped it around my shoulders. "Did they hurt you where I can't see?"
I knew what he was asking but there hadn't been time for them to get that far. I shook my head. He tried to pry my swollen eye open enough to get a look at it, and the tenderness with which he touched me ripped my heart right open.
"I'm sorry," I whispered. A tear streaked down my cheek but I was helpless to stop it. "I thought I was going to die before I got to tell you I was sorry. I wanted to tell you but I didn't want you to throw me away."
"Shhhh," he crooned. "It'll mend."
He let out a sharp whistle and Jeremiah appeared through the trees, dragging two horses behind him.
"Can you hold on and ride?"
Well why the hell not? I'd been dragged behind one of the giant creatures and it hadn't killed me or even kicked at me once. Why not try my hand at riding one like a normal person. "Sure."
He slung himself gracefully into the saddle and grasped my elbow as Jeremiah hoisted me from below. I didn't look so elegant, but at the moment I didn't give a fig about how I looked. After I was upright and had my arms around Luke's taut waist, he made a clicking sound with his tongue and kicked the horse under us. He held my arms in front of him like he thought I would fall asleep and slide off. Wise man.

Chapter Nine
Luke

K ristina's face was seven shades of blue by the time we arrived back home. I wanted to slit her kidnapper's throat all over again every time she winced. Evelynn French, whoever she was, would pay for the injustice done to Kristina's body, and that was a promise. The warning wouldn't be enough. Not for a woman who'd sanctioned this kind of torment, and sooner rather than later, I was going to have to handle Kristina's past personally. If I didn't, we'd never be free of the threat.

She was white as a corpse when I lifted her from my horse and carried her into the house. Jeremiah hadn't said a word since we realized she was missing, but I'd seen the ghosts in his eyes. Kristina's treatment likely conjured memories of Anna. My brother wouldn't sleep for days. It'd probably be best he run as an animal until he could repress the pain again.

Kristina shivered violently against the cool air of the morning and I started a roaring fire in the stone hearth. She emerged from her room in the navy dress but it wasn't lost on me that she left tiny pools of bloody footprints in her wake and stepped with a significant limp. My hands shook with the anger that promised to drag me down into the mouth of hell. She sat in the chair I'd pulled in front of the warmth of the fireplace and I checked her ravaged feet as gently as I could. I had to focus on her needs and then I could let the beast take me over. I could run and kill things and relieve the red savagery that scorched me from the inside out.

She pressed her hand tenderly on the side of my face and the touch of her quelled the darkness roiling inside.

"Thank you for saving me," she whispered.

Her pooled blue eyes were so earnest I had to steady my breathing. Sighing, I slid a hand over hers and said, "Anytime," and meant it.

I warmed a pan of water over the stove and set it beneath her to wash her feet in. Once the dirt was washed away, the damage was easy enough to see. Long gashes and punctures dotted her skin and a small rock still clung to the depths of one of the slices nearest her big toe.

"Best if you don't watch," I said before pulling it out.

Such a brave little thing she was. The arms of the chair gave an uncomfortable creak under her white knuckled grasp, but that was the only sound she gave the entire time I tended her wounds. And I'd seen the fierceness in her face when she spat on that man. No matter what, they wouldn't have broken her, and a swelling pride filled me up like an underwater spring feeding a well. My woman was a stouthearted one. Maybe she'd be able to handle my dark secrets yet.

Her wrists were rubbed raw and would likely scar, but there was nothing to be done about them but keep infection away. Her face was an awful sight and she could only open the one good eye, but it just needed time and tenderness.

The tiny hairs on my ears warned me of the sound a split moment before the wolf's howl rang out, a long and lonesome cry that told of pain and sorrow. With my brother changed, I couldn't leave Kristina alone to satisfy to my own animalistic needs. With Jeremiah out of commission, the running of the ranch fell to me. My wolf would have to wait, so I accepted that the pain in my bones wouldn't find relief for a while yet.

The rain pelted on the window glass as I pulled a blanket over her lap. "You can't be moving around too much for a while, you hear?"

Even the slight nod she gave seemed an effort. Stouthearted though she may be, invincible she was not.

****

Kristina

The pounding rain was relentless in the days that followed my kidnapping. Jeremiah had disappeared with the sunshine and left Luke to run himself ragged with the daily chores that came with running a ranch. I was no use at all as he wouldn't let me stand on my feet until they were healed. He checked in often, but it was easy to see the strain etched into the weariness in his face. On the second day, he placed a book on the small table beside my bed, and though I smiled my thanks, unless it was a picture book, it wouldn't keep the boredom at bay.

Unless I felt like finding all the letter M's from cover to cover. I dog eared the pages in a different place each day and said a silent prayer every evening that Luke wouldn't want to discuss the storyline. I wouldn't admit it to him, but I'd happily found something else to occupy my time. The sewing basket Jeremiah had dragged in for me to ruin that dress was actually a well of knowledge. It housed unsewn quilt pieces and needles and every thread color you could imagine. It held thimbles and measuring ribbons, and yarns, and most importantly, in the bottom of the basket I found a small picture booklet that illustrated the different stitches. Now here was a book I could wrap my head around.

My pride was wounded with the maiming of that first dress and the sewing basket presented a tantalizing challenge. If I couldn't be of any use around the ranch until my feet healed enough, then by golly, I was going to teach myself to sew if I had to prick every inch of skin my fingers possessed. By day four, I'd successfully sewn together six quilt pieces and mastered every stitch and knot in the booklet.

Luke would be in at any time to eat a hurried lunch before heading back out, and I sat staring at the door like a cat hunting a mouse. The miniature quilt was pulled taut in my hands as I tested and retested the strength of the stitches. By the time his boots sounded on the porch, I was so strung out, I hobbled excitedly to the door before he could even lift the latch.

I threw open the barrier between us. "Look what I did!"

"Whoa," he yelled, putting his arm up defensively. "Woman, you scared the dickens out of me. Ain't you supposed to be resting?"

"My feet don't hurt very much anymore. Look!" My voice actually squeaked.

"Did you sew this?" He fingered the stitches and the corner of his mouth turned up in the most delicious smile.

I breathed for that smile. "Mmm hmm."

"Is this what you've been doing while I'm out?"

I couldn't even control my smile if I wanted to. "Yep!"

"Well, Ms. Yeaton. We may make a frontier woman out of you yet."

"Eeee," I squealed and jumped into his arms.

No doubt he was surprised, but he recovered nicely. The sound of his laugh was a sweet vibration against my chest and he hugged me soundly. "I have something I want to show you."

"Well, sir, I'm sorry to say you may not be able to top a partly sewn quilt."

"Probably not. Wait here." He disappeared around the edge of the house and I limped to the stairs to strain my neck after him. What could that man be up to?

What he brought around that corner topped my tiny quilt a hundred fold. In his hands lay a slack, simple rope and behind him walked the most beautiful horse I'd ever laid eyes on. She wasn't as big as Luke's great black beast, but she was slim, muscular, and made for speed with a fine little head. Her face was completely white, but from the neck on, she was the most appealing red chestnut color that shone in the sun. Four white socks made a beautiful contrast, and the red in her coat ran until it stopped suddenly at a white snowcap blanket that cloaked her hind end. And in that snowcap were perfectly round spots of chestnut fur.

Luke had tracked down a polka dotted horse for me.

His eyes never left my face. "Do you like her?"

"She's beautiful. Where'd you find her?"

"Traded with Kicking Bull for her. He brought her in a couple of days ago, but I needed to work on riding her with a saddle. She's been ridden bareback since she was big enough and needed to get used to the extra weight. She still won't take a bit though so you're going to have to steer with a rope until we get her used to it."

"Did Kicking Bull breed her?"

"No, he's Ute. The spotted horses come from the Nez Perce but they trade them pretty regularly. They call her a Palouse horse, for the river that runs through their territory." He fluttered his fingers toward her red mane that lifted in the wind. "I tried to take the feathers out, but they're tied in there to last a while."

A long, three feather bunch hung from wisps of her hair. "Leave them. They suit her."

"You ready to get on her?" he asked.

He was a tricky one. I really hadn't any intention of learning to ride a horse other than the buggy. I thought if I gave him some impossible task such as getting me a spotted horse, I'd never be pressured to ride one on my own. And here he showed up with this magnificent creature and exactly what I challenged him for in just a few days? *Impressive, Mr. Dawson.* "Is she gentle?"

"She's got a sweet disposition, but she's used to being ridden fast. She'll go when you need her to go."

Tendrils of uncertainty filled my stomach. "Right. Just let me put shoes on."

By the time I was back, the mare was tied to the rail out front and Luke was nowhere to be seen. I hobbled back into the house and snatched a carrot out of the root cellar. If she was to be my horse and mine alone, I had to make a good first impression.

She whinnied and tossed her head as I approached, and though my muscles tensed with an edge of fear, I stepped in front of the rail and offered my bribe. She crunched off a good bite and wiggled her lips at me for more. I couldn't help the delighted giggles that came from me at her silly face. I petted her while she finished the treat and spoke softly. When she was finished, she nudged around my dress pockets for more, then left her head resting close to my body as I stroked her.

"What are you going to name her?" Luke asked. He pulled his great black horse easily behind him.

"What did the Nez Perce call her?"

"Something you won't want to pronounce. Best if you pick a new one for her."

Her coat was a shining deep red, and I ran my hand down the side of her to touch the spots. "She looks like a Spotted Rose to me. I'll call her Rosy for short."

"That suits her fine, I think. Let me help you up."

After showing me how to use the stirrup and the proper side to mount from, he hopped on his own horse in a graceful arch. With a few instructions on steering, stopping, and going, we were off on a delightfully unexpected trail ride. Rosy was content to walk side by side with Luke's mount, and before I knew it, my muscles relaxed and I eased into the gentle rocking motion of the saddle.

We followed a well-worn path amongst the thick trees. The rain made everything muddy and darker somehow, but the cease in drizzle also made the leaves and moss a brilliant shade of green. The earth smelled of moisture and storm clouds, and the air was quiet, as if even the bugs and birds were suspicious this was only a short break in the torrential downpour. Even the sound of the horse's hooves against the soft ground were muffled. The rhythm chanted for me to put us out of our silent misery. It was my burden alone to bear.

My mouth went dry as the Texas desert with what I was about to say, but the conversation had been my silent torture for four dreary days. He'd been man enough to let me find my words, and never asked, but I owed him an explanation. "You ever been in love?" I asked.

"No."

"Why not?"

Luke pulled his horse around a tree stump that stood in the middle of the trail. "Because it's a dangerous game for a man like me to play, caring about a woman like that. Have you ever been in love?"

My heart pounded louder than the noise of the horses under us. "I was. Well, I thought I was, but when you're seventeen you think you know everything. My mother had always been a maid to the highborn of Chicago, and when I was old enough to earn a wage, she took me with her. And for a long time, we made a great team, Mother and I.

She'd been wonderful in raising me and gave me the best childhood of anyone I'd ever met. We didn't have much, mind you, but we had everything we needed, and we had each other."

A deep and hollow ache welled up inside of me at the remembering. "When I was seventeen, the widow we worked for invited her son home from university to stay before he started work. I didn't pay him much mind at first, but he seemed taken with me, and when a man so powerful takes an interest in a little nothing of a person, it's hard to fight an attraction to that feeling of importance."

Luke's eyes pooled with regret. "How old was he?"

"He was only a bit older than me at twenty-four. He would sneak me presents. Just little things. Tiny trinkets he'd found shopping he said reminded him of me, and eventually he'd meet me places and kiss me. It was all very exciting. His mother was an awful woman and she wanted him to marry a certain class of lady. She had him go to lavish parties every time one came up and she tried to make a match for him…oh, it must have been a dozen times, at least. But Barron wouldn't bend to her. He said he only wanted me." I swatted a fly and slid a glance to Luke. "Imagine how I felt, a simple girl with barely a loaf of bread to share over dinner, and this man was turning away beautiful ladies of pedigree with hefty dowries for me. My mother warned me time and time again nothing good would come of it, but I couldn't hear anything from anyone. I must've been something special to turn such a man's head, you know?"

I swallowed down the yellow bellied coward in me that wanted to stop the story here. It had to be said if he was ever to really know me. "So one day, I met Barron in the place he'd begged me to, and his mother caught us. He was bedding me good when she walked in."

I tried to smile but my lip trembled instead. It didn't matter though because Luke was lost in a faraway look.

"She said everyone already knew by then that he'd been sleeping with the maid and that I'd ruined them. She said nobody wanted to make a match with a whoremonger. They searched the house I shared with my mother and found the trinkets Barron had given me. I didn't know it at the time, but some of them were valuable. His mother, Evelynn French, told me my mother would hang for thieving. She knew those trinkets were really gifts from her son, but she needed a way to control my future. She said I could change my mother's fate if I lived the way she demanded."

Not even the startling movement of a rabbit that jumped the path up ahead could stop the words tumbling from my mouth now.

"I wasn't to see my mother anymore. Ever. And I was supposed to live the life of a whore in retribution for what I'd done to her son and to their name. My mother was everything, you understand? I would've died to save her from a whipping. She is the best, most pure person you could ever meet and I had to save her from what I'd done. So I told her I never wanted to see her again, because if I didn't, she'd find me and hang for it. I packed my things and left to the room Ms. French found for me. It was in one of the filthiest brothels in the underbelly of Chicago, and after the week of rent she paid, I had to start working men to earn that lousy room. And every two weeks she would drive in with her fancy carriage, and fine, frilly dresses, with a handkerchief over her nose to keep the smell of rot and sex and sewage away and make sure I was down in the dirt where she'd put me. And Barron never came to save me. He didn't visit even once. He married a lady as proper as would take him and moved on."

Luke cursed softly and pulled his horse to a stop beside me. Rosy halted with a small tug on her rope.

"How'd you do it?" he asked with furrowed brows under his hat. "How'd you come out laughing on the other side of all of that?"

"I'm quite determined nobody's going to break me, sir. And besides, you should've seen Ms. French's face when she realized I was making a fool of her. I talked more like a whore, and joked like a whore, and said crass things to the woman, and anyone with a lick of sense saw the fury building in her eyes every time she came to visit. It was quite an entertaining sight to see and it got me through some tough nights. Despite everything she'd done, she was still losing part of the game and it was burning her up inside."

I giggled and tried to stifle it with my hand. Really nothing was funny about my story, but good lord if Luke had seen the look on her face the time she walked in on me with one of her acquaintances giving it to me right, and I'd just waved and said, 'doing just fine here, Ms. French. See you again in two weeks,' with a toothy grin, well he'd be laughing too.

Luke leaned against the saddle horn and rubbed the two day scruff on his face with a thoughtful expression. "I understand the reasons you didn't tell me. I get it. You were looking for a way out and a man to protect you and you just so happened to land here. This don't scare me off, woman. I'll be your protector if that's what you need from me." The horse under him turned with his able direction and headed back where we came from. Luke turned in his saddle and pointed to me. "And I won't let anyone ever do that to your face again, you hear me?"

And as I sat there watching him go, I fell in love for the first time. Real love. Not the kind dependent on secrecy or fear like what I had with Barron, but the kind that's warmth hit you in the gut and made your heart beg for more.

If he was my declared protector, I'd do everything in my power to protect him back.

Chapter Ten
Luke

I had a time trying not to look back at Kristina while I led her to the house. The fear of what she'd see in my eyes left me too skittish to ride side by side with her like I'd preferred. That evil woman, Evelynn French, and all the horrid things she'd done to a sweet soul like Kristina gave me a slow burning fury to rival the deepest fires of hell. I knew evil existed in the world. You couldn't be a creature of secret and not understand that the potential laid within every man. But never had its taint landed on our homestead. Thanks to that black hearted lady, whose dark tendrils of hate swung far and wide, two evil men dragged a woman, my woman, behind a horse and laughed about it.

A wolf could sense evil. Most dogs could, in fact, and my wolf had been screaming to kill both of her kidnappers and make the world better for it. She didn't know it, and I wouldn't tell her, but someday, despite her saving his wretched life, I was going to kill Matthew Streider. The wolf inside of me would enjoy snuffing out the remaining evil that clung to my territory.

Unable to help myself, I snuck a glance behind. She was beautiful, sitting on that Indian pony with her pretty posture in that deep blue dress of hers. She stared off into the forest with a faraway look. It gave me a good view of her neck, long and slender, that led to curves well hidden by the modest cut of the dark fabric.

She was a natural rider and it surprised me how attractive I found it. I'd tested her time and time again to see how she fared with new people; different people. In every situation, she'd been open to them. I could've removed the feathers from her horse's neck or just cut them out if I had a mind to, but a quiet place inside that I didn't fully understand yet wanted to see how she'd react to riding an Indian horse.

She hadn't even flinched. She'd gone further and told me to leave them in and asked what the horse's name in Nez Perce was. Yes it was a long shot but maybe, just maybe, she'd accept all of me as well.

All the admission to her past did was intrigue me. She'd weathered much in her short life and still, she was fighting to hold onto the best parts of herself. I'd seen able men give up under less dreary circumstances.

Drawing up short, I inhaled. The smell of unfamiliar horse and cart filled my nose, but when I scented the humans who'd brought them, I relaxed. Trudy and Elias waited patiently on the porch, swinging their legs off the side and talking easily.

"Got company," I said, and watched Kristina's face light up. How could another person's happiness bring me such pleasure?

In haste, she jerked her knees and the mare responded. "Oh!" Kristina said as the spotted pony pulled into a bouncing trot. She looked jostled at first, but settled into the rhythm fast enough.

Kicking my own horse, I rode beside her as she laughed breathlessly. "Doing good, just let her have some rein so she don't slow down on you. That's it. Flex your legs every other bounce and hold onto the saddle horn if you feel unsteady."

As with the stitching and quilting, she proved a capable student and quick learner and when she pulled the mare to a stop in front of the house, the uninhibited grin on her face had my insides turned upside down.

Elias took the reins of the mare and calmed the excited creature while I helped Kristina down. She didn't need it, but I wasn't about to pass up the chance to put my hands on her waist. She smiled slowly when I left them there longer than I needed to. She shivered curiously under my fingertips and when I gave her a questioning look, a blush crept right into her fair cheeks.

To Trudy's obvious surprise, Kristina turned and nearly tackled her with a hug. Elias and I tied off the horses as the woman slowly hugged her back. Trudy gasped at the sight of Kristina's green bruised face, and the sound had me panicking at some unseen danger.

The dark-skinned woman pulled Kristina behind her and graced me with an infuriated glare. "What have you done to her?"

Shocked, I didn't have an answer ready. I guess if I'd been able to get to her sooner, those men wouldn't have beat on her, but I hadn't known she was gone. I'd been trying to scramble and get the horses back in the downed fence. By the time I knew she'd been taken, the scent trail had been washed out by the rain.

"No," Kristina said, pulling the woman to face her. "Luke didn't do this. He saved me from this."

Trudy frowned. "I don't understand."

"Come on in and I'll tell you all about it."

Kristina's coffee was still a little on the bitter side, but she was making strides for improvement. At least it likely wouldn't poison us. When she'd told our company all about the kidnapping, Trudy pulled Kristina's shoes right off without a question and poked each healing gash. Likely she was looking for infection, and not finding any she turned to me.

"I'm sorry for accusing you earlier," she said. "It looks pretty bad though. Now you boys go on out of here and tend to them horses while we chat."

Elias put his hat back over his blond hair as soon as we were outside. "That's a pretty little filly you got there."

"I traded for her. Kristina told me she wouldn't learn to ride unless I found her a polka dotted horse, so imagine her surprise when I found one so quick."

"Trudy still won't get on one. Says she don't trust them but she'll drive a wagon without a worry. Maybe I should try to find her a spotted horse too," he said with a wink.

With the horses untied, I pulled them both behind me. "Did you come up to deliver that dress Trudy's been working on?"

"Yeah, we hadn't see you two for a few days and Trudy was wanting to show off her work." Elias looked back at the house and lowered his voice. "I'm here for different reasons though. Trudy told me what you are."

"Trudy sounds like she's making assumptions."

"I've seen you fight men in town. You're too fast to be human and you haven't been all that careful concealing that fact. I ain't here to string you up, Dawson. I'm here to ask for protection if ever there comes a time me and my wife need it."

His face was perfectly earnest as his blue eyes sought mine. This was a first. Normally, if people figured our kind out, they'd be there with pitchforks and torches by the next evening.

"What's your game?" I asked suspiciously.

Elias held his hands up in the air. "No game, I swear. We'll never tell your secret. Hell, we'll even try to dispel the rumors swirling around town. But Trudy isn't exactly safe living here with me and I want to know that if we got in a bind, you'd help us out."

"Why don't you move if you don't feel safe?"

"Move where? Where is our marriage ever going to be accepted? Where will we be safe?"

The man had a point. And really, it couldn't hurt to have friends in town. Kristina seemed to get along with Trudy real well and I'd hate to see any harm come to them.

"If it don't put my family in danger, I'll have your back."

The deep line of worry in Elias's forehead smoothed. "Much obliged."

I threw the huge wooden door open and the barn owls went to flapping their wings sleepily above us. "You want to stay over for dinner? Kristina ain't much of a cook yet, but you're welcome to whatever she comes up with."

"Thank you kindly. And don't worry overmuch about that. Trudy will have her whipped into shape in the kitchen in no time. She's taken a liking to your young wife."

She wasn't my wife quite yet, but I wasn't about to correct him.

I liked the way it sounded.

****

Kristina

Trudy showed me how to do properly a whole lot of things I'd been doing very wrong in the kitchen. Thankfully we had some time before dinner so she taught me how to make a fruit preserve pie with some peaches she'd brought with her in a jar. And when that was in the oven, she took me out back to the vegetable garden and we picked everything we'd need to make her famous beef stew.

"Your man's got to eat more than a normal man and it's up to you to feed him right."

I guessed he was taller and more fit than most men I'd ever seen so that made sense. Frying eggs was definitely not going to keep him satisfied.

"All we lack is meat. You got a smoke house?" she asked.

"Out this way." I led her to small log building some short distance off. Luke hadn't been hunting since Jeremiah left, and now all that remained was a row of smoked venison jerky and a leg of beef.

With a practiced hand, Trudy grabbed the beef and hefted it to the house while I trailed behind with the basket of vegetables.

"You know how to use one of these?" she asked, sliding a large knife out of a sheath at her belt.

"No," I said in wide-eyed wonder. It was almost as big as Luke's hunting knife.

"Well, you ought to learn. It's good in the kitchen and you never know when knivin' skills will come in handy."

A vision of Luke pinning Streider's hand to a tree with one had me slowly nodding my head in agreement.

"Honey, are you okay?" she asked, squeezing my arm gently and searching my face.

I couldn't think about that night any more than I had to, and I definitely couldn't start feeling sorry for myself. "I'm fine. I've had worse before."

Trudy's face grew very serious as she unlaced the buttons to her dress. "So have I," she said as she shrugged off the sleeves and turned for me to see the welled scars that ran in a criss-cross pattern across the expanse of her back. "But I also know it takes its toll."

I sucked air through my teeth in shock and ran a light finger over one of the healed marks. "Men can be cruel, horrible creatures," I breathed.

"Yes." She pulled her dress back on with a dreamy look at the door. "But they can also be caring creatures if you find the right one."

My own eyes were drawn to where I imagined Luke would be, brushing down the horses in the barn with Elias for company. "Yes, they can be. Makes them more special when you've seen the darker bits of men."

"True," she said as her last button was redone. "We're the lucky ones and the coddled women don't even know it," she said with a smile.

I'd never thought of it like that. My experiences made it easier for me to see the true and honest good in people. In Luke. I always knew I was lucky, I just hadn't figured out in which way until now.

"How did you and Elias meet?" I asked as I poured cornmeal into a bowl.

"He was the foreman at the plantation I worked for. I was a house servant because I was pretty and I talked nice. Learned fast too and was handy in the kitchen when the girls in there needed help for dinner parties. Elias oversaw the slaves in the cotton fields, and never have I seen a worse foreman. He was too soft. He didn't have it in him to punish anyone and I fell in love with him the day he saved my niece from a lashing. He lied to the other men. Said she was going to grow up right pretty and be a comfort slave if they didn't mar her body. Said they'd ruin her skin and she'd be worthless. Now my niece was many a thing, but she wasn't ever going to be no comfort girl. Half rabid, that girl would bite their manhood off before any white man even got close, but Elias talked and talked until they was convinced. A few months later, the Emancipation came and Elias took me in the night to avoid any violence that was coming as a result. I was a freedwoman, but that wouldn't do me any good if I was dead. He tried to get my family to come too, but they had different plans. I get a letter every once in a while from my sister, who has the words, and Elias reads them to me as they come in. They're making their way up north."

"Do you miss them?"

"Of course, but Elias is home."

"I think I know what you mean. This place feels like home to me, too."

"Because of Luke?" she asked.

"Because of Luke."

"He really treats you all right?"

"Oh, yes, better than any man I've known. Granted I haven't known many honest men," I said as I waggled my eyebrows, "but he carries me over mud, and offers me an arm, and he's been taking real good care of me while I've been hurt. And, Trudy, you should've seen his face when he killed the man that dragged me behind the horse. That monster was pissin' on my legs when Luke tracked us down and just as I thought I was going to die, he came in like some avenging angel come to earth. They were mine to kill and he took the burden." My voice trembled like a leaf in the wind. "I think I love him."

Trudy grabbed my hands and squeezed. "That's different than what I thought then. I won't be asking you about his treatment of you anymore. I just wanted to make sure you was safe, and you sound safe enough to me."

Chapter Eleven
Kristina

E lias and Luke came in just as the last rays of sun stretched across the clearing that cradled our house. They talked and laughed amicably in front of the fireplace while Trudy and I put the finishing touches on dinner. After days of nothing but the patter of rain against the roof, it was good to have a house filled with the sound of conversation.

My favorite time of day came with evening. Luke removed his hat, jacket and the holster for his pistols. He was completely relaxed in his space, with all of that dark hair tumbling around his face, those glorious eyes that followed me as I worked looking even brighter and greener somehow. Like the moss we'd seen on the trees, engorged with the rains and nearly glowing with vibrant, healthy color.

Elias was a tender man who touched Trudy's back often just to let her know he was there. They had the ease of time, and the comfort of an obvious love that taught them to move around each other as if they were dancing.

Someday, I wanted to be able to touch Luke in such a way.

When we bowed our heads to say grace over the steaming plates of food lying before us, an electric current traveled up my arm from where my fingertips touched Luke's. I snuck a glance at him and he was smiling at me in a way that made my insides want to open for him like a spring flower.

"Amen," they all said in unison. I was just a little behind on account of being caught swimming in the depths of Luke's liquid eyes instead, but no one seemed to notice.

Dinner was a relatively quiet affair as we filled hungry stomachs, but the hum of conversation slowly returned with the men's second helping of stew and cornbread.

"I've been having some trouble with cattle disappearing." Luke seemed to speak only to Trudy. "I really need to spend the night out there and make sure the stock's not being rustled."

Trudy's eyes landed on the window behind me, but when I tried to follow her gaze, all I could see was the moon outside, full and bright against the clear, star freckled sky. I turned back around but she was engaged in a look with Luke again.

"Well now, Mr. Luke, I don't feel comfortable you leaving Kristina out in this house all alone with trouble afoot. Would you mind terribly if we stayed the night here with her?"

Luke smiled and said, "I was just getting around to inviting you."

The chair creaked as Elias relaxed into it. "I suppose that's best. I'm not terribly familiar with these parts and I'd rather not take my wife back into town in the dark."

"You can use my room," Luke said. "I'll be out all night and won't have any use for it."

"I'll get some clean linens," I offered. Finally, something of use I could actually do.

After the last sheet was tucked snuggly under the cotton stuffed mattress, I found the dishes already clean thanks to the likes of Trudy and Luke. They talked quietly while Elias plucked on the banjo that usually hung from the wall near the hearth.

Though I was excited with the prospect of overnight company, Elias yawned widely and said he was beat. I tried my best to hide my disappointment when Trudy squeezed my hand and headed to bed with her husband. Tiredness hadn't quite settled over my bones as it often did so late, and the restlessness inside had me stalling for more time with Luke.

He was busy packing provisions for the night and redressing in the clothing that would protect him from the wilds he'd sleep in. He seemed very busy avoiding my gaze, and burying the tiny hurt it brought had me scampering for the bedroom to protect myself. On a whim, I turned. "You be careful out there tonight, Luke Dawson."

He froze with his back to me, then turned his head just far enough for me to see his profile. The lines in his face were grim. "I'll be back in the morning." His voice sounded stiff and strained.

Whatever I'd done, I regretted it. The night had been pretty near perfect and now he was cross with me. He couldn't just leave without an effort on my part to smooth things out. I approached slowly and the apology left my lips as I slid a hand up his back.

Luke flinched away from me but not before I felt the stiff tension in every knotted muscle in his shoulders. Frowning, I watched his steady retreat. "I'll be back before you wake up," he said before he shut the door behind him.

In desperation, I ran for my room and jumped on the bed so I could see his silhouette in the moonlight from the window. He lumbered heavily as if he held a horse across his shoulders and when he stopped and turned, my heart hammered away at being caught spying. His face was dark in the shadow of his hat, but the moonlight illuminated the rest of him.

He watched me there in the window for eternity, or what felt like it. I was a frozen picture on a canvas, and as susceptible to his penetrating gaze as a mouse to some exotic snake. My insides would burn me right through if he didn't release his hold on me. And then, slowly, he lifted his hand in a small wave. I flicked my fingers and a little piece inside that had tensed up with his retreat loosened once again. A tiny sign of forgiveness and acceptance between us was enough to right my world that had teetered on its axis for just a moment.

He disappeared into the night and I sank onto the bed with my fingers to my lips. Dawn was a very long time away, and the best way to pass that time was to sleep. Ambling into the kitchen in my bare feet and night dress, I blew out the lanterns and let the dark strands of sleepiness drag me under the fighting waves of my momentary insecurity.

He'd be back by morning.

****

Luke

Leaving Kristina alone in light of everything that happened wasn't an option I was willing to fool with. But a plan had been hatching in my mind since the moment I smelled Trudy and Elias.

No, leaving her unprotected wasn't something even my wolf was desperate to push for, but leaving her with Elias, one of the best gunslingers I'd ever met? Well, that was the best opportunity I was going to get to change until Jeremiah managed to make his way home. If the damned fool hadn't gone off and got himself shot already.

So from the moment I thought there was a chance to relieve the pain of going so long in one form, my body revolted in anticipation. My bones were drilled until it likely looked like Swiss cheese, and my flesh was fileted. Sure, I looked okay from the outside if I didn't move around too much and give myself away, but my innards had to be ripped to bloody pieces to bring such agony.

Trudy was a quick woman who picked up immediately on what I was really asking. Would she stay and protect my mate while I ravaged the wilds as an animal? Her offering to remain at the house sent my wolf to howling inside of me.

I hadn't meant to hurt Kristina with my hastened goodbye, but Lord knows from the soft look on her face as I left, I had. Loyal creature that she was, she'd watched me go from the bedroom window.

Even with my exceptional night vision, her face was shrouded in the darkness from the candle flickering behind. I'd searched and searched the dark for her full lips, in hopes of a parting smile to hold onto while the human side of me ripped into pieces. When her graceful fingers fluttered in response to my wave, that was enough. It would have to be because like it or not, the time had come to die again.

The barn owls were out hunting the rodents that roamed the forest at night, and the only noise when I opened the door was the welcoming whinny of one of the horses. The sound was a screech against my sensitive ear drums and I hunched forward.

Jeremiah liked to change in the woods, in a different place each time. To him, the newness of the environment brought a tiny element of variety that helped him through the pain.

It didn't work so well for me. My wolf became frantic to claw out of me if I dared to put him in a new place he didn't know. The farthest corner of the barn, behind the last stall in a dusty pile of hay was my death bed a hundred times over. The nerves that washed over me in waves at the sight of my changing place clenched my stomach with nausea.

I wished the change was like the legends said. Enchantment, speed and power. No magic dust floofed from my skin at the moment of conversion. The transition from man to beast took ten minutes at least, and there was no less powerful creature in existence than a turning werewolf. Any ancient, frail man with a cane could walk up and slowly bludgeon me to death with it and I wouldn't be able to lift a paw to stop him.

I was faster and stronger than most human men and the animal that tore out of me was a force of nature to be reckoned with, but the cost was the pain. Eternal anguish.

Kristina lay in bed just a short way off, and though I'd likely scared her enough the first night to thwart her itch to go exploring in the dark, I'd have to be quiet. If she thought I was in trouble, she'd come running, of that I was sure.

The thick leather strap had layer upon layer of my teeth marks on it and the color had faded with time and wear. I'd used it since I was sixteen—since my first change. It was a gift from Da to match the gift of the wolf he'd put inside of me the day he decided to give my mother the children she so longed for.

Would I give in someday and burden Kristina's children with this curse?

The pain drew me to the floor, and on hands and knees I shoved the strap as far back against my teeth as it would go. I wouldn't scream this time. This time would be different and I'd die silently. I could do it to protect Kristina. There it was. I needed that thought to focus on. Protecting Kristina. I'd do anything to keep her safe, so swallowing my screams shouldn't be impossible.

My fingers went first. Every tiny bone broke and snapped and reformed into something else. Blunt, harmless nails turned to sharp, black claws, and the fur that sprouted from my body was a million tiny needles shooting through my skin in the same moment. Every vertebra in my spine snapped and reshaped until it was shortened and made for running on four legs instead of two. I slid to the ground to accommodate my leg bones being ground to dust, and I groaned in a fight against the pain as my neck tilted back until I couldn't breathe. The sound of my death was a popping reverberation against my elongating ears, and the muscles above my bones ripped and reformed into something completely animal.

After my near-silent torture was finally finished, I lay there for a while until the dizziness subsided. I stood and stretched every muscle and tendon out until my new spine cracked into place. Shaking my body to rid myself of the last tingles of the change, I trotted out of the open barn door and found myself sitting below Kristina's window.

A soft whine escaped my throat as I thought about what a relief it would be if she could finally see me—all of me. But whether she was ready or not, I wasn't. The risk of her running and leaving me to mourn what could've been for the rest of my miserable existence was just too great. Until I was certain of her feelings, she'd have to stay in the dark about the beast that lived inside of me.

Turning, I bolted for the woods. I had until dawn to run and hunt and be wild. I had told her I'd be back before she woke, and I intended to keep my word.

Sniffing along the edge of the clearing, I searched for any fresh signs of Jeremiah, but anything I picked up was days old. Likely he'd left our territory altogether. Running so long as a wolf would make him nearly feral by now.

I ran through the woods, as fast as a leaf in the hands of a twister. Faster and faster I went until the trees whipped by in a blur and my feet barely touched the ground. I was as close to flying as a man could get and it was my favorite part of being the wolf. I rushed until all thought left my mind, and all that was left was instinct for where I'd next place my paw. My nose twitched when I picked up a scent that put shudders of excitement into my stomach.

Fresh venison was my favorite food, but I veered off the trail before the hunt even began. Hunting deer as a single wolf was likely to get me nothing but exhausted. If Jeremiah and Gable, my other brother, were here with me, we'd hunt them down using pack tactics. A single wolf though? Unless the animal was injured, I'd never catch up to its throat.

The scent of cattle, sleeping and quiet reached my nose but still, they weren't what I wanted. There was no challenge in hunting the slow moving creatures, and tonight I needed to keep my mind off of Kristina. A movement jerked to my right and rushed away with a lifting of leaves. Rabbit was what I wanted. An agile and cunning distraction. The muscles in my hind legs bunched as I leapt into action after the tiny animal. When it was limp between my paws, I lifted my head and released the triumphant howl that had been tearing to get out.

I hoped she heard me.

I hoped some tiny instinct deep down inside of her heard me and loved the sound of my voice caressing the night air.

Even if she couldn't see me yet, it was essential to my soul she be touched by my secret in some way.

Chapter Twelve
Kristina

The faint morning light against my eyelids was enough to stir me. I stretched and searched for cool pockets under the covers with my legs, then blinked my eyes open. The room was just as it had been last night but with one difference. Luke sat in the chair near the door with his face resting against the palm of his hand and his eyes closed. The pillow was warm under my cheek and I fluffed it upward to give me a better view of him.

His cotton shirt was half-way unbuttoned and his sleeves rolled up. Save a pair of dark cotton pants, he wore nothing else. A small pile of clothing graced the floor beside him and my eyes were pulled again to the opening of his shirt. The skin there was smooth and dark, and the outline of his stony musculature was visible even in the thin light of dawn.

"Come here," I said.

Immediately, his brilliant green eyes were on me.

"Come lay beside me until the rooster crows," I whispered.

I rolled over and faced the wall and the bed groaned under his weight as he lay on top of the covers behind me. His hand rested tenderly on my hip but it wasn't enough. I pulled it over my waist and held it with my own. Such a contrast, our skin was. His palm was rough with callouses and strong from the labor of running a ranch. A man's hands, while mine were soft and miniature against his. His arm relaxed over me as his breathing slowed, and I fell asleep once more to the warmth and safety that washed over the space between the sturdy wall and the able body of my man.

When I woke up for good, the bed beside me boasted only Luke's indentation in the pillow. The covers under my hand were cool and I squinted at the bright sky to try and gauge the time—a pointless endeavor because I'd always been awful at it. Shrugging into a robe, I padded down the hall to Luke's half opened door.

Luke stood over his washbasin with a bottle of cream and a straight razor, and a half shaved smile lit up his face when I peeked my head into his room further.

"Mornin'," he said cheerily.

"Where are Trudy and Elias?"

"They left at first light. Trudy's working at Cotton's today and had to be there early. She said to tell you bye and she left you that." He twitched his head in the direction of the bed. On it lay a brown wrapped package held together by twine.

"My dress?"

"I imagine so. Now go put it on and get ready. Since you can ride now, you're coming out with me today."

Now if the prospect of spending an entire day with Luke and finally out of the house wasn't enough to send me skittering for the package, then I didn't know what would. I rushed to get ready, pausing only to admire the fine dress of gray and red floral calico in the small mirror above my washbasin. I fixed my hair in a casual braid so long it tickled my tailbone, then rushed for the kitchen to find leftover cornbread from last night's dinner. Two tightly wrapped pieces plunked into my dress pocket and my shoes were pulled on before Luke even entered the big room.

"Did you already eat?" he asked.

Amusement danced in his eyes but what did I care? I was getting out of the house! "I put two pieces of cornbread for us in my pocket already."

"Eat one while I finish dressing. I ain't gonna leave you."

Only slightly disheartened we weren't leaving right this millisecond, I inhaled a slice of the golden, buttered bread and wiped my mouth with the back of my forearm.

Luke was taking his sweet time fastening up the holster for his weapons, so I snatched his hat off the peg and handed it to him with a cheery smile. "Trudy said I need a knife."

"What kind of knife?"

"One for cooking and gutting a man I suppose."

His eyebrows flew up. "Oh. All right, I guess it wouldn't hurt for you to have one." His eyes danced. "In case you need to gut a man."

I slapped him on the arm soundly. "Luke Dawson, don't you make fun of me. I could've used a knife when those men took me. I didn't have a single weapon on me."

"Oh, you had weapons and you used them. Teeth and claws. I saw the man you let go. He was all torn up. Seems you bit through half his hand."

I tipped my chin and straightened my spine. "Well, he would've got a whole lot worse if I had a blade on me."

Luke dug through a chest in the corner of the room. "Here you go. Don't go sticking yourself now. Best to keep it sheathed until you need it."

The knife wasn't as big as his but it fit my hand. The handle was made of some sort of animal bone or antler and the blade gleamed in the sunlight that streamed in through the window. I could see my own grin in the steely reflection. I slid it back into its leather sheath and stuck it in my dress pocket. The weight was a comfort. I had all kinds of hidden weapons now.

Luke didn't bother with his jacket. He wore a dark sleeveless vest over his cotton shirt. Cow leather pants met worn, spur shackled boots that went almost to his knee. A trim man like him was made to wear these sorts of clothes.

The leather string that tied the belted holster steadily to his thigh made a zipping sound as he tightened it. His eyes met mine like he knew I was watching. "You like the way I look?" he asked with his head cocked to the side.

If it hadn't been obvious from me staring at him like he was a jug of water in the desert, it was a surprise to me. He didn't have to know I'd been undressing him with my mind, but even a confident man needed reassurance every once in a while. That much I'd learned quick at the brothel. "You suit me just fine," I said.

His fingers reached out to brush the fabric against my waist. "I like the way you look just fine, too."

My insides melted like butter in an iron skillet. How could a rugged country man who could slit someone's throat so easily say such sweet things to a woman like me?

"Come on now," he said. "Today you're going to learn the ropes around this place and we're starting with you saddling your own horse."

Rosy was in a good mood, probably because of the bucket of oats Luke gave her to munch on while he taught me the ins and outs of brushing her hide to shining. The saddle blanket was well in the realm of what my flimsy arms could hoist over her back, but the saddle was a different matter. It took several tries and copious amounts of grunting to get it over.

Rosy looked back at me in annoyance several times, but Luke said she'd get used to the saddle the more I used it. He taught me how to tighten it as the horse exhaled to keep the saddle from slipping. When Rosy was all done up, he saddled his own horse in the blink of an eye. Lifting the saddle proved difficult but I would adjust as I did with everything else in my new life, and already I could mount her by myself.

The cows sounded furious we'd missed their milking but Luke said we'd have to take care of the barn animals when we got back. The grazing herd of cattle were getting too close to Old Man Murphy's land, and apparently that grumpy old son-of-a-gun would right out thieve them from under us if they ate so much as one blade of grass from his property.

Rosy wanted to run, and though I held onto my saddle horn for dear life, I couldn't help the breathless giggles that escaped me. If I could balance with my hands straight out to catch the wind that caressed my body, I would've done it. With Luke's eyes on me and an easy smile that lit him up like the moon, I'd never been freer.

"Whoa," I said as I pulled Rosy's rope to my chest. She slowed to a skittish walk as we ambled the edge of the large herd of Dawson cattle.

Luke pointed. "You see that ridge over there? That's Old Man Murphy's land. We need to push them back closer to the house."

We were almost spitting distance to the property line. "Okay, what do I do?"

"Go around them wide. Don't spook them and then when you get your back to the property line, you start hollerin'. When we get them moving, we'll come up around the sides and keep them from scattering."

Sounded simple enough. If the cows had been let in on the plan, maybe it would have actually worked. Instead, as I took one side and Luke took the other, the cattle bellowed and moved of their own accord, and straight in the direction of Murphy's land.

"Aw piss," I said as I kicked Rosy. I ran wide and tried to cut them off with Luke on the other side mirroring. After what had to have been half an hour of coercing the beasts, most of them got going in the direction we wanted with just a handful of stragglers escaping the herd to frolic onto Murphy's side of the line. Great.

"I'll get them," Luke said easily. "You keep the rest of them moving as best you can and I'll catch up." He pointed toward the steadily rising sun. "Take them that way, in as straight a line as you can manage."

With him out of sight, I could use the filthy vocabulary I'd picked up from my whoring days. "Come on you lily livered nugget lickers!" I waved my arms and yelled and threatened and it seemed to work for the most part if one ignored the small trios of cattle that tended to wander away from the rest before I could get to them. Luke would have a time rounding all of them up, but he was a capable cowboy who rode his horse like it was an extension of himself. I doubted there was much he couldn't do if he put his mind to it.

Luke rode up some while later with an older gentlemen whom I could only guess was Old Man Murphy himself. All the cursing tipped me off.

"Mr. Murphy, my wife," Luke said formally.

Mr. Murphy spat on the ground and looked none too impressed with the likes of me.

"Nice to meet you," I said cheerily.

"If I find a single one of my cows in your herd, I'll shoot you my danged self," the man said in a frail but firm voice.

"You're welcome to look like I said, but we ain't cattle thieves, sir. In fact, we already have as much as we can handle. We don't need any more than we've already got."

Murphy grumbled in a manner that said he didn't believe a word Luke said and kicked his mount hard. Scattering the cows in all directions, he searched them with a critical beady eye.

"What's he doing?" I asked.

Luke rubbed his hand over his face and leaned on the saddle horn. "Making more work for us."

"But why?"

"Cause that's what crazy people do. He lost three cows and he's convinced they're in here somewhere. Except his herd is on the other side of his property and I can't see three cows wandering all the way over here just to make some new friends."

Murphy skidded to a stop so close to Rosy, she reared up before she skittered to the side. "I don't know what you done with my cows, Dawson, but somethin' ain't right around here and I know it! I can feel it in my bones. I never lost a cow to nothin' but natural causes and predators but since you Dawson's moved in here, fourteen of my cattle have just vanished into thin air." He snapped his gnarled fingers. "Just poof! I'm callin' on the sheriff next time I'm in town. You can bet your boots I will." In a flash, the old man rode for his own property.

Luke's eyes churned as he watched him leave and with a grumble that sounded suspiciously like 'Jeremiah,' he turned and rode after the scattered cattle to the east.

He was preoccupied with the goings on in his mind for the rest of the day. I worked without complaint for fear of burdening him further, but likely he'd forgotten I wasn't used to such backbreaking labor. By the time we had the cattle moved near a watering hole out back, the chickens fed and chased from the coop, the cows milked, the horses fed and watered, the stalls mucked, the garden tended, slops chopped for the pigs, and the eggs, milk, and water hauled in, I was drenched, exhausted, and had more blisters than fingers to count them.

If I wasn't a country woman yet, Luke was whooping me right into shape for it.

I made biscuits and gravy the way Trudy told me and it only turned out half burnt and a little salty. Venison jerky was the only side dish.

"Luke?" I asked warily as he finished off his plate without a word. He hadn't spoken other than to direct me in hours. "We're almost out of meat in the smokehouse."

He leaned back into his groaning chair with an explosive sigh. "What do we need?"

"Beef, deer, catfish. It don't make no matter. So long as its meat, I'm sure I can figure out a way to cook it."

He stood and took the dishes to the sink. "I'll go hunting first thing in the morning." With a soft brush of his lips against my forehead, he said his goodnight and disappeared down the hall.

I leaned my chin on the table and frowned at the darkened hallway. My fingers traced the patterns in the wood grain while my mind reeled like a leaf caught in the currents of a whirlpool.

He was a confounding man to be sure but there had to be something big I was missing. Maybe he was unhappy with me for not catching on fast enough to his way of life, or maybe he was second guessing a marriage to me. My throat went dry. Where was that damned circuit preacher? Waiting was a risk in a situation such as ours. I'd sworn never to let anyone break me, but if Luke Dawson ran me off, I didn't know if I could hold that kind of hurt and not be affected.

And with as hot and cold as the man had been as of late, I really didn't know where I stood.

Chapter Thirteen
Luke

If Jeremiah took that many cattle on his wild streak out of the territory, Murphy wasn't the only rancher around here he hit. I kicked my horse into a trot and scoured the woods in the early morning light. Trouble was he would've left behind some evidence. Wolves didn't eat bones after all, but where'd he hide the damn carcasses?

The sickly sweet scent of rot hit the sensitive lining of my nose and dread slammed against me like a storm wind. I kicked my horse again and shortly came to a clearing. The dead animals were covered in swarms of flies and two of them hadn't even been eaten. They'd been killed just for the violence of it.

I cursed and pulled a red handkerchief over my nose. Jeremiah was off the rails. What a fool I'd been to think he should let the wolf take over. Anna had been tortured, and of course Kristina's treatment would trigger a break. And the wolf was the one who couldn't let go of his mate.

The men who'd killed Anna got away with it. We'd never been able to track them down, and it created some deep darkness inside of Jeremiah I hadn't any idea how to tame. For as levelheaded as Jeremiah the man was, his wolf was an uncontrolled monster. The day Anna died was the day we stopped changing together. He didn't feel it was safe for me anymore. I'd bet my hat that was why he was searching so hard for a new wife. He was trying to give his broken wolf someone new to love.

For the millionth time I wished our oldest brother, Gable, was here. He always seemed to know more about the wolf than even the wolf itself. He was the only werewolf I'd ever met, who reveled completely in the power that came with being one. He loved everything about it, and somehow, someway, he'd even managed to embrace the pain. That trick he hadn't shared before he became patriotic and left for the War Between the States. If anyone could yank Jeremiah from the roiling darkness his wolf had plunged into the day Anna died, it was Gable.

I squinted at the half devoured cattle. I'd have to bury the bodies or burn them and neither could be done this close to Murphy's property line. Had the danged fool even know he'd chased them onto our property? Maybe he'd done it on purpose, but I was at a loss as to why Jeremiah would do such a thing.

I had rope to drag them, but not nearly enough. I rode a good mount that'd never balked at what I asked him, except if it was to drag a dead animal too close to his back end. I'd need more length.

"Hup," I said, as I flecked the reins against the shoulder of my horse and the loyal beast obeyed with a flash of speed.

The tension eased as the house came into view. I didn't like being away from Kristina for too long. Not after what happened to her, knowing the danger was still very real and in no way over for us.

A flash of annoyance washed over me at what that woman had done in such a short amount of time. From the day she arrived I'd become tethered somehow, like a rope hung from me to her, and the farther I got away, the more it hung me. The relief at seeing her feeding the chickens was so thick I could almost touch it, and just like that, my annoyance was gone.

It wasn't her fault I felt so strongly. If she wouldn't have come in here all mysterious, and knowledgeable about the world, intelligent, and funny, why I'd have never fallen like a sack of flour for her. She couldn't help her alluring nature. She couldn't help how danged pretty she was. I knew that because the way she lit up like a sunrise every time I gave her the barest compliment said she didn't even know she was beautiful.

Jeremiah was an idiot for passing her up.

She looked up warily as I approached and her hesitation stung. What had I done? Sure I hadn't felt like talking much last night, but I had more pressing matters filling up my head, like a slow boiling rage at my brother and a rampaging werewolf attack I was going to have to somehow cover up.

Everything was on me to keep this pack safe, and Kristina was included in it now. It put a disconcerting fear in me I hadn't known before. I knew my brothers and I would be burning or hanging on our way out. That was something we accepted young in this life. No one was perfect all the time, and one misstep from any three of us, and we'd die for it. But Kristina was an innocent, and her fate clung to mine now.

She stood with her apron full of chicken feed. The sunlight lit up her hair and from where I sat above, it looked like pure spun gold. Her lips were full and pink and her little nose flared with questions she seemed too afraid to ask. Probably best.

"You were gone when I woke up," she said. "I didn't know where you'd run off to but I made breakfast. It's still warming on the stove if you want it."

My stomach lurched at the thought of what I was about to have to do. "No time just now. I have a problem I have to take care of quickly. I'll be back in for lunch though." I turned for the barn but spun back around. "Stay close to the house while I'm gone. You find trouble, use the pistols by the door."

She clutched the apron tighter to her stomach like a shield and nodded. The chickens clucked and pecked around her feet like our entire world wasn't in danger, as I rode my horse straight into the open barn. The rope I needed was hanging over the railing of an empty stall. I pulled my work gloves on and slung it over the saddle bags. Before I even let myself see the disappointment in Kristina's face, I raced for the dead cattle's resting place.

"Whoa," I said quietly as my senses picked up something the man in me couldn't understand. I searched the woods but all had gone quiet except the soft sigh of something I couldn't put a finger on. My skin tingled and my horse skittered to the side in reaction to my discomfort. The danger wasn't close enough to draw a pistol, so I slid quietly out of the saddle and tied my horse to a sapling. Inching forward as quietly as a man could, I stopped in another fifty yards and listened. This time the sound was plain as day—men's voices. One of them was Murphy and the other two I didn't recognize.

Crouching down, I got as close as I dared. The gun wasn't necessary as they weren't on my land to trespass or poach. They'd found the dead cattle. My blood went cold as a snake's in winter. I hadn't been nearly fast enough. Damn Murphy, that relentless old coot. He'd made good on his promise to call on the law.

The sapling my horse was tied to bent under his restlessness but I wasn't gone long enough for him to break it just yet. I slid into the saddle and kicked him in a rush.

Kristina's head snapped up at the sound of a horse running full out. She was in the process of gathering a wire bucket of eggs out of the coop while the chickens were busy with their breakfast.

Before my mount even stopped, I jumped off my horse and ran for her as fast as I could pull him. "There're going to be men here any minute. Don't say anything unless they talk to you and don't tell them I've been out. If they ask, I've been here all morning, okay?"

She stood frozen with wide eyes as blue as the pools at Clear Creek.

"Okay?" I asked a little louder.

At her nod, I ran my horse into the barn. As quick as I could, I pulled his saddle and blanket off as one and pushed him into the last stall. The gate to it clicked closed just as the sound of faint hoof beats headed our way.

****

Kristina

Three men on horseback rode up the dirt road to our homestead. I hadn't done anything constructive since Luke successfully confused the daylights out of me a minute ago. I glanced behind me but he was still in the barn. What was I supposed to do? He said not to talk to them but then he left me directly in their path. Ridiculous man.

"What can I do for you?" I asked as they slowed down in front of me.

One of the men was Mr. Murphy but I didn't know the other two. One was tall in the saddle with an impressive mustache that curled on the ends. Big feathered eyebrows covered expressive brown eyes. A gold star on his pocket told me he was the law in these parts. "Who're you?" he asked.

Mr. Murphy sniffed. "Ain't you heard, Sheriff? Luke Dawson's gone and found himself a bonafied whore to marry."

"Mr. Murphy!" I couldn't even control the anger that clenched my hands at my side. "I ain't a whore anymore so you can bite your tongue! Right off and it would please me."

"Eeeeewey!" The other stranger said with a grin. "This one here's a spitfire."

"Enough," the sheriff said. "Where's your husband?"

I blasted my fists onto my hips and glared. I should definitely stall. If Luke wasn't out here already, it was for a reason. "Now sir, I don't claim to be lady of the manor right yet as I'm not married. We're waiting on the circuit preacher, you see. Now as to the whereabouts of my betrothed, I'm sure you understand the needs of a working ranch and with only the two of us to man it at the moment, he could be doing a number of chores."

"Where's Jeremiah?" Sheriff asked.

"How the devil should I know the business of that man? He could be at the saloon in town, but from what I gather, he's an honest and decent man. From my experience, not too many of his breed show up in those kinds of establishments."

The sheriff closed his eyes and sighed deeply like my guesses were boring, but I kept right on.

"But if I had to guess, I'd say he's in Denver on business as he's been gone the broad side of a week."

"What kind of business could he possibly have in Denver?" Mr. Murphy asked in a tone that dripped with condescension.

"That I couldn't venture a guess at, Mr. Murphy." I leveled a glare at him. "On account of me being just a whore."

"What's going on here?" Luke asked from behind. He balanced a sloshing bucket of milk and stood as if he were completely shocked at their being there. He could have rivaled the actors I saw in a traveling theater once in the city.

"Three of Murphy's cattle were found dead on your property, Mr. Dawson," the sheriff drawled.

"Oh." Luke cocked his head to the side. "You know I can't control where your cattle wander off to die, don't you Mr. Murphy?"

"They didn't wander off to die!" he yelled shrilly. "Somebody's gone and killed them."

"Why would I shoot a cow? Unless it was snake bit, that seems like a pretty big waste."

I stood clutching my basket of eggs as Luke came to stand beside me. He rubbed the small of my back lightly with a finger and heat ran up my spine at his touch.

"Now, if you'll excuse us, gentlemen, I can't help you with your cow problem. I don't know anything about them."

"Where's Jeremiah?" the sheriff asked again.

"Probably up in Denver. I can't be for certain because I'm not my brother's keeper and he wanders from time to time."

Huh. I'd apparently been right in my guess.

The smaller man, a young deputy of some sort, said, "Mr. Murphy's cows weren't shot, Mr. Dawson. They were torn apart by something and on your land. You seen any predators that could take out three cows?"

Mr. Murphy snarled, "Seen any? He's the damned predator. Whole town knows it; they're just afraid to say it out loud."

I was shocked into action by his accusation. "Excuse me. What are you saying? That Luke went running around in the night and killed your cows with his bare teeth? That's absurd! My fiancé is here with me every night! And if he did have a hankering for beef, why on God's green earth wouldn't he just go harvest one out of our own substantial herd? You gentlemen are welcome to go hunt down the actual animals that chased your cattle onto our land, which is something I assure you we cannot control, and do with them what you think is necessary."

"See, that's the thing, ma'am," the sheriff said. "I can't name any predators capable of killing three cattle right next to each other, and then only eating on one like the others were just for fun. And there's wolf prints all around the kills but the problem is, while wolves used to cover this area before we showed up to settle it, there are only a few hundred left and we've pushed them farther into the wilderness. Haven't seen any of them in years."

A cold stone just thawing from winter settled in my gut. I'd almost been ravaged by a wolf so I'd seen the animal to blame for the killings. Dryly, I said, "That sounds just like what you did to the Indians. It seems you've missed one."

I turned for the house but there was a warning in the sheriff's voice. "Oh, we didn't miss him. He's just become very cunning at hiding." He stared levelly at Luke before he turned and led the men back down the road.

A chill started in my arms and worked its way up my neck. What was he saying? I knew it had to mean something, some secret they were hinting at, but all I saw was a man holding a pail of milk. He couldn't kill cows like a wolf. The sheriff would do best to organize a hunt and find the real culprit.

Luke grabbed my hand. "You done good."

I spun on him. "If you've got secrets, I understand. I kept mine for reasons, and you've got your reasons too, I know it. Don't get me hurt over them, though."

"I won't hurt you."

"I'm talking about others." My voice dropped to an anguished whisper. "Don't you hurt me over your need to keep secrets. Trust me, it's better when you own them."

His green eyes searched mine and his mouth opened like he would confess his soul. But he didn't. Instead, he walked past me toward the house. "I ain't got no secrets to share, woman. Wish I did so you'd leave off about 'em."

"Luke Dawson!" I screeched. I had nothing else to say, I just wanted to scream his name so when he threw his free hand over his ear and hunched toward me, I had enough satisfaction to make up for him dancing around my questions.

"What?" he snapped.

For lack of anything better to say, I smiled cheerily. "If you want me to cook you dinner tonight, I need meat."

His narrowed eyes were nothing shy of suspicious. "I said I'd hunt this morning didn't I?" He lifted his face to the sun. "It's too late for deer to be moving and I don't really feel like beef all the sudden."

"Will you take me fishing with you?"

His chin dropped and his eyebrows disappeared under his hat. "You want to go fishing?"

Honesty was the best policy. "I want to spend time with you, and my best chance to do that is if I go fishing with you."

A slow smile took over his face and filled his eyes. "If you saddle your own horse, you can go."

"Take my eggs in, then. I need a head start."

Chapter Fourteen
Kristina

I managed to wrestle Rosy's saddle on. Thankfully, I'd been able to do it before Luke walked into the barn. I didn't need his ribbing at the ungraceful way Rosy spun to the side and just about pressed me on my backside in the hay. I was in the middle of tightening up the cinch when he strode through the door in a plain shirt and thin, cotton pants over his boots.

The sunlight was behind him and he walked with the confidence of a capable man. His face was dark, but still his eyes shone such a bright color, they seemed to glow in the dusty light of the barn. He stopped so close to me, the warmth of his body brushed my skin and my insides opened up in ways I'd never experienced before. He was going to kiss me and it would be the first that meant anything in a long time.

He leaned closer with a delicious smile and I closed my eyes in wait, lips throbbing with the want to touch them to his. When nothing happened, I peeked one eye open to find him checking how tight my cinch was. Embarrassed, I spun away from him as burning heat crept into my cheeks. The last mortification I needed was for him to see me blush over him. Infuriating man.

I was a saloon girl and one highly sought after if my earnings said anything. I hadn't a problem with men throwing themselves at me and paying me handsomely for it, so why was it so hard to pry some warmth from my fiancé? He seemed like a man who enjoyed the company of a woman. I could nearly smell the strength and virility permeating from him, so why didn't he want me?

He placed his hands on my waist but it only maddened me. "I don't need your help," I snapped.

His hands went up in surrender and he saddled his horse in the back stall while I tried and tried again to hoist myself up in the stirrup. In desperation, I dragged Rosy closer to the gate and climbed it to get a better angle. Success. It hadn't been pretty, but it got done.

"Don't you need a fishing pole?" I asked him. I was no expert, but unless I was mistaken, fish didn't just jump in a bucket.

"We do it a little different around here," he said before kicking his horse into a gallop.

If I wanted any chance to keep up with him, I was going to have to push Rosy faster than I'd ever gone. Holding on for dear life, I kicked her and the response was instantaneous. Luke was right. This horse had been born to run.

Trees whipped by and Rosy jumped over logs and rocks that graced the thin trail toward the sound of rushing water. Flushed and breathless, I pulled her to a stop when we reached a gently rolling river. The countryside was hilly and long grass waved like ripples in the water itself. Yellow and purple wildflowers dotted the lush landscape and I pulled Rosy toward a giant shade tree near the water. The sun was high in the sky and my heart pounded with the exerted energy of the race. Luke took the make-shift reins from me, then led both horses to the meadow behind us where they munched grass in companionable silence.

When Luke returned, he pulled his shirt over his head. "Avert your eyes," he said halfheartedly.

Like hell I would. Instead I crossed my arms and leaned against the giant tree to enjoy the show.

"You know, most ladies would look away."

"I'm not most ladies."

His eyes dared me to look and he stood to his full height and waited as I raked my eyes down the length of his shirtless body. I'd known he was a well fashioned man from the way he filled out his clothes, but I hadn't an idea just how tight his musculature was. He looked like one of those Greek gods I'd seen in a picture catalogue once. His arms were big, but not overly so, and they led to well-muscled shoulders that had tanned in the sun. His chest begged for my fingers to trace the taut outline and his flat stomach tapered at the waist and disappeared into his loose fitting pants in a way I found truly tantalizing. I'd never been so desperate to see more of a man.

My breath trembled slightly but he couldn't know that. He wasn't close enough to hear. A naughty smile touched his masculine lips and he backed slowly away from me until he was in the water.

I arched my eyebrow. "I said fishing, not swimming."

"The way I fish is a little of both. My Da taught me and my brothers to catch them with our hands. Come over here and I'll show you."

The low hung branch behind me gave a tiny complaint under the weight of my elbows. "I can't."

"Well, why not?" His grin was growing wider by the moment and he splashed a handful of water in my direction.

"I told you I could shoot, sir."

"Yeah?" He splashed me again. "What're you gonna to shoot me with?"

I cocked my head and waited. The look of realization on his face made my insides dance.

"Wait," he said. "You telling me you have a gun on you?"

"Yep. You want to see it?"

He stood as straight as a razor while tiny waves lapped at his hips. "Yes," he breathed.

The roots of the tree were aged and gnarled and I set my booted foot upon the highest one. Slowly, careful never to take my eyes from his face, I slid the hem of my dress up my leg. Higher and higher it went until it reached my thigh where a red garter holster nestled my Derringer. It was a tiny one-shot that fit perfectly into my hand with a detailed ivory grip and a floral etched hammer.

Luke inhaled sharply and dropped down into water up to his chin. "Where'd you get that puff pistol?" he asked in a very nonchalant tone.

"From a regular client. He said every good whore needed one. He was a wealthy man, and gifted it to me the last time he came to visit. Does it bother you?"

The water rippled as Luke shook his head. "You know how to use it?"

I wouldn't tell him just how well, as he didn't need to know the number of hours I'd spent practicing. Or that one day I planned on my little Derringer being my sword of light against the woman who'd taken everything from me. My heart didn't harbor revenge, so Luke shouldn't think that it did. It only harbored a calm knowledge that someday, in some way, justice would come to Evelynn French. Instead I told him, "I can shoot well enough."

"Come here," he said quietly.

"Now, Mr. Dawson, a lady can't go swimming with a man she hardly knows in her finest dress."

"I don't care about the dress and you know me just fine."

I frowned. He might not care, but I did. I only had two dresses, besides the one I whored in, and they were my prized possessions. Besides my Derringer, they were the only material things with any meaning to me. Saucily, I repeated his words. "Avert your eyes."

"Hmm mm," he said and kept right on watching.

Fair enough. I untied my apron and lay it across the tree branch before slipping out of my dress. I had my thickest cotton shift on underneath and left that secured snuggly to my body. It was sleeveless and came up to my knees but he'd just seen much more of my leg a moment ago, so I didn't fuss over that much.

"It's cold," I complained as my toe graced a lazy wave.

Something akin to a growl rumbled from Luke's throat, throwing my tiny hairs on end. Before I could retreat, he was out of the water with little care to splashing me and I was scooped up in his arms. He dragged his feet through the waves as he took me deeper and the shock of the cold against my bare legs and arms made me gasp. I squirmed and exclaimed, "Luke!"

"Give it a second and you'll get used to it," he rumbled next to my ear.

We hung there, frozen in the moment and closer together than we'd ever been. I clung to him with my arms around his neck and his breath tickled my throat where his jaw was nestled. The temptation to feel his face against my neck was too great and I leaned in just enough to touch my skin to his lips. My breathing was ragged, but it could've been from the cold. His lips moved against the tender skin of my throat as he kissed it. And by the time he'd left a trail of burning fire up to my mouth, I was clay in his capable hands. I held him closer and turned, ready for the connection I'd been hoping for since the day I saw his alluring profile in town.

His kiss was warm and so sweet, it melted the hardened parts of me that'd gotten used to not really *feeling* the adorations of a man. Where I had expected violence, I instead received an unexpected tenderness. He sucked gently on my bottom lip and to my great embarrassment a groan escaped my throat. I hadn't even forced it. It bubbled forth like he'd drawn it from me.

He paused at the sound but then his hand cradled the back of my head and he parted my lips with his, deepening the kiss. My body floated downward into the water as his arm released me, and when I was vertical, he pulled me to his chest with a grasp so strong it was shocking. If I didn't stop us, I'd give him everything—every little piece of me right here in the running river. Never again would I have a chance to do this right.

"Luke," I gasped, but he'd moved his lips to my collar bone. The sun was so bright as I threw my head back, I closed my eyes to save them. "Luke, please," I tried again. His hand moved to pull my shift to the side but I held it still with my own. "I want to be more."

His body tensed and he stopped. "What do you want from me, woman?"

I kept my eyes closed against the disappointment I knew would be swimming in his face. I'd fold if I saw it. "I don't want to just be a whore to you. I've had a mind to do this right and I aim to."

He didn't say anything so I cautiously opened my eyes. He still held me against him and his hand brushed my back rhythmically in a distracted manner. The green in his eyes had faded and left some other lightened color I couldn't put a finger on in its place. They seemed to glow from the inside out and I blinked my eyes, once. Twice. It had to be a trick of the sun reflecting off the water or something. But as the color stayed, I frowned and stroked his face with my dripping finger.

"Your eyes," I whispered.

He turned away as if I'd burned him and I went under. He was much taller than me, and while he'd been standing on the rocky bottom, my feet had been floating far above it. Gasping as I swam to the surface I made my way to shallower water. "Luke Dawson!" I yelled when I was able.

He was already some distance off with his back to me. The river ran around him like a protruding boulder was in its midst. Immovable and accepted, the water parted for him and continued its journey downstream. His back glistened with tiny water droplets and his hair was wet from where he'd apparently submerged himself while I was floundering for a footing. The grass swayed in a dance around the river and the sky was so blue it looked like some painting that belonged in a fancy city gallery. He looked very lonesome standing there all by himself. It struck me that maybe he'd grown up a lonely soul because of some demon he wrestled within himself.

My heart reached for him and I let the current pull me closer. The skin of his back was smooth and tense under my hand. "Hey," I said softly. "You don't have to hide. Not from me."

When he turned, his eyes were back to green. Maybe my eyes looked a strange color too in the sun soaked water.

"I respect you wanting to do this right. I'm going to town tomorrow to send word to the circuit preacher again. I don't know what's keeping him, but we'll find out, okay?"

"Can I come, too?"

His hands were strong and enticing as they found mine under the water. "You want to see Trudy?"

I nodded until the water lapped at my chin.

His gaze was steady. "I have to tell you something."

This was it. This was the moment he'd let me in.

"Trudy's going to have a baby."

Well, that wasn't at all what I'd expected. Granted, I hadn't any earthy idea what he was going to say, but this certainly hadn't been in the realm of possibilities.

"What? Why didn't she say anything?"

"I don't think she knows yet."

"Then how do you know?" I asked with an odd sense of wrongness churning in my stomach.

"I can just tell these things. When she realizes, she'll share her excitement with you. You'll be her confidant while she grows, and you'll get feelings like you want the same experience. It's like boys with pistols. The first boy in our school to be gifted a pistol from his pa was Blaine Green and he had the rest of us clawing our eyes out to get one."

"You're afraid Trudy's pregnancy will give me baby fever?" I couldn't see the problem. "Why is that a bad thing?"

"Because I don't want children, Kristina. Not just now. I mean, I don't ever want children. I've never wanted them and never will. I won't be a man you can talk into it either. I want you to think about it really hard before we go in front of a priest because it means you're committing yourself to a childless life."

Something ached deep inside of me. I'd never once in my life thought about children or being a mother, but him telling me he'd never give me one was a loss I wasn't equipped to deal with. I would never hold a child with his green eyes in the cradle of my arms. I'd never feed his babe at my breast. Never would the noise of children echo in our home.

"Is it because I'm a whore?"

Emotion roiled within the depths of his eyes. "I don't want to talk about why's and why not's."

"You don't think I deserve a reason? I don't deserve an answer when my friends look at me with pity years from now, and wonder what's wrong with me? When they talk in hushed whispers about what a failure of a wife I've been because I couldn't even give you a child. You don't think I deserve a weapon against that gaping hole you'll shove me into?"

His mouth was set in a grim line but he said nothing.

Anger was a whiplash against my skin. "Fine. I suppose that's the catch then isn't it. I get to bed a fine and handsome man and fall under his protection, but I won't have the whole family." I fled the water as fast as my dragging legs could go. "What with my past, why did I ever expect to have some perfect ending?"

I needed to escape before I cried. That would be the push that sent me over the edge if he got the satisfaction of seeing me cry over him. I shoved my feet into my shoes and threw my dress and apron over my shoulder before I turned. "I'll marry you still, Luke Dawson, because damn you, you made me love you before you enlightened me of your rules." I stomped off in the direction of Rosy with the back of my hand pressed to my eye like it would help keep the tears inside of me.

Why was I so emotional over something I didn't even know I'd wanted? Never had the thought occurred to me that I'd want a child with any man. Not after seeing the darkest parts of them. But then Luke had come and cared for me, saved me, touched me, and all the sudden, him taking this away felt like a betrayal.

I thought he'd give me anything. The assumption was so stupid because no man I'd ever met had been honorable, but Luke was. The treacherously hopeful corners of my heart thought he would find a way to fix everything. What a fool I'd been. He didn't want a child with a saloon girl. He didn't want a child who would bear a whore's blood running through his veins.

My fury helped to hoist me up onto a grazing Rosy in one motion. I gathered my clothes in my lap and nudged the red-hided animal away from the prying eyes of that insensitive man. The wind whipped through my wet hair and raised gooseflesh on my skin as it caressed the moisture on it. The sound of the lonesome breeze comforted me and dried my eyes.

Maybe he was right.

What chance did the child of a whore have in such a cruel world?

Chapter Fifteen
Luke

Maybe if I brought enough catfish home with me, she'd be less angry. *Idiot.* That wouldn't work at all. *You just told her she couldn't ever be a mother if she marries you, and you think bringing buckets of fish home that she has to cook will piss her off less?* It was impressive how dense I was with women's actual needs.

I hefted the string of catfish over my shoulder and pulled my horse's reins in irritation. Gorging on meadow grass had him taking his sweet time behind me.

Okay, but if I didn't give fair warning before she married me, what kind of man would that make me? The kind that don't care about honor or integrity, that's the kind. I wasn't tricking her into marrying me. I wanted her to know what she was getting herself into. Well, most of what she was getting herself into anyway. The werewolf stuff we'd have to deal with in time, when I was sure she wasn't going to scatter.

But still…the devastation in her blue eyes flashed across my mind again. Honestly, I hadn't expected that reaction. She was a whore and I hadn't ever met one that was the mothering kind, but Kristina was different and I was a fool to forget it.

The familiar smell that belonged in those woods hit me long before I took the time to realize its meaning. I was too lost in my own churning thoughts to pick up on something that was at home with the scent of the native trees and grasses of our little hideaway. It wasn't until I was much closer that it drew my conscious attention.

I smelled Jeremiah.

"Come on," I goaded the horse as I pulled him behind. My sensitive nose led me right to his crumpled body.

If it weren't for the struggling movement of his chest, I'd have thought him dead. His body was mangled in the in between state that said he wasn't completely with me yet. At least his fur already retracted and he had smooth, human skin again. He grunted as one of his fingers snapped back to its human shape. It was happening so slowly. I was watching my worst nightmare come to life.

"You stayed wolf too long," I scolded him, unsure if he could even understand my words or not. The rumble that came from his throat said not.

The smell of predator was pungent against the forest. I couldn't just leave him there. He'd likely been changing for hours and the smell of his struggle and sound of his pain was bringing in critters that would eat him alive.

"Sorry," I whispered as I hoisted him over the saddle. He screamed and my horse shied. "Steady there, boy," I crooned. "It's just Jeremiah."

The rest of the journey back to the house lasted hours. Likely it was twenty minutes or so, but every labored breath and groan from behind me brought the memory of pain to my bones. My hopes of Kristina being safely inside when we arrived were dashed the second I pulled through the trees that edged the clearing. Her gaze plowed into mine and her eyes went as wide as dinner plates.

"Is he dead?" she asked breathlessly when she reached us.

"Nope, but not for lack of trying. I need you to get back in the house."

Jeremiah screamed again amid the sound of cracking bones.

"He needs a doctor!"

"What he needs is you not staring at his naked body. Get on inside, you hear me?"

Stubbornly, she said, "I'm riding to town for a doctor."

"No! No doctors. He's fine. The best thing you can do for him is fry up these fish. He'll need something to eat." I handed over the string of fat catfish and pushed past her.

"I'll get his bed ready," she said quietly.

"He's sleeping in the barn tonight," I called behind me.

With a furious screech that rattled my eardrums, Kristina stomped for the house as I threw open the barn door. Jeremiah, for all the trouble he'd caused, could finish his change in my own little private corner of hell in the back. I dumped his body and unsaddled my horse before I headed for the house.

Da had taught me there were things in life that a man didn't want to do, but if he was man enough, he'd do them anyway. I was headed into a hailstorm, and there was no help for it but to keep on going.

I ducked when I opened the door as the smallest of the catfish I'd pulled from under their nesting rocks sailed through the air at my head. Another one followed.

"Dammit woman, would you stop that?"

"What in hells bells am I supposed to do with whole fish? I know you don't think I'm going to fry them up this way, do you? Your brother's dying and you hand me fish and tell me to cook them? You've lost your ever-loving mind, Luke Dawson, and you'd better find it again, quick."

I sloughed my reserve off and grabbed her hand before she could throw another. Her eyes were frightened but my speed did the trick. She wasn't lobbing things at my face anymore. "I'll clean the fish. Just let me get a clean pair of clothes for Jeremiah first."

"I'll get them!" She ran for the room and as we both got stuck trying to shove ourselves through it, she burst out into a fit of giggles.

Leaned up against the doorframe with her pink cheeks and smiling eyes, she looked right harmless from the screaming banshee that had been throwing fish a second ago. I relaxed against the other side of the door and huffed a surprised laugh at the absurdity of the last five minutes.

Moving a strand of hair out of her face, I waited until she was calm enough to hear the truth in my words. "I'm sorry about earlier. I wasn't trying to boss you around, I just needed to get him off that horse so he can start feeling better. Jeremiah will be fine, I promise. And what he's going through right now? That man deserves it and more. He'll be back to his normal, intrusive, overbearing self again by morning. You just have to trust me, okay?"

The smile faded from her full lips. "No, you have it wrong. It's you who has to trust me." And with that, she retreated from the door.

She retreated from me.

****

Kristina

Jeremiah obviously had too much drink in him and hurt himself coming home. Luke thought he was protecting me by keeping his drunken injuries in the barn, and while it was sweet that he was trying to be a gentleman, I'd seen more drunk men than sober in the past year. I was basically a professional at men who'd consumed too much of the rotgut whiskey, but if Luke wanted to squander my abilities to sober up a man, so be it. Their loss.

I strained the bucket of milk through the thin cloth again and

97

frowned when Luke called my name from the yard.

"What?" I yelled testily. If the cream didn't rise off by dinner, there'd be no milk with our food.

"You need to learn how to do this," came the muffled reply through the front door.

The empty bucket made a thud as I set it in the sink to rinse. I'd go outside out of curiosity, but I'd take my time about it.

When I hopped off of the bottom stair of the front porch, it was obvious what Luke wanted me to see. He sat at a small wooden table, stained darker in the center, with two filleted fish and one in process. Disgusting.

"I'm all for cooking them. You clean them. That's the deal."

"This is a valuable skill to have in case I'm not here someday and you get a hankering for fish. Come on, woman. I'm waiting on you."

"Fine," I groaned. With my eyes squeezed tightly shut, it wasn't so bad.

"You won't learn anything with your eyes closed, now come here."

I glowered at the back of his head. How did he know?

"You still have your knife on you?"

Out of my pocket my new deadly friend slid, and Luke nodded his approval.

"Good, now watch me this first time, and on the next one you can do it."

I eyed the still catfish and swallowed a gag. "This don't seem like women's work to me."

Luke sighed and wiped the back of his arm across his forehead. "It ain't but I thought you said you weren't like other women. You're going to learn stuff other women don't know, because I want you to be prepared out here. If you want me to go back to treating you like you're helpless, say the word and I'll coddle you. You didn't seem too happy when you weren't contributing though. I respect that, but if doing all the extras is too much, I'll dial it back."

Well, that sounded not at all like what I wanted. It was nice that he wasn't treating me like some woman who stayed in the kitchen baking pies all day. He'd been okay with me going fishing, and bought me a horse so I could learn to ride. He'd even mentioned me learning to shoot a pistol. He was making me his equal, and if cutting up a fish kept him on that path, then so be it.

"Okay, show me."

Luke did show me, and then after I'd done a hack job of fileting my fish, he showed me how to make the batter to fry them too.

"I thought Jeremiah did all the cooking before I came along," I said to the sound of popping grease. The smell of cooking cornmeal was enough to set my mouth to watering.

"Nah, we took turns. My Da was the one who cooked when we were growing up. Ma was a self-proclaimed terrible cook so if we wanted to eat, Da or us had to make it."

"What did your mother do?"

"She did all of the other mothering things, just not that. She helped Da out a lot with his work as well so we didn't ever mind it. My brothers and I didn't know any different, so it wasn't strange. Like this," he said, leaning over my shoulder and tossing a strip onto the hot grease.

The rasp of his jawline against my cheek was a gentle reminder of the closeness we'd shared in the river and my heart hammered so hard, surely he'd be able to hear it from where he stood.

In search of somewhere to place my focus other than his glorious face against mine, I asked, "What happened to your parents?"

"They're both still alive, living happily in the city where my mom was born. She doesn't like the wilds as much as the men in our family do, so Da told her if they got all three of us grown and on our own, he'd buy her a place in Boston. Someday we'll go and see them. They'll be mighty surprised to see me settled down."

If he kept touching my waist like he was, I was likely to burst into flames at any moment. "I guess I wasn't in your plans, was I?"

"Making a home has always been Jeremiah's thing." He paused before he said, "Speak of the devil and he shall appear."

A moment later, the front door flung open and Jeremiah staggered in. His face was haggard and his hair mussed. Heavily, he sank into one of the dining chairs and groaned as if he'd aged a hundred years in a week.

In a move I found so surprising it caught my breath, Luke kissed my neck before he left me to finish ladling the fish from the oil and onto a cloth covered plate. I glanced at Jeremiah to see if he'd seen the daring affection, but he only had eyes for the corner of the table. He looked haunted.

As I lay the plate of food in the center of the table, Jeremiah put his hand over my wrist. "Can you forgive me for leaving you in such a state?"

"There's nothing to forgive. I'm fine."

His dark eyes searched every facet of my face before he nodded. "You do look like you're healing. I shouldn't have left until I was sure though."

I sat beside him as Luke watched us from the front where he poured milk into a pitcher.

"Jeremiah, why did you leave?" I asked. Sometimes it was easier if a man just said the vile thing he was going through—if he spat it out like poison before it turned his soul to rot.

"My wife, Anna..." He swallowed hard. "She was abused before she was killed. I couldn't watch another woman in pain like that. It was too much."

I'd figured it was something along those lines so I patted his hand with little surprise. "I'm sorry for your Anna. Thank you for coming with Luke to save me. If you two hadn't come..." My voice trailed off to a feeble little sound. "If you hadn't come, I would've died too, so thank you."

His smile was as dry and frail as a barren desert, but it was a smile and a start nonetheless.

Chapter Sixteen
Kristina

"Trudy isn't here today. She's feeling poorly so it's just me here to serve all these people until tonight," said the harried girl at Cotton's. Leslie, I remembered Trudy calling her.

Okay. An inkling of suspicious excitement lit my gut. Maybe Luke was right. I hadn't a clue why he'd venture a guess like this, but he had, and now I couldn't put it out of my mind. "Thanks and good luck today," I rushed before I slid out the busy front door. Breakfast was booming at Cotton's.

The street was still muddy, but I'd wised up and found a thin trail of plank boards someone thoughtfully floated across the muck at the end of the street. The general store was nearly empty when I wandered in. A man behind a cluttered counter smiled from behind his glasses.

"I can't say I've seen you around here. You new in town?" he asked.

"Pretty new. I just arrived last week."

"Ah, welcome. What can I do you for?"

"Do you have any ginger to sell?"

He pointed his finger at the roof like he might just have what I needed, then rifled through a row of jars until he came to one with two pieces of ginger in it.

"You're in luck, little lady. We got some on the stagecoach two days ago."

Beaming, I slid a coin across the wooden surface of the counter and waited for him to fold one into brown paper before I all but danced out of the store.

With a quick rap on Trudy's door, I glanced around to see if Luke finished his errand at the post office yet. He stood leaned against a post, watching me with an indecipherable expression. I waved but he didn't seem to notice.

The door opened and Elias stood with a worried look in his blue eyes. "Trudy's feeling poorly this morning, Ms. I'm worried she's got the grip and I don't want it spreading to you and your men."

Poor Elias looked disheveled and pale. "Don't worry. She doesn't have the grip and I've got the cure for what ails her."

His shoulders relaxed noticeably when he saw the brown wrapped thing I carried. "Come on in. She's in the back room."

Trudy was pale faced, shaking, and clutching onto an empty washbasin when I pushed the door open. Maybe I should've bought up all the ginger the general store had.

"Mr. Elias," I said with an edge of worry. "Could you heat up some water?"

Immediately the sound of banging pots rang out.

"I don't want any water," Trudy said. "I don't want anything."

"Well you're going to have to drink something sometime. It won't help anything if you lose your strength."

Trudy's lip trembled. "I'm real sick, Kristina. I think I'm dyin'."

My heart lurched at her fear. "Oh, Trudy, you aren't dyin'. You're with child."

Her dark eyes grew as round as the full moon. "How do you know that?" she whispered.

"For one, Luke told me you are, because apparently he's some sort of magical midwife—"

"Luke told you I'm pregnant? But how…" A toothy grin spread across her face and some of the color returned to her dark cheeks. "He'd know, I suppose."

"I suppose," I said doubtfully. "And second, what you're doing now with the shaking and nausea is exactly what I saw one of the girls I used to work with doing when she was accidentally with child. Now, whores know a thing or ten about avoiding pregnancy, but those tricks don't work all the time. She, Gretta was her name, was sick from the day she found out until the day she delivered, and nothing would help her keep food down but warm ginger water. And you need to eat so that baby can grow big and strong. I brought you a present." I opened the corner of the wrapping and let her see the fragrant spice.

"Don't tell Elias," she said with an excited tremor in her voice. "We've been trying a long time."

I zipped my mouth and whispered, "This is your news to share." Squeezing her hand, I swished into the kitchen and pulled the knife from my pocket.

The water was boiling by the time I was finished chopping a piece of the root as finely as I could manage. When the ginger water was steaming in a tin mug, I brought it in for Trudy to sip. A dreamy look had settled on her face and she smiled from time to time for no apparent reason. I was so happy for her I could cry, but a tiny part of me pulled into itself protectively. I would never have this moment. That moment of realization that my body was making a miracle and I was creating a child as a woman was meant to do. I wouldn't dare let my loss show on my face though because I wouldn't ruin Trudy's moment in a million years.

She gasped. "Kristina, no midwife is going to take me and there aren't any other freedmen around who would deliver me either. What am I going to do?"

"Can you send word to your family up north? Could they come down when you get closer?"

"No, they won't travel this far. It wouldn't be safe here for them either."

"Okay, we have some time to figure all of that out. Even if we have to send for a midwife from up north, between Elias and me, we'll get it done. Don't you worry."

"Do you have any experience midwifing?" she asked.

"No, not me. I've been in the room on a couple of births, but I don't know how to get those babies to air like someone trained would be able to."

"Will you be there anyway?"

I tried to keep the emotion out of my voice just in case. The sheer potency of my excitement had a tendency to frighten people. "Do you want me in the room?"

Her delicate eyelids were lined with the shining jewels of unshed tears. "Yes."

Raw emotion made my throat close up, so I swallowed hard before I answered. "Then I'll be there."

****

The ginger seemed to do the trick and when I closed the door to Trudy's house with a happy heart, I looked up to find Luke in the same place he had been. He was joined by Elias, who leaned heavily against the post talking quietly.

"Is she all right?" Elias asked the moment I was close enough.

"She'll live," I said with a wink at Luke.

I stopped him from jogging back into the small home. "Elias, she needs ginger. I've left some in the kitchen for you, but she may need more and I have it on good authority the general store has another root of it. Buy it up so they'll order more. When she needs it, boil water and chop a small piece finely. When it's good and mixed in the hot water, give it to her in a tin mug. Give her bread or something hardy right after, you hear?"

"Thank you, Kristina." He kissed me on the cheek before he switched directions for the general store.

"You okay?" Luke asked as I watched Elias walk away.

Inhaling deeply, I said, "I'm fine."

Luke's fingertips brushed mine as he pulled my hand into the crook of his arm. Our shoes made very different tones as we walked across the wooden planks in front of the shops.

"In my experience, when a woman says she's fine, she's usually not."

Clever man. "This isn't about me. It's about Trudy now. She wants me in the delivery room, you know."

"Really? Do you want to be?"

"Very much."

His eyes tightened. "You're changing the subject."

"I'm hungry," I said with a tremulous smile.

A grunt more animal than man escaped his mouth as he picked me up in one impossibly fast, impossibly easy gesture.

Gasping, I said, "Luke Dawson, people are watching."

He pulled gently at the tender skin of my neck with his lips and a deep velvet chuckle reverberated against it. "I don't care about what they think."

I smacked his shoulder halfheartedly as he strode across muddy Main Street. "You should. Maybe you'd get accused less of cattle thieving if you looked like a semi-honorable man while you were in town."

"People will talk either way. May as well enjoy my life."

That seemed like a sound argument to me, so I didn't object when he kissed me fiercely before he set me down on the other side. Just as we were heading into Cotton's, Jeremiah ducked under the shorter door frame and pulled his hat over short, dark hair.

"Did you already eat?" Luke asked.

"I tried but the sheriff and his new deputy are in there and they just gave me an earful in front of half the town." He smiled politely at a family who walked by and lowered his voice. "I think we might have a problem."

Luke clapped him roughly on the back and said a terse, "Welcome home."

Rosy waited patiently in between the Dawson brother's black horses with her back hoof propped up like she hadn't a care in the world. I petted her neck as Luke and Jeremiah argued quietly in front of the cabinetry shop.

"What're we going to do with these boys?" I asked.

Rosy gave a tremendous snort and shook her head until the feathers in her mane flapped back and forth.

"Me either."

"That's a mighty pretty horse you got there," a man said as he ran his hand along Rosy's hind end. "Is she an Indian pony?" He looked to be young, around my own age, with light brown hair and friendly hazel eyes.

"She is. I wanted a horse with polka dots, so we traded for her."

"Do you trade often with the Indians?"

His question was strange but his eyes held an openness I hadn't seen in many men. He seemed genuinely curious, but I didn't know what was unacceptable to talk about in these parts. "I'm not sure, sir."

"Ezra. Call me Ezra."

"I'm not sure, Mr. Ezra, as I've only come to town within the last two weeks."

He petted Rosy gently and leaned his head to the side. "You look familiar. You came in on the stagecoach last week, you said? Might you have come in from Chicago?"

Something akin to a snake slithered down my spine. "Who wants to know?"

"I'm just making conversation, Ms. Yeaton. Don't take offense to a friendly question."

My voice dropped to a whisper. "I didn't tell you my name."

"You didn't have to. I'm from the Chicago area myself and never forget a face. Especially not one as pretty as yours."

"Get away from my horse," I growled.

He pointed lazily at me and leaned against Rosy's saddle. "I see your face is healing from a pretty good beating."

My heart hammered like the pounding of a drum. He knew Evelynn French. I just felt it in my bones. He was here to finish the job the others failed at. I wasn't safe at all. One step backward and my shoulder blades landed against a very solid wall of man.

As I sucked air to scream, Jeremiah said, "Kristina, is this man bothering you?"

Luke appeared behind Ezra like he was an apparition back from the dead for revenge. His moss green eyes seemed to glow when I said, "He knows Evelynn French."

Without a word, he wrapped an incredibly large hand around the stranger's neck and dragged him bodily into an alleyway between buildings. Strangled sounds came from the man, and he made smeared lines in the mud and across the wooden floor with his flailing boots.

Jeremiah stood watch at the mouth of the alleyway, and not more than a minute later, an empty handed Luke was back and headed down the street. Jeremiah and I exchanged a questioning glance before scurrying after him.

"Where're you going?" I asked.

"To get you something to eat," Luke said, holding one of the swinging doors to the saloon open for me.

Jeremiah grabbed my arm before I could follow him in. "This is no place for her."

"Actually, I'm quite comfortable eating here." I'd skipped breakfast in hopes of a meal from Cotton's and about now, I'd eat a barbecued armadillo.

"You heard the lady," Luke said as he pulled my other arm. "And besides, the only other place to eat is Cotton's and since you pissed off the sheriff, I'd say that's out because I sure as shit don't think we should be fighting anymore in public today."

I wrenched my arms free from the two iron grips "Unhand me, both of you! I'm going inside to eat. You two can squabble at each other all you want out here."

"Men and whores only," the old bartender sternly said over the noise of the drinkers and gamblers.

"Pipe down then. I'm whore enough."

A group of men nearest the door arched their eyebrows and one whistled.

"Fresh meat," another one with missing teeth and a long scar across his neck said.

"Sorry, lads, I'm on a break of sorts. Carry on." I sat at the furthest table and moments later the towering Dawson boys came through the swinging doors at a slow and deliberate spur-jangling saunter.

From my seat, I had a fantastic view of the show. If my entrance had caused a scene, theirs brought the saloon to an absolute standstill, one they didn't seem to notice. In a frozen room, Luke tipped his hat to the bartender.

"Bucyrus," he said in greeting.

The trio of saloon girls sitting around an old piano were the first to react. "Oh, Mr. Luke," the blonde-haired one squealed.

Jeremiah made his way to my table and tossed his hat onto it. "It ain't right for you to have to see him carrying on with these whores."

"As long as he don't take one in a back room, I'll be fine." I leaned forward. "Listen, Jeremiah, you're a real gentlemen, and it's mighty kind of you to treat me like a lady, but you don't have to worry overly about Luke hurting my feelings. He has experience with my kind and besides, if he offends me, you know I'll tell him about it. He has to learn his way around me just like you'll have to learn your way around whoever answers your advertisement."

After a long, hard look at me, he sighed in apparent resignation. "What do you want to eat? I'll go put our order in."

"I don't know. Just get me whatever you're having."

He palmed my head and shook it slowly as he got up. While he was at the bar telling the bartender what to get the kitchen started on, my attention drifted like a leaf in the wind back to Luke.

Slowly but surely he was making his way to our table, but the whores weren't making it easy. One wore his cowboy hat with a flirtatious grin shining up at him, another had both arms looped around his elbow and talked as if they were taking an afternoon stroll, and the last was running her painted claws up his thigh suggestively.

Was that what I looked like when I was trying desperately to get a paying customer? I scrunched up my face. I didn't think so. My clients had come to me willingly enough. The only time I went after someone was if I knew he was kind, or tipped well, or on a rare occasion, was an excellent lover.

Hmm. My oh my, Luke Dawson was becoming more intriguing by the minute.

"Ladies," he said. "I'd like you to meet my wife. Or soon enough she'll be my wife. Kristina, meet the only three whores left in town after old Bucyrus over there shipped off the other two on account of them getting the pox."

The ladies went silent. "Wait," the redheaded one said with a drawl of disbelief in her voice. "Luke, are you settling down on us?"

"Sure am."

Blondie shot daggers at me with her eyes and I smiled happily back. "Nice to meet you, and thank you for keeping my husband happy in my absence."

"Minny, it's okay," the short, dark-headed one said. "Luke can still come by and visit after he's married. Lots of men do it."

Luke pried his arms out of Minny's grip and shook his head in what I fervently hoped was *mock* sadness. "Sorry girls. Dawsons take marriage vows seriously. Kristina will be enough for me."

Minny snorted unbecomingly. "That's what you all say in front of your wives."

"Do men bring their wives in here often?" I asked out of rampant curiosity. I'd never seen it once in my year at the brothel, but maybe Colorado Springs was a different sort of place.

"Well, no, actually," the little dark-haired woman said. "I think you're a first."

Luke sat, but Minny followed and wrapped her arms around his neck as she floated into his lap. The red and black lace corset did little to shield her ample cleavage from Luke's line of sight, but she was just being territorial. She was probably losing her nicest customer. I'd always hated when that happened.

The bright red of her lipstick matched perfectly the color of her dress, and her blonde ringlets hung down over Luke's chest. The oddest sensation stirred inside me, watching that strange woman lay across my fiancé like an ornament. Even as he was trying to gently pry her from his lap, a little knife blade cut at my understanding and released something seething and red to match the woman's dress. I kept my face perfectly placid but even a returning Jeremiah had a sense that something was wrong, because he took one look at me and shot a warning glance at Luke.

Minny never took her eyes from my face as she snuggled against Luke with a tiny groan of pleasure.

"Don't," I warned casually.

"Okay, Minny," Luke said in a stern tone. "You had your fun." He grabbed her arms and gently pushed.

The crimson smile that spread across her face was nothing short of wicked as she clutched his jaw with both hands and kissed him soundly.

Well, I'd warned her. The tiny red smoke trail that opened with the first feelings of jealousy burned into a bonfire in an instant as I rocketed across the table and yanked her hair back.

Her scream was angry as her fingers flew to try and pull my hands from her tresses, but the lack of pain in her voice said my instincts were right. I gave another stout yank, and Minny's wig came right off.

Luke was already in the midst of pushing her upright and out of his lap and the low curse that Jeremiah uttered behind me was downright amused if I had to guess.

Bucyrus held three plates of food across his arms and was in the process of setting them down on the table. "Hey! Careful with her now. She's my best whore!"

I threw the wig in Minny's infuriated face and leaned back comfortably. "Well, now *she's* your best whore," I said, pointing to the redhead. "And your smartest."

Red Hair smiled boldly like she'd actually just got a promotion. Minny stood with her tiny fists clenched and her netted, short, brown hair for all to see for a moment more before she snatched her wig and disappeared with a wild animal shriek up the stairs.

I took a bite of fried potatoes and gave my very happiest grin. "Sorry for the inconvenience ladies, but Luke's off the table now. I'll take good care of him for you, I swear."

"Well," Jeremiah drawled. "That'll teach you to bring her into a saloon."

Maybe he was right. Perhaps too much of me had changed for the better and this wasn't my scene anymore. Luke stared at me like I'd lost my mind, but by the time half of my food was devoured, he was restraining a smile.

It really was quite difficult to feel guilty about my actions when my man found them so amusing.

Chapter Seventeen
Kristina

"Did you kill that man, Luke Dawson?" I asked
Rosy answered the pressure of my knees and moved beside his horse at a trot. Jeremiah seemed happy to stay right where he was—in the back.

"Well, did you?" I asked again.

"No, I didn't kill him. We were right in the middle of town. Where'd you think I stashed his body? I was only there a minute."

"What did you do?"

"I put the fear of God into the man. He wet his pants and then told me what I wanted to know."

Irritating silence followed until I took the bait. "Okay, and what did you want to know?"

"If Evelynn French sent him, which she did. How many she'd sent this time. Two. The other man was across the street watching. And lastly, what they'd been sent to do. They weren't here on a kill mission. Just to scout and keep you scared. Evelynn wanted to make sure you weren't skipping town." The leather in the saddle creaked as he turned to me. "She's going to have to be stopped eventually. You know that, right?"

"I know. I was kind of hoping she'd end up out here to finish the job herself and give me a shot at her. I couldn't touch her in Chicago."

His dark eyebrows shot up as if he were surprised. "You want a shot at her?"

"If it comes to that, yes."

"Huh. You're a violent little creature, aren't you?" The way his eyes raked across my collar bones and neck said he didn't mind that trait so much. "Circuit preacher will arrive on the morning coach tomorrow. You sure about going through with this?"

"You sure about giving up your whores?"

He pulled his horse closer until his leg brushed mine. "Well, I ain't givin' up all my whores, now am I?"

"You're a wicked man," I said as his horse danced out of my swatting range.

His laugh was booming and deep and my heart locked away the sound to cherish. The trail narrowed and Luke pulled back to let Rosy go first. Lurching forward, I cried out as she reacted at once to some unknown threat and bucked in panic. Unready, I was tossed from the saddle and landed on my side as she ran off at a frightened gallop. I groaned in soreness and as I glanced up, saw a viper curled on the trail, not a foot from my face. The sharp gasp that filled the clearing was my own as the snake reared up and stared at me with its flicking tongue tasting the air around me. I was going to die just a day before I married Luke, and the unfairness washed over me in the second it took to accept my doom.

"Don't move," Luke breathed. In his voice was something I'd never heard before. The confidence had washed away, and in its place, the tremble of fear immersed itself in his tone.

A sharp hissing sound came from the small serpent and just as it was about to strike, I held my breath in the last few moments of pain free life. Luke, in a move faster than my eyes could comprehend, whipped the snake out from in front of me just as he pressed forward to strike. He came so close, the wind from the poisonous little creature's movement brushed across my cheeks and a tiny drop of venom landed on my nose. Luke launched it far into the brush and fell onto his backside with the force of it.

It was as if everything played in slow motion. He sat there leaned back against his hands in the dirt with a look of absolute petrifying fear. His green eyes were wide and his mouth slack. Something about his expression made me feel empty. It was as if something important about my life was changing for the worse in this moment, and I was helpless to change the outcome.

"Luke," I whispered. Even I could hear the pleading in it and I didn't even know what it meant.

And then I blinked and he was gone. My rescuer was already up on his horse and running like the wind before I could even sit up in the grass.

"What's happened?" I whispered breathlessly as Jeremiah lifted me by the arms.

"Nothing good." He wiped the drop of poisonous moisture from the tip of my nose.

Standing here, looking up at Jeremiah's stoic face, I could see the worry in his midnight eyes as he watched his brother ride away.

****

Luke

The wind whipped me and sang a mournful song as if it could convince me to go back to her, but I kicked my horse again in defiance. I couldn't do it. I couldn't sink any deeper into quicksand with Kristina than I already had. The wolf inside of me howled in fury at my fears, but they'd always been the same. Nothing had changed from the moment before I met the woman until now.

Giving a woman's love to a creature like me would destroy everything. I'd bring hell to earth to protect her, and I'd known her less than two weeks. What would happen when I knew her a year? When I shared her bed and her sadness over our childless home? What would happen when I bound my wolf completely to her protection and she died on me, like all fragile humans did in our violent world?

I'd drown in flames of agony, that's what would happen.

My wolf would be broken like Jeremiah's. I'd be tormented for years until I convinced myself I needed another woman to love, just like my brother was doing in a horrible, vicious cycle that would bring nothing but suffering.

I'd be the death of that perfect, beautiful woman. Only the most selfish creature on earth would put her in the crosshairs of this life and when she was gone, I'd have to live with a pain worse than dying.

One snake bite was all it took for her life to be over.

It was dangerous in the untamed wilds of Colorado and not a place for a woman like her. It wasn't a place for a woman at all. Only men made of gristle and bone and too tough for this life to chew up and spit out.

We'd be the death of each other, and I had to save us both.

Nothing changed since I met her.

Nothing but my blinding love that would burn us both up like the sun.

****

Kristina

No way was I going to lie down while Luke talked himself out of marrying me. Not when we'd come this far and were this close. Rosy could run, he'd been right about that. Her speed was a breathless ride that bordered elating and terrifying all at once. She was sure footed and quick as lightning, and gave me more when I asked for it. My grip on the saddle horn was relentless as I steered her pounding hooves down the road that led home.

Home. My home and I'd be damned if Luke messed that up for us. Jeremiah yelled from behind me but I couldn't understand what he was saying, nor did I really care. I couldn't tell the sound of my heart from the rhythmic force that was my Indian pony's hooves. She reared with a scream when I pulled her to a sudden stop in front of the barn, but I was ready. I held on until all four of her hooves brushed the earth again.

He'd be putting his horse away and he'd be cornered in that old, rickety building. Luke wouldn't be able to escape the tidal wave of pleading emotion that was about to barrel down on him. I'd beg for his love if I had to.

"Kristina, don't!" Jeremiah yelled from the clearing but I ran for the door and threw it open.

"Luke!" I spun when I couldn't find him. "Luke, where are you?"

His horse was loose and came running with a terrified sound for the door. I pushed out of the way and clutched onto the nearest stall. He had to be in here. He wouldn't leave his horse out and saddled. Jeremiah was getting closer and he'd keep me from degrading myself—from begging his brother to keep me.

My panting breath was deafening as I searched each stall, every corner, every dark hiding place he could be. A soft noise came from the back of the barn and I ran, lifting my skirts as I rushed for him. In a back stall, one dilapidated with a lack of use and care, Luke's crumpled body lay bent and broken.

I slid into the musty hay beside him and waved my hands over his skin helplessly.

"Get out," he growled around a leather strip of hide he held clenched in his teeth.

"I can't leave you like this. Did you fall from the horse?"

An inhuman bellow burst from his throat as his neck snapped backward with a deafening crack.

"What's happening? What do I do?" I chanted, like the incantation would give me an answer somehow.

His face elongated with a crunching of bones and sharp teeth grew from his opened mouth. Hair sprouted through his smooth skin in a burst, and the blood in my veins turned to ice.

He wasn't dying. He was changing into a monster.

In a fit of self-preservation, I backed as far as I could against the next stall. Unable to take my eyes from the horrific event unfolding just feet away from me, I watched as the Luke I loved melted into the beast that'd tried to kill me the first night.

The panicked sounds, I came to realize, were mine. As his transformation into the wolf of my nightmares was completed, the fear loosed its hold on me just enough to let me run. I tripped on my skirts in the afternoon sunlight and fell with a tremendous crash outside the barn. The wolf was on my heels and when I turned, the snarling beast was on me.

His teeth shone white, and his crystalline blue eyes were so light, they were almost the color of bleached bone left out in the sun too long. I screamed in terror as he lunged. With his paws on either side of my body, his lips lowered over his teeth in a look of uncertainty. His eyes grew serious and clear.

I'd never seen heartbreak in an animal before now.

And then he was gone. He was just the back of a wolf running for the woods, leaving me to lie in the dirt, gasping and crying.

I lay there a long time. It wasn't an option to convince myself I'd imagined it. For the rest of my life I'd never get the vision of his breaking body out of my memories. I slammed the back of my head into the dirt and tried to get a handle on my breathing. Tiny stars dotted the edges of my vision and, blinking hard, I swore not to pass out in the yard. I stood and stumbled toward the house.

Jeremiah sat on the porch steps with his hands clasped under his chin. The saddest look I've ever seen danced in the depths of his dark eyes.

"Are you like him too? Do you turn into a wolf?" My voice sounded very small and had a tremor to it.

"Yes. And so does my other brother, and so does my father, and so has every man in our family tree since the beginning of humans."

My knees would buckle beneath me if I didn't sit, so I climbed past him and collapsed into the old wooden rocking chair. "What about your mother?"

"Human."

"Have you brought me here to kill me?"

"No. I brought you here to marry me. To soothe my wolf after losing his mate. I haven't lied about that part."

Nodding slowly, I said, "Not that part, just everything else." I touched my lips. "Luke kissed me. Will I catch it?"

"No, it isn't catching. If he bit you as a wolf, you'd die a slow and painful death though."

Jerking my head toward him I said, "Are you trying to frighten me?"

"No, Kristina. It wasn't ever our intention to scare you."

"Then why," I yelled, "did Luke attack me that first night? If it wasn't to scare me, then why'd he do it? Was he going to bite me and kill me? Was he that determined not to marry me?"

Jeremiah's patient voice was strained and loud. "Luke was a damned fool that night. He thought if he scared you, you'd stay out of the yard after dark and inside where you'd be safe. In his own way, he was trying to protect you."

"I've dreamt about the wolf and the fear I felt almost every night. How could that be protecting me? What am I supposed to do with this, Jeremiah?"

"It seems to me you have a choice. You can accept him, all of him, or you can pack your bags and leave knowing if you ever say a word about what we are, we'll be killed. Our futures are in your hands now. You have to decide your real feelings about Luke and if they're enough to overlook the nights he has to change into an animal."

****

That night, I cried until I had no more tears left to shed.

Somewhere, deep in the stillness of dark, a wolf howled. *My* wolf howled. The subtle shift in my way of thinking had me searching for him out my tiny window. The yard was still and shrouded in the midnight blue that accompanied an eyelash moon.

I fell asleep with my back against the wall, waiting for my wolf's song to touch my ears again.

Chapter Eighteen
Kristina

I slept fitfully, and time after time, my dreams careened back to the look in Luke's eyes when I screamed and cried in terror.

No wonder he hadn't told me.

After I was washed and dressed, I found breakfast still warming on the stove. I ate it on the front porch, but neither Dawson brother was around. The homestead was eerily quiet without the sound of them working. Even the animals seemed melancholy.

Finished with breakfast and thoroughly full, I rinsed my dish and the others in the sink before I headed out to the barn. It seemed to echo with emptiness, though all of its inhabitants were still here. Jeremiah and Luke's horses were missing, so they must've been out with the cattle. If I had any idea where the herd was, I'd head out after them. They'd been moved since last I'd seen them though, and I hadn't a guess where.

An ache bloomed in my chest the longer I went without seeing Luke. A quiet desperation to make it right washed over me. But my wants went unanswered as the morning sun rose in the sky to hang over a hot midafternoon.

I finished every chore I could think of and landed in the garden tugging ruthlessly on giant weeds that had sprouted after the rains. If I spent the time to make the boys a huge feast, Luke would have to let me say my piece. I'd make Trudy's stew and the cornbread she'd showed me how to make.

I pulled oddly shaped carrots, snap peas, green beans, squash, and onions too. Tomatoes hung from their mother plants so numerous, the limbs were weighed down with the red orbs. When the garden looked immaculate and my basket was filled with the vegetables I'd need, I dragged my haul inside and washed my dirt riddled wares. Someone had put beef in the smoke house, so I cut enough for my stew. When the kettle sat boiling over the fire, I took the sewing basket out to the rocking chair on the front porch, and busied my mind while my eyes searched loyally for Luke.

He couldn't avoid me forever.

It was Jeremiah who rode slowly through the edge of the woods. His hat shadowed his eyes, but the grim set of his mouth was telling enough. Whatever news he bore, it wasn't good.

"Where is he?" I asked as he tied his horse to the post out front and dismounted.

Removing his hat, he leaned his foot against the bottom step. "Luke's gone. The cattle are gone too, so I suppose he's driving them to Denver." His eyes never left the toe of his boot while he talked.

"By himself?"

"He's capable enough." His eyes found mine. "He's a werewolf, after all. I tried to catch up but he must have left in the night." His jaw clenched and unclenched with some hidden emotion.

"I don't understand. When's he coming back?"

Jeremiah shook his head and reached into his pocket before handing me a folded piece of parchment paper. "Found it on the table this morning."

The edges of it were warm and soft in my grasp. Upon opening the letter, dark scrawled handwriting flowed across the page. It must've been his and I traced the first word with the tip of my finger before handing it back. "Can you read it for me?"

I followed Jeremiah inside and melted numbly into a dining chair. The lantern battled the evening light and flickered across the table, sending scurrying shadows dancing across the floor. I picked at the edge of my apron as Jeremiah's deep voice resonated against the cabin walls.

Dear Kristina,

I'm leaving so you'll have plenty of time to find your own way without me there. Jeremiah will give you money for the train and you can go anywhere. You're young and will find another man. One more worthy of you. I don't want a wife and never have, but if we lived in a different world, I'd want a woman like you.

Be happy.

Fall in love with a man capable of loving you back.
Live.
-Luke

I wanted to throw the letter into the fire before Jeremiah even uttered the last word. I wanted to shred it into a million pieces so it wouldn't be true. I hated the letter more than I've ever hated anything in my entire life. How dare him cast me away before I'd even had a chance to talk about what I'd seen.

I didn't want to leave. Where in the entire world could I feel this safe? This taken care of? He'd given me a taste of what it was to have love returned, then he'd ripped it away from me with that blasted letter.

I tore out of the house as the roiling anguish threatened to drown me. At the edge of the woods I dropped to my knees and screamed his name until my voice was battered. A selfish and dark piece of me wished he could hear the sobs in my voice and somehow feel the pain that ripped at my soul. This hurt so much more than anything physical ever could.

Exhausted and defeated, I stumbled into the house.

"I can take you to the stagecoach tomorrow if you'd like," Jeremiah said.

With the back of my hand I wiped my tear stained cheeks, then straightened my spine. "You'll do no such thing. Luke is mine and I'm not going anywhere. This is my home."

****

Luke

It'd been five days and I already missed everything about her.

The long hours of slowly driving cattle weren't any help for the ache in my chest that grew bigger the farther away from her I rode. The drizzle that fell in waves from the dark storm clouds above did nothing but dampen my mood. I pulled my hat further down over my face as the steady *drip, drip, drip* of water fell in front of me. I couldn't name a more miserable time in my life.

I'd have to sell the spotted horse if she didn't take it with her. I couldn't see the animal in the barn and invite that kind of loneliness every day. Maybe I'd give her to Elias and Trudy. If Kristina was kind, she'd take everything that would remind me of her. My life had to be cleansed if I was to move on.

My wolf revolted and the animal slithered and snarled inside of me in desperation to get out and run back to her. I couldn't change until I knew she was gone into the world where I'd never find her again. Where my wolf would never find her.

The look of terror on her face when she saw the real me was

something we'd never get over, even if I wasn't already leaving. Too much was stacked against us and if she was to have a life, one without fear, it was going to have to be one without me. It was best we cut our ties now before we got any more attached.

She'd find a normal man who'd give her all the babies she wanted. She'd never have to hold her withering daughters or cry over their graves. She'd never have to wish for boy children so they'd survive. She could be pregnant and not be afraid.

The thought of her blooming with another man's child buckled me into myself. I shook my head violently and kicked my horse until he was running after a few cattle who'd wandered into the brush.

We hadn't a huge herd, but driving them one-manned still wasn't ideal. It seemed a fit punishment for me though. Every difficulty I'd found along the way, and they'd been numerous, felt right and justified. Maybe they would balance the wicked things I'd done.

Through the thinning trees, the edge of Denver was visible. The sight of it should've brought me excitement that the drive was almost done, but it was only the first leg of my journey.

I wouldn't see home again for a very long time.

People in Denver knew enough to move out of the way when cattle were driven down the rustic roads that led to the pens beside the train. My herd, weary from the journey, were easy enough to coax as I rode from side to side, keeping them in line and in the right direction. Once they were loaded into the pens, looked at, and given a head count twice over, I was paid.

In years past, Jeremiah and I would cut loose at a saloon up here in the city, but this year, our money wouldn't be squandered. I paid an advance to the Denver Bank that would get our homestead through the winter, and made arrangements to get Jeremiah his share of the leftover funds. With part of mine, I bought a train ticket.

"Where you headed?" the ticket master asked.

"Chicago bound, sir," I said over the pounding rain.

If I was leaving Kristina to make her way in the world, I was leaving her safe.

Evelynn French didn't know what kind of hell was coming for her.

Chapter Nineteen

September
October
November

Chapter Twenty
Kristina

Winter was relentless in the hilly forests of Colorado Springs. Snow was a daily burden, and predators, desperately hungry in the weather, grew bolder in coming close to the house at nights. The biggest chore was keeping warm, especially when my heart felt so very, very cold.

Jeremiah had agreed to take up where Luke left off and teach me to survive in the wilds of the place I was so determined to make my home. Trudy picked up the slack when Jeremiah was too busy trying to keep the ranch running.

Trudy had bloomed, and the first signs of a growing life inside her could be seen through even her loosest of dresses. Elias was ever the doting father and waited on Trudy like she was a queen. At first it had hurt so badly to see them together that I'd withdrawn. It was Trudy who'd got me living again with a firm lecture on independence and creating one's own happiness.

She was right. I had a warm bed and a strong roof over my head. I contributed to a ranch and had become a decent cook. I had companionship in Jeremiah, and even though it wasn't romantic, I still had someone to talk to. And someday, I'd see Luke again. Until then, I just needed to keep moving, and living, and breathing.

For all the hate I'd felt for his letter the first time Jeremiah read it, something had changed over the lonely months. Now I looked over the letter before I went to bed every night and slept with it tucked into my pillow case. It was my only connection to the man I loved and mourned for. From time to time, on the snowiest days, Jeremiah would offer to read it to me, and I could almost imagine Luke's voice through the sound of his brother's.

Through the months, I'd grown used to what the Dawson boys were. Jeremiah had set a rule that he'd tell me when he was changing and I was never to venture outside, no matter what. His wolf was shattered and he didn't have any logic when he turned. He assured me he'd bite me with little regret until he turned human again, and I believed him.

Sometimes, after he changed, the wolf would claw at the wall of my room to get in, and the snarling tearing sounds that would drift through my window said he was crazy. At first I'd been terrified, but now I'd press my hand against the wall he was trying to rip through and my heart ached with sadness for him. The loss of his Anna had fractured him, and a big part of me understood the loss. Maybe the biggest part of me now.

The cabin smelled of cherry preserves, golden flakey pie crust, and sugar. I wrapped the pan of desert tightly in a clean cloth as Jeremiah pulled the buggy around front. Trudy had developed a craving for pastries and the weather had cleared enough for us to ride into town. Buffalo hide blankets covered our laps as we raced the whipping wind over the miles that separated us from civilization.

"I've been wanting to talk to you about something," Jeremiah said as he steered the thickly furred horses around a dip in the road. "What do you think about marrying me instead?" He slid a dark-eyed glance my way but it took me a minute to recover.

"I'm waiting for Luke."

"I know you are. You're a loyal woman, Kristina, but I don't think he's coming back. He's left like my brother, Gable, and I can't seem to track him down anywhere. He doesn't want to be found."

My world shifted under my feet. "Do you love me?"

"No," he said shortly. "You're like the sister Ma always prayed for."

"Do you think you'll ever love me?"

The breath he exhaled froze in front of him. "No."

"Then why would you want to marry me?"

"We get along all right. We run the ranch well together. You know my secret."

"And every two days or so, the animal half of you tries to kill me. I'm not your cure, Jeremiah. You need love to fix your wolf."

"I want you taken care of. I'm so mad at Luke for the way he left, I can't even see straight, but someone has to fix this."

His duster jacket was cold and coarse against my cheek as I rested against it. "You're a good man, Jeremiah, but you don't have to tether yourself to me. We work well just as we are."

"Will you at least think about it?"

I frowned, but nodded. "I will."

I could see his loneliness growing. Anyone with eyes could see he needed a woman, but I didn't soothe anything for him. He needed a woman he could love. A woman his wolf would see as a mate and attach himself to. He belonged with Anna like I belonged with Luke. Two spare parts wouldn't work if they weren't built to complement each other.

Jeremiah dropped me off in front of Trudy's house before tying the team in front of the post office. I watched him go with a heavy heart. I didn't want things to change between us, but we were on the cusp of destruction.

Trudy opened the door and hugged me harder than I'd been held in a while, and the tensed muscles in my shoulders relaxed. "Cherry pie," I said with a knowing grin, and she lit up like the candles on a Christmas pine.

"Eat a slice with me," she merrily demanded.

I pulled a fork out and handed it to her before checking her ginger jar. "You need more," I noted, but she shook her head.

Around a bite of sugar coated crust she said, "I haven't been nauseous for the better part of a week. I think it's finally over."

"Jeremiah asked me to marry him." I said it with my back to her because I didn't know if I wanted to see her reaction. She was as mad at Luke for leaving as his brother was.

The clink of the fork hitting the side of the pan was the only noise in the kitchen. I turned. "I told him no, but he's asked me to think about it."

"I think you should wait for Luke."

I sat gratefully down beside her and took my own bite of pie. "Why do you say that?"

Trudy wiped her hands on the edge of her apron and leaned forward. "Luke is your Elias. It's been clear from the start you're in love with him, but you and Jeremiah?" She shook her head. "There is no spark there. I'm mad as a hornet at Luke for putting you through this, but I don't think marrying his brother, no matter how logical it seems, is going to fix what's been broken."

"Maybe Jeremiah will get a response to his advertisement in the post today and forget all about his proposal," I said hopefully.

Elias came through the door, stomping snow off his boots. "Hey, Kristina," he greeted me with a kiss to my cheek.

"Elias, you're freezing!" I said, rubbing my cheek to bring warmth back into it.

He laughed unapologetically and kissed his giggling wife. "Saw Jeremiah at the post office and figured you two would be in here eating somethin' good."

Trudy spooned him a heaping bite of pie and he disappeared into the back room, mumbling compliments to me for my improved baking.

Turning back to Trudy, I said, "Listen, I don't think you guys should be coming to our place anymore until the weather warms up. The roads are getting really bad and I don't want you stuck out there in your condition."

There was a slight pout to Trudy's full lips. "Okay, but I won't get to see you as much."

"I'll come into town as much as we can manage. It's not so scary for us." I winked. "I have a werewolf driver."

"Mmm, speaking of, is he still trying to kill you?"

"Every change." I rolled my eyes to the rafters.

"Men," we said in unison and burst out laughing.

Elias came back in with a worried furrow to his brow. "You're sleeping with a gun just in case, aren't you?"

"Yep, my trusty old Derringer. Jeremiah made silver shot for it and everything."

"Good. Anything you need, you come to us, you hear?" he asked.

"Loud and clear," I said.

"Okay, ladies, I'm back to it. Gotta get back to the shop. You and Jeremiah staying for dinner?"

I licked cherry deliciousness from my fork. "No. Oh! That reminds me. Jeremiah said we're about to get slammed with a big storm. Blizzard big, so visit the general store for anything you need before everyone buys them out. We're heading back to our place before the weather rolls in."

"Eee," Elias said. "Okay, I'll go to the store before I get back to work."

Trudy rattled off a list of necessities as a knock sounded on the door. That would be Jeremiah. I squeezed her tightly and waved to Elias before I let myself out. The wind picked up and I held my skirts as I teetered over the icy wooden boards. The buggy was half full of Jeremiah's latest order from the general store and the horses were antsy and pulling against the reins in anticipation of the long ride home.

"Did you have a good visit?" Jeremiah asked with a steadying hand on my shoulder.

"Yes, but it wasn't nearly long enough."

He hoisted me into the seat and I rearranged the buffalo skins to let him in.

"I've considered your offer, good sir," I said grandly as we pulled out of town.

"That was fast. And what say you?" he played along.

"Luke is the one for me and besides, I like us the way we are."

"Fine, I won't mention it again."

"I'll make a pot roast for dinner to make up for rejecting your proposal."

He chuckled. "Well, that's better then."

And just like that, I'd managed to stop the winds of change.

Chapter Twenty-One
Luke

K ristina had been right about a lot of things, but this was the biggest. Evelynn French was nearly impossible to get to in Chicago. I'd been a very patient hunter in my pursuance of avenging my almost wife, but still my soul was clean and my hands empty of the gratification that would come with making her safe once and for all.

I'd acclimated to life in the city as I had to, and procured an entry level job in one of the many lumber yards the French family owned. Quickly, I'd moved up to foreman and was being eyed for a numbers job at a desk. Why? Simply put, because no human could do the amount of work I could in the same amount of time.

My big break came yesterday when I'd been invited to make an appointment with Mr. Barron French, the man who started it all. He was gathering under him a small group of professionals to break out on his own and open a lumber yard under his name, and rumor was he wanted me working for him, not his mother.

Dissention in the ranks only boded well for me.

So with the last of my cattle money, I'd purchased a dark suit and top hat and here I stood, eying the mansion of the man who'd seduced Kristina. It must be nice sitting up in his fancy tower while his spoils were hunted like dogs.

A butler answered the door and took my hat and coat before leading me to a parlor where four men sat around a table playing cards, drinking fine scotch, and smoking giant, hideously fragrant cigars.

"McClinton, you're the last one here," said a man who stood to shake my hand. "Barron French."

"Brian McClinton. Pleasure," I said, shaking his offered palm firmly. I'd used that false name so much in the past months, it'd become natural for me to answer to it.

The man stood shorter than me with thick brown, wavy hair and dove gray eyes. I supposed he was a well-built man if you ignored his slight paunch and the stagnant smell of one who smokes too much. Maybe it was a new habit he'd formed after his fling with Kristina.

"Sit down and have a drink before we talk business, McClinton," he said. "Refreshments are over there." He pointed to a long table piled high with pastries and meat pies, exotic fruits and silver platters of sliced roasted meats.

His snack table was richer than the best Christmas dinner in all of Colorado Springs. Damn, I missed home.

I sat between two older gentlemen who were dealt into a game of poker. Introductions were made, but I didn't catch their names. I was too busy trying to figure out what a seventeen year old Kristina had seen in such a pompous man.

Scotch would hamper any plans I had, so I sipped it slowly and tried not to gag on the smoke that stifled any chilly breeze that flew in through the open window. Chicago as a whole stunk mightily to a man with a sensitive nose, such as myself. Any city did. I didn't know how Da managed to live in the city limits of Boston.

An hour into our conversation, the door behind Barron opened and the man who walked through it could've been the one to ruin everything. Matthew Streider closed the door gently behind him. I stood in a rush and turned for the refreshments table. Feigning interest in the wide assortment of colorful pastries, I strained my sensitive ears and listened attentively to the long haired man who whispered to Barron.

"Sir, she's asking for you. The baby is keeping her very sick and—"

"What does she want me to do about it?" Barron interrupted in a furious whisper.

"Nothing, sir. She just wants you to come to her. She hasn't seen you in days."

"Surely you can quiet a fretting woman, Streider. If you can't figure that out, then maybe you should go back to work for my mother." A long and pregnant pause was filled with the unwitting laughter of the other guests. "Fine," Barron hissed.

Streider's boot steps retreated to the door.

"Gentlemen, you'll have to excuse me," Barron said in a put upon tone. "I have a wife who apparently needs me to tuck her in at night. Helpless little creatures, aren't they?"

I stifled the growl that bubbled from my throat. Had he talked about Kristina in such an inconsiderate manner when they were together?

Stacking food upon my plate, I pretended not to hear their exit until I was sure Streider was out of the room and unable to identify me as the murderer of his former boss' hit man. That would definitely complicate things.

Eventually, Barron returned and the evening dragged. I was unable to find an opportunity to talk with Barron in private, so I had to make my move at the end of the night, when the rest of the company said their goodbyes.

"What do you say to my proposal," Barron asked. "It would pay a good amount more than you're getting right now."

"That's the truth, Mr. French." I smiled at the last two gentlemen as they headed for the door. "But I like to know what kind of people I'm working with. Now your momma, she's an honorable woman."

Barron snorted. "Not so much."

"What I'd like to know is if you're an honorable man."

"Well enough. What exactly would ease your mind, Mr. McClinton?"

Steadying my pounding pulse I lowered my voice. "Now I've heard a disturbing rumor or two around town that says you kept a mistress a couple years back. A pretty little thing who was a housemaid to your mother."

Barron's face went pale and his eyes darted around like he was nervous. "That's not appropriate talk for mixed company."

I made a show of looking around. "Ain't nobody here but me and you," I said, letting the comfort of my natural drawl come out. "So how I heard it, you had quite the torrid affair and when your mother found out, she tortured the poor girl."

"I wouldn't say tortured her, but she sent her away, yes."

"To a brothel, to work as a whore."

"What? What're you saying to me right now?" His voice shook with fear or shock or maybe a little of both.

"Evelynn French, your mother, sent your young mistress to work men, and every two weeks, she'd come and make sure she was still there. And if ever she stopped whoring, your momma would have her killed or her mother framed as a thief. Am I close?"

To the man's credit, he looked completely taken aback. "Kristina?" he whispered.

I struck while he was still dazed. "Hers is a happy ending for now though. She escaped your mother's spies and made her way south. And just when she thought she was safe from the ruin you'd clouded her life with, your momma sent men to torture her. They took her in the night, and beat her face until it was unrecognizable, and then they tied her to the back of their horses like some animal and dragged her through the mud, barefoot, for nearly six hours. You can ask your man Streider all about that. Ask him where he got that scar on his hand."

Barron's nostrils flared and his voice shook. His rapidly racing heart was the easiest thing to hear in the room. "I thought you said it was a happy ending."

"It is," I growled. "A man saved her, but your mother sent more and more men to hurt her because she had to ruin the life of the servant who almost ruined her family's name. But now the girl's disappeared into the world where no one can find her but your mother and her spies."

Barron slumped into a great oak chair propped in the shadows of great tufts of priceless curtains that adorned a towering window. His green color said he needed a bucket.

"If you ever had a tender feeling for Kristina," I growled, "you'll find a way to call your mother off her trail and let her heal. Let her live a life you came so close to ripping away from an innocent because you couldn't keep your pecker in your pants."

Barron shook his head slowly back and forth. Back and forth. "I can't call that woman off. She'd kill me, her only son, if she thought it would bring her a profit. I can't help you." His voice dropped to a tremulous whisper. "I can't help her."

"Then tell me how. How do I save the girl?"

A fine sheen of sweat dotted his brow and he dropped his voice even lower. "There is a way."

****

The click of the lock on the door wasn't the only noise on the abandoned street, but it was the loudest. The butler had handed me my top hat and jacket, and I stood here, staring at the closed door, pondering what possible reason Barron could have for throwing his mother to the wolves, so to speak.

It was likely a trap. Family didn't give over family this easily, even in the cutthroat world of Chicago society.

I turned and made fresh footprints in the falling snow down the walkway to wait for one of the servants to bring my horse around front. Reaching out to catch an oversized snowflake on the tip of my finger, I leaned against a towering stone lantern post. I had no choice but to walk right into that trap, but I didn't have to do it alone. The time had come to use the gifts the animal inside of me offered. If I couldn't use them in a time such as this, there was no benefit to being a werewolf. The McCall family was an impressively large pack of five brothers and their father. Why they'd decided to settle on the outskirts of a thriving city like Chicago had always been beyond me, but to each his own. Now, the McCall family was friendly with Da but they didn't run things like the Dawsons did. They weren't a careful breed and if I had to guess by the way they acted, I'd say their wolves ran their lives and pushed their human nature to the smallest crevices of their mind they could manage to shove them.

I'd contacted Mr. McCall the moment I came into town. It was a common courtesy to let packs know if you were in their territory and why. I'd given him my reasons, and he'd all but salivated over the prospect of a hunt. Not an animal one, mind you. The McCalls, on occasion, were man-eaters—the monsters that generated legends and conjured nightmares.

I'd told them I'd have to see where my hunt led, but if there was need enough, I'd let them in on it. With a foot in the stirrup, I mounted a horse with a coat as dark as the moonless night, and thanked the servant.

If I was going to willingly walk into a trap set by the French family, a clever werewolf would invoke the help of a pack.

The ride home was a long one at our slow pace, but my longing for fresh air outweighed the chill. I'd been in the city way too long and changed only when the pain grew so great I couldn't stand it anymore. Far out in the woods I'd run, giving my wolf a night before I locked him up again and caged us both in the big city. My soul longed for the mountains and the empty dirt roads and the endless woods that surrounded home.

It longed for the last place I'd been with her.

A penniless couple huddled together against the gate of some giant house. Through the windows a party could be seen with eating, drinking, dancing, and merriment. I stripped out of my jacket and hat and handed them to the man, who immediately gave the coat to the woman clutching his arm.

I told them, "Wear these tonight, but sell them first thing in the morning so no one accuses you of thievin'."

"Thank you, sir." The man's voice and uncovered hands shook with the cold.

The woman leaned forward. "Won't you get cold tonight?"

"Won't need a jacket where I'm going," I said with a wink. Hell was probably plenty warm. "Take your woman to an inn and get a room for the night. It's only getting colder out here." After I dropped the rest of the money from my pocket into his outstretched hand, I tipped an imaginary hat and nudged my horse toward the other side of town.

As I rode along, the houses changed from the upscale mansions with gables and stretching porches on pillars with perfectly manicured yards and winter rose gardens, to modest homes where small families worked their fingers to the bone to survive.

I lived beyond that.

When I'd ridden into town, I'd tracked down a room above a shop where the rent was cheap and the neighbors rowdy. Flickering oil lanterns on posts tossed shadows over the filthy streets and drunkards who lay passed out in shallow alleyways. And down the street from my temporary home was a brothel. Kristina never told me the name of her previous home, but I liked to imagine it was here, just a few buildings down from where I slept at night. Even if it was out of my way, I always rode an extra street to turn around and pass by the brothel after work at night. There was always a raucous crowd of drinkers, and the piano played at an almost constant volume, and it gave me comfort to envision being close to a place she'd touched.

One day. I frowned and rubbed warmth back into my cheeks with the palm of my hand as I passed the brothel. One day to plan what I'd wanted to accomplish for months. Avenging her torment had been the only thing to keep me focused on anything other than the gut wrenching agony that tore at me whenever I gave my loss a voice. A sliver of fear snaked through me. What if I accomplished my task, and all that was left was the heartache? What if I could never be happy again?

After handing the reins over to an underfed stable boy, I climbed the rickety stairs and opened the door to my cage. The room was small, simple, and square as many cages are. It smelled of wood rot and I could never quite get the feel of filthy moisture off my skin no matter how hard I scrubbed. A small, bug infested bed took up the corner under the window and a wooden chest rested against the foot of it, just waiting to be opened. Tonight was its lucky night.

The lid whined as I lifted it and when all of the clothes from my old life were laid across the bed, I touched the leather of my holster with a sense of relief that covered me like a warm blanket.

Finally, I'd feel like myself again.

Only after my pistols were belted to my hips where they belonged did the gravity of what I'd do become real.

Whatever happened tomorrow, I was either leaving this world or leaving this town.

Chapter Twenty-Two
Luke

That rat, Barron French, had lied.
The jingle of my spurs was the only noise in the still, snow dusted woods. Miles from any trace of civilization, he'd sworn on his unborn child's soul that Evelynn French was escaping the city by way of back road tonight, but so far, the only ones in these woods were me and the McCalls.

Lennard McCall, father of the pack of ruffians, spat. "They ain't coming, are they?"

Curses of disappointment sang out from the brothers behind us but as a low whistle sang out, the woods grew silent again.

"That'd be Eustis," Lenard said with a gap toothed grin.

"I don't have a mind to kill a woman, no matter what she's done," I said for the fifth time. "Scare her and be thorough about it but let her live."

Lennard stretched his neck and rolled his shoulders. "You heard him boys. Unless Mr. Dawson here tells you, don't kill her. It's his hunt. We're just here for the chase."

The stagecoach that floated through the trees was as black as pitch but even from where I stood, bright pink silk like the first streaks in a morning sky pulsated from within. A high falutin' coach for a high falutin' lady.

With a wary ear on the woods, my skin prickled with goose flesh. If this was a trap, it'd be set any moment now. Instead, the coach pulled closer still until I stood in the road and pointed my Peace Maker at the driver.

"Whoa," he told the four horse team.

"One of two things is going to happen tonight," I said loud enough for him to hear over the rearing, prancing team. "One, you're going to try and be heroic for a woman that don't deserve it and you'll die. Or two, you can drop Mrs. French and take the stagecoach, and your life, back to town without a word of what went on here tonight."

The man lifted his arms slowly into the air. "Please, sir. I work for Barron. I knew you was going to be on this road tonight."

I followed him with my pistol as he climbed down and opened the door to the coach. "I'm sorry, Miss," he mumbled before pulling her bodily from the back.

I'd be damned. Barron French really gave over his own mother.

"I demand to know the meaning of this!" she shrieked.

"Ms. French?" I asked.

"Who wants to know?"

I'd seen black and white photographs of her plastered all over the paper so her acknowledgement meant little. It was her all right.

"Luke Dawson," I answered.

The set of her mouth drooped into a grim line. She fluttered her hands helplessly as the carriage turned and escaped the way it had come. She was a statuesque woman with a railroad tie posture that said she'd been well-bred and well-kept. Her face was covered in the deep wrinkles of one who'd frowned much more than smiled in life. Her eyes were so dark you couldn't tell where her pupil ended and she had the nose of a great eagle. Not the noble kind, but the kind that dined on the carcasses of the weak. Her dress was a deep red to match the tiny hat pinned to her dark curls, and the first signs of gray showed at her temples.

I could smell her fear and my wolf bathed in it.

"You remember Kristina Yeaton?"

"Oh," she said with a clucking sound against her tongue. "Don't tell me you're the poor sod who's fallen for the little whore. You've killed one of my men, and scared another into worthlessness and for what? A little trollop not worth her weight in pig shit."

A snarl ripped from my chest as, for the first time in months, I didn't push the wolf down. "Here's how this is going to go, Ms. French. I'm a man of honor and I don't like the idea of hurting women, so I'll give you...what do you think boys? A ten minute head start?"

The grumble of agreement sounded from behind me.

I pointed east. "Chicago's that way. Now run for your life before I let my dogs loose on you."

"I see no dogs."

Lennard stripped off his shirt to expose a chest full of mutilating scars. "You will," he said in a voice not entirely human. Glowing eyes of a demon never left their quarry.

The brothers had already dropped to all fours and the crunching of bones could be heard over the whispering wind of the woods.

Evelynn stood still as a stone with wide, frightened eyes.

"I'd run now," I advised.

She picked up her skirts and bolted in the direction I'd pointed and I leaned against the nearest tree to wait for the McCalls to make their change. Her panicked panting echoed off the forest and had the animal inside me howling to be released. I winced and doubled over as it ripped me up from the inside out. Staying human was imperative. I needed to finish this.

The McCall boys' wolves were a myriad of colors. One was black, another gray, one a brownish red, and two were white. I hadn't a guess what color Eustis was, but somewhere in these woods, he was changing to join the hunt. One by one they recovered and charged forward with excited yips. When the last one was done, I pulled my horse from the trees and kicked him into a run.

The fresh trail the pack left was pungent and mixed with Evelynn's own scent. If I hadn't my nose, I'd have an easy enough time seeing their newborn tracks against the thin layer of snow. She'd made it about a mile when the howls broke the silence of the forest.

True to their word, the McCalls hadn't mauled her, but it was close. She was pinned against a great oak and inch by inch, the wolves came closer as if their human sides were slowly losing the battle to their bloodlust. The snarling snapping predators lashed out at her ankles as she scurried closer to the tree. Out of the dark I came, walking between two wolves without an ounce of fear, only knowledge that it would be done soon. I knew what my eyes looked like to her as she stifled a scream at my approach. They weren't human eyes anymore, but there was little to be done about that. She was meant to see her doom before I released her.

Wrapping my hand around her neck, I pushed my hat out of my face so she could see how badly she'd underestimated me. Her face morphed from frozen fear to grim acceptance. And then the corner of her mouth curled up.

"You're dead and you don't even know it yet," she whispered through rasping breath.

The hairs rose on the back of my neck and a growl sounded long and low from my chest. "Why were you fleeing Chicago?"

"I was running from you. I got your message that you'd kill me if I came after you. I knew you'd make good on it."

I slid my knife out of its leather sheath and pressed it against her neck until her pasty flesh dripped red. "Speak English."

"I always know my opponents, Mr. Dawson. It wasn't hard to figure out what you were. Even after you kill me, I'll still have my revenge. Your entire bloodline will burn for you protecting that little whore from my reach."

I pressed harder on the knife and she gasped before a bone chilling cackle left her mouth. "I've sent Hell Hunters to your home, Mr. Dawson. They left on the train yesterday. As we speak they're headed to Colorado Springs to burn your home and hang your family."

I shook my head in denial of the vial thing she said. "Jeremiah can take care of himself." I said it to sooth myself as much as to deny the woman her treachery.

"Maybe. But can your whore?"

"No. She left months ago. I let her go. She's not there anymore."

I'd never seen a more satisfied look on any human being's face than the one that settled on Evelynn French. "That's not what my spies tell me."

"No!" I yelled, standing up.

My body went numb, like I'd been covered in snow for too long. I knew all about Hell Hunters and what they did to families accused of being supernatural. Women and children burned alive in their beds while men, good men, were dragged to the nearest tree and hanged for what they were.

And Evelynn had sent a hoard of them for my home.

I'd never seen true evil before, but standing here, with her laughter filling every thought, I knew the Hell Hunters were hunting the wrong kind of villain. Tears of happiness filled her eyes as I stood there looking down on her, and her crowing stretched on and on.

"Kill her," I said and the laughter turned to screams as I ran for my horse.

Telegram would be the fastest way to reach them but what could I say that wouldn't tip off the town what we were? Winter months meant long stretches of time where the roads were inaccessible. How could I be sure Jeremiah would even make it to town to receive the telegram before the Hell Hunters were in his backyard? If there was a chance for me to catch up, it wouldn't be by rail. Not from a day behind them. The trains made stops in every town to load and unload, and I needed that time to reach home.

It would be close but it was doable.

I had days of travel ahead of me and though my horse was fresh, he wouldn't last forever. Not at the speed I needed him to.

"Hyah!" I yelled as I hunched down against the saddle. I'd try to spare his life, but I'd have to trade horses in the small towns I came across.

The wind wailed against the exposed skin of my face. *You're too late*, it sang. *Too late, too late. Too late to save them.*

Kristina had waited for me. She'd waited all these months for me to return, and I'd left her unprotected. I'd left my brother without a pack to fight the ones hunting him. *Faster*, my wolf pushed, as we flew through the woods.

Branches and trees sailed by as the full moon lit our way and soft, powdery snow flew up around my horse's thundering hooves.

Hold on, Kristina. I'm coming.

Chapter Twenty-Three
Kristina

I sat up to the crack of a gunshot and gasped. Cold sweat trickled between my breasts as I kicked free from the heavy blankets that'd ensnared me. I couldn't remember the dream that woke me, but it had to have been a bad one to wake up like this.

Another gunshot echoed across the clearing.

"Hells bells," I grumbled, lunging for my warmest dress. The laces weren't even done up by the time I was running out the door, hopping on one foot as I pulled my other shoe on.

The snow was up to the middle of my calf and I trudged through it, half hopping with experience. Jeremiah's horse skittered constantly as he shot at the full grown black bear that was raiding our smoke house. Trudging faster, I took my shot as the bear turned for Jeremiah. Holding the pistol as steady as I could manage in the howling wind, I closed one eye, held my breath and pulled the trigger as lightly as the brush of a butterfly wing. The blast before impact gave a short echo as the enraged bear turned on me. The hammer was hard to pull even if my hands weren't numbing from the cold, and he bore down on me faster than a falling tree.

Jeremiah was doing his best to distract the bear, screaming and firing, but in one smooth motion I lifted the cocked pistol and aimed to kill. The bear fell and slid across the ground until it lay inches from my feet.

"Ho!" I exhaled, expelling all of the air from my lungs like it would rid me of the fear that throbbed through my veins.

Jeremiah looked nothing short of furious and I smiled brightly.

"Now we've got bear meat." I turned and trudged back into the house while his eyes likely bore holes through the back of my head.

Back in my room, I took my work dress from the tiny closet and pulled on the boots Trudy gave me for Christmas. After my hair was pulled tightly out of the way with a thin strip of leather, I slid into my jacket and turned to find Jeremiah leaning against the door with wolf-bright eyes.

"What in the hell am I supposed to tell my brother when you get yourself killed by a bear?" His voice was too quiet and set me on edge.

"Easy. You tell him he should've showed up earlier and prevented it."

He scratched his bottom lip with a thumbnail before saying, "You were screamin' a lot last night again."

"Bad dreams."

His dark eyebrows lowered. "You know my rule."

In a deep, very Jeremiah-like voice, I said, "Harvest what you take." I slid the top part of my hunting knife out of my pocket and arched my eyebrows.

Sighing, he said, "Let's get to it then. And thank you for bringing the pistol this time instead of your little pea shooter."

"My little pea shooter's going to save your life someday, Jeremiah. Just you wait and see."

He stopped so suddenly in front of me, I ran into the back of him. On his face was the most peculiar look, like he'd never seen me before. "Did you feel that?" he asked.

"Yeah, that was me running into the back of you."

"No." He shook his head slightly. "I just got the strangest feeling." He rubbed the back of his neck like he was putting warmth back into it.

I shoved past him and grumbled, "You're turning as crazy as your wolf."

His horse didn't like dragging the bear to the hanging post outside of the barn, but he did it anyway. I still remembered that feeling of uncertainty when I'd made the first cut fileting the fish Luke gave to me months ago, but the hesitation had disappeared with experience. His brother, determined to do it right, made me watch him harvest every animal I had the time to. And when I didn't gag at the sight of blood anymore, Jeremiah stuck a knife in my hand and told me to do it myself.

"I'm glad it's dead," I quipped. "He's raided us more times than I can count. We can't keep feeding a bear if we're barely feeding ourselves."

"Well, I'm sure he feels differently about the whole thing." Jeremiah tied a rope around the bear's legs and hoisted him up with a pulley system with one strong yank. Werewolf strength really was beneficial at times like these. "I'm going to round up the horses. Holler when you're done."

"I can't reach the top of him." It wasn't an excuse. I really wasn't tall enough.

"There's a step stool over yonder. Hurry up, I feel like bear for lunch."

I glared at the back of his receding duster jacket. We'd been bickering a lot lately, probably due to the fact that we'd been snowed into our homestead for a week and a half, and our starkly different personalities tended to get us fighting even in the best of situations. He didn't appreciate my filthy humor, which only made me try harder, and made him get madder. His patience with me had officially worn thin as spring ice. I suspected it had something to do with his unanswered advertisement for a wife, but I couldn't mention it to him anymore without him biting my head off. That man needed a lady like the crops needed rain.

With a growl I'd adopted from the constant noise coming from Jeremiah's throat these days, I stabbed the bear and pulled down with all my might. And for the four-hundred-thirty-seventh time, I missed the way Luke smiled with his eyes when I was being sassy.

I took my time on the bear, careful to tan the inner hide to make a blanket. It was tedious work, but in the end it was worth it to have a warm material of such high quality. It would fetch a pretty price at the general store next time we were in town.

"Finished," I said in a quiet voice. I'd learned my way around the ears of a werewolf long before now. He'd hear me.

Like magic, Jeremiah appeared around the corner of the barn and dismounted his horse. "That was fast."

"Funny." It had taken hours but the meat was just about frozen by the end, making it difficult to cut. "Haul this out to the smoke house but leave a leg for the kitchen, all right?"

"Yep." He grunted as he lifted the bulk of my work and headed for the shack out back. Squatting, I rinsed my hands in the snow as best I could before heading inside to the warm fire.

"Caw, caw."

I turned to the unfamiliar bird that rested on the ledge of the roof. It was fluffed up against the cold. It was large, with feathers so black they almost looked blue. He turned his head from side to side and watched me with a round, shining eye. "Caw!"

I jumped at the loudness of it. Movement against the trees made me jerk my head. With my hands on my hips I squinted to see better. Kicking Bull sat on a painted pony just inside the tree line. I waved but he made no motion to wave back. Strange. He usually came right up when he wanted to visit or trade.

With a great flapping, another bird landed beside the first.

"He won't come any closer," Jeremiah said from behind me.

I clutched my chest. "Jeremiah Dawson! What've I told you about stalkin' up on me so quiet like?"

"Those are crows. The Ute think they're a bad omen." Jeremiah waved to the old Indian, then followed me inside.

Unease had been building in me all day. An unsettled feeling crept slowly into my bones and it all started with the dream I couldn't quite remember. "What do you think?"

"That old man knew what we were from the first time he set eyes on us. If he thinks those birds are bad magic, I'm inclined to believe they are too. I want you to stay inside for the rest of the day."

"What're you going to do?"

He tipped his hat and opened the door. "Shoot the crows."

His plan to shoot the crows sounded fantastic up until the point I realized he planned on aiming a pistol in the general vicinity of the house he'd just confined me to. At the first shot I slithered right on to the furthermost room, which happened to be Jeremiah's. In all these long months, I'd never actually been in his bedroom. It was tidy with a bed and small chest of drawers under his washbasin.

What caught my eye was what stood beside the empty bowl and pitcher. There, just to the right of it, stood a framed photograph. A light haired woman stared back at me from behind the glass. I couldn't tell exactly what color her hair and eyes were in the black and white picture, but she was quite a stunning woman—high-bred to be sure with a pretty set to her nose and lips. This must've been Anna.

Another shot rang out.

"I wish you were here," I whispered to the photograph.

With the picture clutched tightly to my chest, I imagined their relationship. Jeremiah didn't laugh much anymore, but maybe he used to before he was broken. Definitely, she would've been the opposite of me to catch his interest, but was she funny? Quiet? Did she have the iron will Jeremiah seemed to demand from the people he surrounded himself with?

When the front door opened, I rushed to put the picture back where I'd found it. I didn't know if he would mind me touching her, but I didn't want to test him to find out. If he knew, like he did in the uncanny way he seemed to know everything that went on, he didn't let on as I floated into the kitchen.

"Weather's lettin' up. The roads might actually be passable in a day or two."

Well that sounded like the greatest news I'd ever received right there. One more week holed up with his bad mood and I'd probably just let his wolf in one night out of desperation.

"I'm changing after we eat, so don't go outside."

Eh, it was downright creepy when he read my thoughts like that. Another boring night it would be, all alone and working on my needle point. I was beginning to fervently wish something exciting would happen.

The night passed filled with more dreams I couldn't grasp and a deranged wolf clawing at the house. When, by the next morning, Jeremiah was sound asleep in his bed and we weren't covered in pox or locusts or the like, I began to think the crows didn't hold any black magic after all.

Chapter Twenty-Four
Luke

My ears were so strained for the sound of a carriage, I managed to completely tune out the pounding hooves below me. My horse, the fifth that'd carried me so far, was slowing and it was only a matter of time before he was too exhausted to keep up the speed I needed.

Closing my eyes, I took a deep draw of air. I might've been only imagining it, but the scent of human was there if just barely.

There was no way to tell if the Hell Hunters were in front of or behind me, but the urgency of my instincts said it was going to be close. They would've taken the train as far as Denver before jumping a carriage, and whether a four horse team pulled it or six, it made a difference when we were this close in our race to get to Kristina and Jeremiah.

I was weak, and weary, and hungry from the journey, but none of that mattered. All that mattered was the vision of my family engulfed in flames. For the uncountable time, I calculated each of our journeys.

It'd be close. It'd be *so* close.

I steered my horse at an angle to connect with the road that would lead us into Colorado Springs. There were fresh tracks and divots in the snow, but they could be from the stagecoach delivering mail and supplies, or perhaps another carriage full of passengers traveling while the weather was fair and the roads passable.

I had a plan, and as the outline of the town stood out against the waning evening light, that idea became more defined. The horse under me chugged breath and slowed more.

"I'm sorry, fella. Almost there and then you can rest." White frothy sweat lathered his neck where the reins touched his skin despite the cold. I'd run him longer than I should have, but it couldn't be helped. There weren't many towns to trade up between here and Denver and the invisible clock in my head that tick-tock, tick-tocked time away wouldn't let me rest him.

Though the streets were nearly empty, a few townspeople flitting here and there jumped out of my way as I came barreling through town. At the water trough in front of the general store, I slid off of the exhausted horse and didn't even bother to tie him up. The extra second couldn't be wasted.

I wasn't going to be able to take on the Hell Hunters alone. I needed another gunman and no human I knew could sling a pistol quite as well as Elias. Boots skidding across the ice, I barreled down on his door, pounding my fists until the bones in my hands rattled. When nobody answered, I pushed open the door and looked frantically around. Elias and Trudy's dinner sat half-eaten, and their lantern still flickered against the shadows that crept through the darkening window. Where could they be?

On the porch, I searched in vain. Barely a soul walked the main street and shopkeepers had turned their closed signs early. There wasn't time to look for Elias in a ghost town.

I'd have to use plan B. The lanterns were still on outside the jailhouse at the end of the street. Through the window, Sheriff Eugene Hawkins leaned into his chair and read over paperwork by candlelight.

Kristina once told me to own my secrets. I sure hoped she was right.

When I threw the door open, the sheriff stood and in one fluid motion, had a pistol aimed at my chest.

The old wooden door groaned against the cold weather as I closed it gently. "I need your help."

"Why would I help a cattle thief?"

"Has anyone strange showed up in town today?"

The tightening of the wrinkles around his eyes was enough of an answer.

"When?" I asked. "When!"

"Thirty minutes ago. Rough looking crowd in a black carriage. Blasted straight through town and headed up the road your way."

"My brother and I ain't never asked anything of this town, Sheriff. You know that. But I need your help now."

He leaned against the table and his eyes grew as sharp as a snake's. "I don't know what kind of trouble you brung to this town, boy, but I ain't helpin' you wiggle out of it."

I slammed my fist on the desk and let the power of the wolf take over my eyes. Sheriff Hawkins was staring at his end. The smell of his fear was pungent and bitter.

"I don't have time to argue. I need an extra gun. You know what I am, and if you help me save my family tonight, I'll pledge to the law. When you need help someday, and you will, I'll owe you. I'm faster and stronger, and I'll get you back home to your woman alive."

"Why would I trust a thief?"

There wasn't time to persuade him. My wolf was howling to go. "Every animal we hunted from other rancher's herds, we didn't mean to. And slowly, over time, we've replaced every one of them without those ranchers being the wiser. Murphy just jumped the gun before we could make it right. Have you ever known me to murder a man?"

Hawkins eyebrows shot straight into his hairline.

"Who didn't deserve it," I clarified.

"I'm sorry," he said. "I can't be the law in this town and be helping the likes of you."

The wolf lunged inside, but the rest of me was perfectly still. I was out of time. I turned for the door and as the cold whipped against my face, urging me to stay inside and stay alive, I turned in the lantern light. "I wasn't asking for me. I was asking for my woman. She's an innocent." I slammed the door as consuming frustration escaped through my fingertips.

I'd have to go this alone if I wasn't already too late. If the sheriff wasn't going to help stop a bunch of renegades from murdering and unsullied member of his town, the least he could do was lend me his damned horse.

Up and riding again on the fresh mount, I broke for the tree line. I'd have to take it in a straight line and avoid the road if I was going to make it in time. The horse gave me more speed and through the drawing dark, I listened for the screams of my betrothed.

It wouldn't be long now.

****

Kristina

I'd promised Jeremiah a pot roast if he never mentioned a marriage proposal again, and tonight, I was finally keeping my word. Four floofed in the air as I coated a bear meat rump roast in it. While it set on the table, I filled the cast iron pot with the spices that smelled good with it. Basil, oregano, thyme, salt, pepper, and when water had been added and stirred, quartered onions, peeled carrots and the smallest of our whole potatoes from the cold root cellar went into the pot as well. I sprinkled the floured roast with some of the dry mixture as well before browning it in the other iron skillet the kitchen boasted. When it was boiling away, I poked at the wood in the stove until it was an acceptable temperature.

I stood by with my hands on my hips and frowned. Hopefully I'd done the recipe just like Trudy said. I wasn't experienced with cooking bear.

Outside, the snow was still as the wind died down to nothing as suddenly as it had come in on the dark storm clouds. Not even the leaves on the trees stirred, and through the woods came Jeremiah on his horse that was as dark as the coming night. He paused and turned his head to the side until I could see a perfect profile. Not a muscle moved on the man until he reached back and rubbed his neck again. He'd been doing that a lot throughout the day. The gesture left me downright edgy. Nothing surprised that old wolf.

With a gentle kick to his mount, he rode for the house once again and I returned to the kitchen to place a cloth over the rising yeast rolls. He came in a few minutes later, stomping his boots until little clumps of snow skittered across the wooden floorboards.

"You already put your horse up for the night?" I asked in surprise.

"He's in the barn but he's still saddled. Something just don't feel right today. For my own peace of mind, I want him ready to go."

Pity. I'd hate to wear a saddle all night long if I were a horse. "Where've you been all day?"

"Burning the crows."

A chilly breeze brushed against my forearms, but when I checked, the windows were all firmly closed. "Not on Dawson land, I hope."

He shook his head. "Rode them out into the wilderness, far away from here and far away from the Ute."

My voice caught. "How many were there?"

"Seventeen."

Seventeen crows all landed on the roof to caw their last chilling word. My appetite was waning by the moment. "Dinner won't be done for a while yet—"

"Shhh," he hissed with a finger by his lips. His shadow colored eyes were wide as he searched for something far away and not of this world. He'd frozen into place like the garden statues I'd seen near the fancy houses of Chicago.

A shiver of excitement snaked up my spine. Maybe it was him. At long last, maybe Luke had returned to me.

"It's a four horse team. I can hear the jingle of the harnesses. The weight sounds deeper than a buggy. It has to be a carriage," Jeremiah breathed. "They're comin' and they're comin' in fast."

"Luke wouldn't come here in a carriage," I said in a small voice.

My heart slid down to the space between the soles of my shoes and the floorboards. No one I knew would come here in anything more than a buggy.

"Get your jacket on and be quick about it," he said in a hunter's quiet voice while he checked the load in his pistol.

The cloth I'd been holding floated to the ground and I bolted for my room. With my jacket on, I turned at the door. Doubling back, I snatched Luke's letter from inside of the pillow case and shoved it in the pocket of my dress. Something told me I'd need it tonight.

Jeremiah stood on the front porch with the door standing so far open, the cold air rushed in, setting a chill to war with the warmth from the hearth. From the space beneath his arm, the road was visible in the moonlight. Dark treads of the buggy were the only things that separated the road from pasture under the snow. Even I, with my insensitive human ears, could hear them coming now. Four horses as white as the snow thundered through the trees, pulling a carriage as black as tar.

"Kristina, go out the back door and run for the woods. I'll come find you if I'm able."

"Wouldn't it be safer in here?" My whispered voice trembled.

As fast as a flash of lightning, he turned and clutched my arms so hard I gasped in pain. "Whatever you do, do not let them bring you back in the house. Do you understand?"

I nodded. "Come with me," I pleaded. I didn't know who that carriage housed, but there was fear behind the mirrored lantern light in Jeremiah's eyes.

"I have to hold them off to give you some time. Go now!" His impossibly strong hands shoved me toward the back door.

Catching myself, I threw it open and flew down the stairs. The unblemished snow made a chawing noise under my shoes. *Crunch, crunch, crunch* came the frantic sound as I ran for the tree line. I was safer in the woods with all of the trees to hide me, but I'd do as Jeremiah said and run until he found me again. Faster and faster I pushed my legs until they tired and slowed. A horse's trumpet echoed off of the trees but when I turned, not a leaf stirred.

They were coming for me. I just couldn't see them yet.

With a yelp, I slid waist deep into a snow bank and scrambled to right myself. Pulling at the gnarled roots of an old pine tree, I slowly gained ground against the frosted pins of cold that clawed at my bare legs under my dress. I imagined bony hands reaching up for me from the grave I'd fallen into, clawing and dragging me down to hell. Panicked, I kicked and tore myself free and ran toward the moon that sat low in the sky. *This way*, it seemed to beckon me.

Hoof beats pounded the ground, but I couldn't see anyone.

Suddenly, there was a great white horse and a man shrouded in darkness so close I couldn't move out of the way fast enough to save myself.

Like a jouster in some medieval game, he charged me and I screamed as some blunt wooden object hit me at full force in the chest. I couldn't think about anything but sucking air into my drowning lungs. I clawed feebly and lifted myself to all fours, but escape fell secondary to breathing. Choked and strangled sounds pushed from my throat and suddenly my hair was wrenched backward, stretching my tender neck until surely it would snap.

The creature in the black hooded shroud pulled my head back until the light of the moon caressed the frail skin of my throat.

"Breathe, girl," the creature hissed. "You can't die like this. We have plans for you."

Acute and blinding terror froze my limbs into place and as I drew a shallow breath, the monster pulled his cloak back. A man's face appeared out of the darkness. His hair was shaved to smoothness, and his skin was pallid. Four long scars ran from forehead to chin like he'd been clawed by an animal, and the eye that had been run through stared back at me with a milky white film over it. His teeth were snaggled, and the ones that remained were the rotten color of dried, overripe wheat.

I fought like some wild thing, flailing and kicking at anything solid. He turned and dragged me by the hair to his waiting horse. The pain was shocking as each strand on my head started to release its grip in my scalp. I screamed and screamed with every ounce of breath I possessed, but a slow and chilling chuckle was all the reaction that came from the man.

My knife. The Derringer rested on my bedroom dresser, but the knife still sat in my dress pocket. Getting to it meant releasing my desperate grip on his hands to ease the pain in my head, but it'd be worth it to live. The handle was warm against my palm, and in a motion that at once loosed it from its leather sheath and thrust it upward, I sliced the man's arm where he held me.

His yell sounded pained and surprised and I thrust again before he could move to stop me. All I could reach from my disadvantaged position on the ground was his leg just above the knee. Screaming, he pulled the knife out and smashed the hilt of it against my temple.

I held onto the moon as long as I could while the edges of my vision crumpled in on itself. Smaller and dimmer the moonlight grew until I gasped with relieving the effort, and gave into the darkness.

Chapter Twenty-Five
Luke

I'd arrived just in time to watch them die.

Jeremiah, whose face was bloodied and swollen, was already noosed to a tree with a fidgeting white horse under him. A Hell Hunter trotted out of the tree line behind the house with Kristina flung limply across his horse's withers. A thin line of blood trailed down the white coat of the horse where her head rested and I covered my mouth to stifle the anguished sound that threatened to come from it.

I lay on my belly in the snow, loading my Peace Makers. If they were dyin' tonight, then I was goin' with them.

Evelynn French must've found us a real threat to send five Hell Hunters after us. If that woman had been anything, she'd been thorough. One was hauling Kristina into the house, the second was pouring what smelled like lantern oil across the outside. Another was checking the noose around Jeremiah's throat while a man with his back to me stood on foot holding the prancing hang horse, and the last of the hunters stood lookout. It was him who was close enough.

I steadied the pistol over my forearm and took a deep breath, held it, and pulled the trigger. He dropped like a sack of flour and the others drew their weapons. Shouted orders flew this way and that and I pulled the hammer back and aimed for the man who was tightening the noose. Jeremiah was closer to the house and if he were free, he'd be able to get to Kristina quicker.

"You missed one," a deep voice rumbled from behind me.

I rolled over just in time to see the butt of a rifle coming down on my head.

****

Kristina

The smell was what woke me up. You couldn't mistake the smell of lantern oil for anything else. It filled my head. The throbbing that blasted through my eardrums pinpointed into a small space on my temple. With the back of my hand, I wiped blood away from a knot the size of a small egg. It had a pulse of its own. I retched at the blinding pain, and then retched again. Where was I?

I forced myself into a sitting position and my head lolled as I waited for my vision to clear enough to give me any clue on where that awful man had taken me. The fuzzy edges solidified little by little. Home.

A chair stood haphazardly beside me, and I used it to prop myself up. With all of my weight, I pressed against the back door but something had it firmly jammed closed. I stumbled to the front door with my hand shielding my nose from the nauseating smell. It too wouldn't budge, no matter how much I pounded and flung my body against it. At the too small window, I shoved the curtains out of the way and fought for breath when I saw what they'd done to Jeremiah.

He struggled against hand restraints as he sat upon a large white horse by the big tree near the house. A gag filled his blood-soaked mouth and a noose hung around his neck. If my blood ran cold seeing that, the next realization froze it in place. A cloaked man, much stronger than he should've been, carried a man's limp body over to a second horse and forced him into an upright sitting position before another cloaked man punched him across the face.

Luke.

A man on a horse tied a noose around Luke's neck while I banged on the thick paned window and screamed for him.

It only took him a few seconds to grasp the situation before his wolf-lightened eyes swung in an arch to me and held understanding. His hands were already tied and he screamed something I couldn't understand from behind his gag.

The cloaked man on the horse grabbed his chin and forced his face in my direction just as a tiny lick of flame flew through the air and hit the side of the house with a tiny *click*. Such a small and unassuming sound for the destruction it brought. The sides of the house were up in flames in a matter of moments, and I sobbed with the realization of what they intended to do.

A man stood outside with flickering fire reflecting off his smile.

"Did Evelynn French send you?" I screeched in anger.

His laughter grew louder. "God sent us," he said.

They were insane. There was nothing right about these men. I had to think.

Flames licked the wall and smoke billowed into the cabin. I dropped down under the fog of it and scrambled to my room and then to Jeremiah's collecting the Derringer and a loaded pistol. By the time I'd reached the living room, I couldn't get close enough to the window to shoot the man laughing at my slow death. The back of the house was burning too, and rafters of the roof were beginning to splinter and fall. There was no point in screaming. No one would hear me but the people who would find amusement in it. And if my screams reached the Dawson men's ears just before their own deaths, well, I didn't want to send them into the next life with that sound echoing in their minds.

I broke out a back window but it was too small for me to fit through. As I sat on the hot floor and kicked at the back door over and over again, the guns in my pockets rocked with the rhythm of my movement. I scrambled out of the way as a rafter above the back door fell.

I was doomed.

My skin was scorching like I was in the cast iron pot with the bear roast. Sweat ran down the sides of my face and pooled near my breasts as sobs wracked my body. It was a horrible way to die, knowing such pain was coming and with the knowledge the one I loved would die within moments. I'd never even got to say goodbye or that I was sorry.

I covered my eyes as the door exploded inward. With a tremendous crash, it opened completely. Through the flames and smoke, I could see the outline of a man.

"Kristina, give me your hand."

I couldn't breathe anymore because the smoke was so thick. Maybe this was what it was like to die—imagining someone saving you. If I took his hand, would I go to Heaven?

"Dammit, Kristina, move!"

Okay, there was no cursing in Heaven. I squinted through the smog.

It was Elias! In a burst of hope I ran for him but the flames engulfed the floors and wall. I wouldn't make it. My eyes burned from the billowing smoke and I coughed over and over again.

"Jump. You have to," he said.

And I did. The flames gobbled me up, licking at my dress and jacket. I quieted the screams of pain as I fell into the snow. Trudy, with her angel's face, threw snow onto me until the burning stilled and Elias tore the flame riddled jacket from my body.

Luke, Luke, Luke. "You need to go," I cried. "I have to save them, but those men will kill you if they find you here."

Trudy clutched onto Elias's arm. "Help her."

He nodded. "Run for the woods, honey. Stay inside of those tracks." He pointed to the ones I'd made earlier. "Don't jostle the baby." He kissed her hard before she ran.

The shrouded men were all gathered around the horses that held Luke and Jeremiah. Their backs were to us as we ran low to the ground in front of the burning cabin.

The crack of my Derringer being cocked seemed awfully loud in that clearing full of death. I aimed it for the big man—the one with the uncanny strength.

"Traitor," I growled as they all turned around. "You're a werewolf, aren't you?" I didn't need an answer; his bright gray eyes were enough. "Hunting down good families of your own kind. It's what you do, isn't it?"

The devil was in his smile. "You sure you know how to use that, little lady?"

"Doesn't seem to matter much where I shoot you, so long as it's silver shot, right?"

His smile froze in place but dropped its humor.

"Release them, or so help me, I'll blow a hole through you so soundly, I'll be able to see moonlight through you."

"Do as she says. Now," Elias said from behind. I couldn't see him, but I knew he had two pistols up and ready.

The other men drew their weapons slowly. "Now," the wolf said. "Which one is your mate? They can't both be yours, surely. We wolves don't share so well."

"Don't," I said as he moved steadily toward Luke.

"From what I hear, your monster has eyes so green, they'd blind you. At least that's what Ms. French told us, and she heard it from someone he messed up pretty good. What was his name? Stringer? Struden? Streider. That's it. Shame your man wasn't here protecting you, Ms. Yeaton, but understandable. We wolves are also a fickle lot."

He slapped the horse under Luke with an echoing smack and it flexed for just an instant before it thundered off. Luke's body jerked as he dangled from the tree and I made the decision. I'd die if I took my aim away from the wolf, but I had to if I wanted Luke to have a chance at living. I swung my little pistol in an arch and aimed it on the rope that was strangling the life out of the man I loved. The sound was deafening as I pulled the trigger and the rope snapped in two. His brilliant eyes never left mine as he fell to the ground and a great weight pushed me backward into the snow.

Gunfire erupted from everywhere.

So this was what it was like to die. My lungs begged for air that wasn't coming, but I accepted my fate. The end of my life would be spent looking at Luke's face. It was much better than dying alone and burning in the cabin that lit up the clearing. Luke yelled around his gag and ripped his hands out of the tie behind him. He didn't react to the ricochet of bullets that pummeled the tree bark and snow around us. I alone held his attention as he slid closer.

His weight was warm and solid, a comforting safety after all these months of cold. He protected my broken body with his own. "It's okay, darlin'. I'm here," he murmured over and over against my ear until I could finally breathe.

Jeremiah stood over us with pale, unnatural eyes the color of blue morning snow. "The wolf's still alive," he growled.

Luke's mouth took a grim set and he took the pistol Jeremiah offered. The cloaked wolf dragged his bullet riddled body through the snow, leaving a trail of red behind him. He hadn't gotten very far. An eerie chuckle of one not afraid of death echoed against the night air and I turned away as Luke pulled the trigger. It was his revenge to take, but I didn't have to watch.

"Elias!" Trudy screamed as she came running from the other side of the burning cabin. The worry was thick in her voice, but it needn't be. Elias was standing next to the sheriff, talking in a low voice. The sheriff? I blinked hard but he was still here.

"She's hurt," Elias mumbled when Trudy reached him.

"Oh, sweet girl," she muttered over me.

"I don't feel anything," I said. It was true. I was numb to everything except the warm tear that trickled down the outside corner of my eye.

"You will once we get you away from this snow and thawed out. We need to get her to a warm bed. I have a salve at home that'll help, but we need to go now."

"I'll stay back and take care of the bodies," the sheriff said. "I'll get you all cleared of this."

Luke shook the lawman's hand and thanked him before running to the barn to strap the team to the flat bed buggy.

Luke cradled my head in his lap in the buggy while Elias drove and Jeremiah rode his horse. Trudy fussed over me, but really I was fine. I still didn't feel anything but a dull ache on one side and up my neck.

"Jeremiah," Trudy said. "I need you to track me down a possum. We need the fat." He disappeared into the woods without a word and Luke shed his jacket and started to put it over my shivering body.

Trudy caught his arm. "Don't you dare," she breathed. "The

second she warms up, she's going to be screaming and you'll want to be far away for that. Help me keep the burns packed with snow."

Burns. That must've been what caused the dull aching. I must have been burned worse than I thought in the cabin. Luke's eyes were shielded and calm and he wouldn't look at me. I closed my eyes against the pain in my chest. Nothing had changed. He'd come back in hopes that I'd already moved on and away from here. He didn't come back because he wanted me. He'd come back because it was his home.

"Will I scar?" I asked.

The air was filled with the sound of snorting horses, and squeaking wheels, and wood that groaned against shrinkage in the cold.

"Yes," Trudy finally whispered.

I sighed. The breath in front of me looked like the smoke that billowed from the remnants of the cabin. "How will I ever find a husband now?"

No one ever answered, so I lost myself in watching the stars twinkling around their mother moon.

Chapter Twenty-Six
Luke

How was she supposed to find another husband? Those words were a slice across my innards. I was right here! But maybe she'd changed her mind after I left. Maybe she wasn't here for me. Maybe she'd stayed for Jeremiah. The thought of her loving another man made me sick inside.

She'd changed in the months I'd been gone. Winter always changed everyone but she was different in other ways. Yes, she looked thinner, but it wasn't from not eating. Jeremiah would've provided for her so she wouldn't go hungry. Her thinner frame was from being outside and helping with the ranch. I'd bet my pistols on that. Her eyes had changed too. I hadn't ever seen anything but bottomless happiness and humor in them, but now they held the shadows of doubt and sadness.

I'd done that.

Her head was a solid weight against my thigh but this could be the last time she let me near enough to feel the warmth of her shape against my clothes. She shook like the tail of a rattlesnake, and the clatter of her teeth pulled on my heart with every mile. I wanted to lie down next to her and warm her with my own heat, but I was helpless to do anything but watch her suffer and know it was going to get so much worse.

But for now, she was safe in my arms. I could reach out and touch her skin if she'd let me. She was breathing, and her heartbeat was a steady comfort in the dark. It became my lullaby as my eyes drooped with heaviness. I couldn't remember the last time I slept, and with the burden of imminent death for everything I loved lifted, I gave into the drowsiness.

The wagon came to a stop and the rock of it woke me. The shop lanterns had all been extinguished and Elias's home stood stark and lonely at the end of the dark street.

"Kristina, you still awake?" I asked gently.

She turned her head up to me and the moonlight caressed her cheek and neck. Her voice took a dreamy quality. "I'll never sleep again."

"She's in shock," Trudy said. "Get her out but be gentle about it."

Kristina's eyes grew wide, like a frightened rabbit, as soon as we were inside. The lanterns were out of oil from burning so long, but Elias lit candles and started a fire in the hearth.

I lay her on Trudy's bed and squatted down next to it with my hands clasped under my chin.

"Out," Trudy clipped as she pulled tatters of clothing away from Kristina's burns.

"I'm not leaving her. Not until she tells me to go."

Kristina stared at a crack between the boards of the wall.

"You seen her naked yet?" Trudy asked.

I shook my head.

"Then get out."

"Give me a job to do," I begged. "Something to help her."

"Go wake up Buddy and tell him to let you at his general store. I need beeswax, honey, and white cloth. The softest you can find."

"It hurts," Kristina whispered as I walked out of the room. "It really hurts." The panic rose in her voice. "Trudy, make it stop! Please, it's getting worse!"

"Luke," Trudy said quietly. "If the general store don't have no laudanum, best you track down a doctor who does."

I walked out the front door to the sound of Kristina's panic, and her fear followed me down the street like a humming, uninvited companion.

Buddy didn't have any laudanum at the store, but he swore he'd put an order in for it first thing. Until then, he gave me a small vial of his wife's personal stash of it that he claimed she took for headaches.

By the time I arrived back at Trudy's, Jeremiah sat on the front steps skinning a possum. I couldn't for the life of me figure out what possum fat was going to do for her, but Trudy's confidence was catching. I didn't know treating burns from treating the grip so if she was certain, that was good enough for me. And besides, I'd seen our drunken town doctor's work before. He was a big fan of bleeding his patients and that wasn't going to sit right with me or my wolf.

I had to know.

"Did you bed her?" I asked.

"Nope," my brother said void of hesitation. *Scrape, scrape, scrape* sounded the knife.

"Did you kiss her?"

"Nope," he said again. The truth of the word rang clear as a bell, and a little piece of me relaxed. "She's here for you," he said.

"I messed up," I said, like the admission could soothe my agony.

"Yep."

My boots were loud against the front porch and before I could disappear inside, Jeremiah turned. "Did you kill her?" he asked.

I knew who he meant. He might not have bedded Kristina, but it didn't take an intelligent man to see they'd formed a bond over these cold months. He wanted her safe, too.

"Evelynn French is dead."

Jeremiah turned back to the possum. "Good."

The small bedroom had warmed considerably since I'd left. Kristina was drenched in sweat and dressed in a night gown I didn't recognize. Trudy looked up with wide eyes, but I came in anyway.

"I've seen her in a nightdress," I assured her.

The white cotton was loose on her and one of the sleeves was ripped off to expose the burns on her arm. Trudy mixed an odorous salve in a glass jar. She added the ingredients I'd tracked down for her in turn.

"What else is in it?" I asked, refraining from the urge to put my hand over my nose.

"A little bit of everything that'll sooth the burns and help them heal. We used to spread it on the girls who'd been whipped. It takes the fire out."

I sat heavily into a rocking chair in the corner. "I looked for Elias when I came through town. I wanted his gun slinging abilities with me but you were already trying to get to her. How'd you know?"

"I've seen Hell Hunters before." She ripped the cloth into a small strip and dipped it into the salve. "As soon as I seen those men riding through town, I knew they were headed for your place and nothing good was going to come of it."

She knew an awful lot about an awful lot. "Where're you from?"

"The bayous, Mr. Luke. Lots of dark magic out by the bayous."

Huh. I bet I knew the family of werewolves she'd met and her earlier story of the girl who disappeared didn't surprise me. "Thank you for coming for her."

"She'd have done the same thing. Oh!"

I jumped up like I'd been buckshot. "What's wrong?"

She laughed a little breathlessly. "It's the baby moving is all. You mind putting this on her burns. My back's killing me."

Straining my ears, I heard Trudy's heartbeat, strong and steady if a little rushed from her scare. Faintly came the steady, faster rhythm of the life inside of her. "The baby's heart is steady. It's okay."

"You can hear it?"

Hear it? I couldn't take my eyes from the swell of her belly. How many times had I seen Ma swell with child?

"Show me what to do."

"See there? The laudanum has put her to sleep. Best wrap her fast before she wakes up."

We watched her in the dark—the rise and fall of her chest, the nonsensical mutterings on her lips, the bandages that hid her injuries. Time and time again my gaze drifted to the letter I'd left her with, folded neatly on the table next to her bed. She'd carried my abandonment in her pocket. How many times had she read those words?

"Kristina told me about you not wanting children," Trudy breathed. "I know it ain't easy for your kind to breed, but you'd do best not to take the option away from her."

"That was part of the reason I left. I don't want her suffering like my ma did."

"Suffering? You're mother raised three boys to adulthood. Heartache is the burden of every mother, but give her the choice." Trudy grabbed my hand and pressed it against her undulating belly.

Her growing baby kicked and pushed against my palm and the strangest feeling came over me at touching a life so small and fragile.

"Tell her the risks and give her the choice. Don't take growing your baby in her belly away from her, Luke."

The walls of the room were coming to crush me. I couldn't bear the thought of watching Kristina cry like Ma had while burying all of her daughters in their tiny graves. I couldn't bear the thought of her never holding our sons.

I grabbed my hat and left without another word.

No choice kept us from losing.

****

Kristina

My mouth felt like a cotton ball on a cactus. I'd been riddled with fever dreams I couldn't quite escape and in the dark before morning, the burning in my body brought me back.

Trudy lay beside me but I couldn't bring myself to wake her. Luke sat in an old rocking chair in the corner, slumped over with his face resting on his hand. He looked like death warmed over. I didn't remember him being so skinny, and even in the relaxation of sleep, he still somehow managed to look exhausted. Whatever he'd been doing all these months hadn't been good for his health. The moonlit window showed enough jaw to tell me he hadn't shaved it in days. His nose and cheeks were red, windblown, touchable. His neck was raw and open where the rope hung him and his eyes…I gasped. Green pools of color stared back at me.

"I thought you were asleep." Why was I slurring? This hadn't been the reunion I'd dreamt about. That one included less clothing and more sobriety.

His voice was gruff and full of sleep. "I heard you wake up. Are you hurting?"

I tried to be quiet and nod but I sucked air in through my teeth at the pain in my neck. "Does it look bad?" His answer mattered.

"You look beautiful."

"It feels like it looks bad."

A deep rumbling chuckle came from his corner. "Do you want some more laudanum?"

"Is that what gave me all those terrible dreams?"

"Probably."

"Then no, but thank you kindly. I'm thirsty."

The sound of his boots faded into the kitchen and I tried to make sure I was dressed decently. The skin at my neck screamed as I tried to turn my head, so I gave up. Surely Trudy would've covered me up well enough.

Try as I might, I couldn't help the pitiful whimper that burst from my throat when he helped me sit up. I drank more than I needed in an effort not to have to do it again for a long time.

"Can I lie on my good side, so I can see you?"

His eyes traveled the length of my dressing gown. "Your side was burned. The gown will hurt it."

Like I couldn't tell my side hurt. It was screeching. "Please?"

He lay me on my side and pulled the rocking chair close, and then gently, slowly, he slid his hand up the thin cotton of the gown leaving a trail of soothing coolness where his touch met mine. His fingertips brushed across my skin as he travelled from knee to hip to waist and stopped just shy of the burn. His hand rested there, creating a barrier of space between my nightgown and blistered skin.

My voice trembled. "Why'd you leave me?" His face dropped but I wanted to see his answer as well as hear it in the rich tone of the voice my ears had missed so much. I rested my hand on his cheek and pulled him back to me. "Why?

"I was scared. I'd never been scared before and I panicked."

"Scared of what?"

"Letting myself love you. If I lost you, I'd be broken, just like Jeremiah. I thought if you moved on you could be happy, have children, live in the city where you're safer, find a nice human man to keep you out of the danger you'll always be in with me. I thought I'd go find you, years from now when you had a babe on your hip and a man, and I'd be able to see how happy you were and maybe I'd be able to live with leaving you then. If I saw I done right by you." His throat worked as he swallowed. "I saw how you looked at me." His voice caught. "At *it*. When you saw me change, I couldn't get the horror on your face out of my head. You were disgusted with what I was. I didn't want to trap you in a marriage that scared you."

Tears ran little rivers from the corner of my eyes and I bit my lip to stop it from trembling. Quietly, so only he could hear, I said, "I can't read."

He frowned. "So? It don't make no difference to me if you have words or not, Kristina."

"Now we both know the other's biggest shame."

"But…I turn into a monster."

"So?" I tried to laugh but it came out a sob. "Your wolf isn't half as scary as Jeremiah's."

He leaned closer and held my hand in his. "What do you mean?"

"I mean, his wolf tries to eat me every few days. I have to sleep with silver shot in my Derringer."

Luke looked horrified. "Why would he do that?"

"Because his wolf is crazy."

"Kristina, you weren't safe. Why didn't you just leave?"

"Because if I left, I'd never see you again. And because it felt like accepting all of Jeremiah somehow made up for how I reacted to you when you changed. I'm sorry, Luke. I'm so sorry. I was shocked and scared because I'd been having nightmares of the wolf attack that first night, and I panicked. You left before I could think about it or apologize and I thought I was going to burn alive last night without having made it right with you. It gutted me."

He pressed his lips to my hand as he watched the dark, blue, dawn light creep in through the window. "I went to Chicago." His brilliant gaze collided with mine. "That's where I've been. I've been hunting."

My heart gave a nervous flutter. "What were you hunting?"

"Evelynn French."

"And?"

"She'll never hurt you again. You're safe."

Denial was the easiest thing in the world. For too long I'd looked over my shoulder. It couldn't happen like this. Not so easily. "But what about those men tonight? She didn't send them?"

"It was the last thing she did before I found her. She told me about the Hell Hunters she'd hired to kill you and Jeremiah and I rode for days until I got here." His whisper was anguished as it dropped to a ragged breath. "I thought I'd be too late."

That explained why he looked so tired. "Have you eaten anything? Or changed?"

His eyes widened. "We don't have to talk about that stuff."

"We do so. Are you hurting?"

"I'm all right. Let's just worry about you."

"Luke," I scolded. "You've been riding for days with little food, little sleep, in one form for way too long, and you're injured. Go take care of yourself, man."

His mouth hung slightly open as if he didn't know what to say. "What, now?"

"Do you really want to wait until tonight or even days from now with that aching in your bones?"

The corner of his mouth turned up in a wicked grin. He stood and headed for the door but stopped. My blistered skin burned from the absence of his shielding hand but I tried as best I could to hide the regret of his going. He had another part of himself to take care of too. I couldn't stand the thought of him in pain just to stay beside me.

"I'll come back," he said.

"Promise you'll *always* come back to me."

His eyes held the saddest look. "I promise." And then he was gone.

My man went away to turn into a wolf, and I was left with a disconcerting emptiness that was slowly filling with something I couldn't quite understand. I listened until his boot prints faded into the early morning, and then I cried tears of pain, of sadness, of longing, but most of all, of joy.

My wolf would return to me.

Chapter Twenty-Seven
Kristina

Alone with my thoughts and the pain—that relentless, all-consuming pain—the silence turned out to be a good thing. I didn't have to pretend I wasn't hurting and I finally had a moment to process what happened last night.

Luke was in the woods somewhere, Elias and Trudy were working, and I had no guess where Jeremiah was.

I went through last night over and over, owning the fear I'd had when I'd been chased down by that Hell Hunter, when Luke had the noose around his neck, when the horse had loosed him to hang, and the moment I'd been convinced I'd be burned alive.

I groaned as I tried to find a more comfortable position. I wasn't dead yet, but I'd definitely burned.

Evelynn French was finally out of my life for good. I inhaled deeply. I'd often imagined what freedom would feel like. Maybe it would be better when my skin healed and I didn't want to scream.

More important than any of it was the fact that Luke was home. At long last, he was back where he belonged. His admission this morning that he'd been hunting the woman who'd ruined my life meant more than he'd ever know. It was the most romantic thing any man had ever done for me.

A soft knock wrapped on the door and Jeremiah poked his head around it. "Can I come in?"

"Pull up a chair," I said, trying my best to smile. How could the pain actually be getting worse?

An old rocker clunked down closer to me. "You were wrong," he said as he sank into it.

"About what?"

"You said your little pea shooter was going to save my life someday, but it didn't. It saved my brother's."

"You aren't dead yet. There's still time to save you with it."

"Do you know how difficult it is to shoot a swinging rope? Nearly impossible. Why didn't you tell anybody how handy you were with that little puff pistol?"

"A lady has to keep some of her secrets."

"Mmmm," he said noncommittally. "I think you'll do just fine out here, Kristina. You made it through a Colorado winter and you saved a couple of werewolves from the likes of Hell Hunters. Not an easy feat, that one."

I snorted. "All I did was shoot a rope."

"That's not all you done and you know it. If you hadn't come back, we'd be cold and swinging from that tree right now. Sheriff Hawkins and Elias helped, no doubt about that, but you led the attack and you showed no fear in doing it. My brother lives because of you. So, I guess what I'm getting at is thank you."

If I could bottle up the emotional balm his gratefulness brought and rub it on my burns, I'd be healed instantly. "You're welcome."

He cocked his head to the side in a very animal-like gesture and stared up at the window. "Your man is here."

A drunken warmth washed over me and despite my burning body, I laughed an excited sound. Luke took off his hat as he ducked under the doorway. He'd washed up and looked happy and fed. His eyes were brighter, and though the rope burn on his neck was still angry and raw, it already looked better than it did this morning. He sat on the squeaking bed beside me while Jeremiah rocked absently in the chair.

"Better?" I asked.

Luke ran his hands through his long, dark hair and nodded slightly. "You?"

"I feel like someone dipped half of me in boiling tar. Did you go by the cabin?"

"I did but there's nothing to salvage."

My eyes drifted slowly to Jeremiah. I'd lost my precious dresses but he'd lost so much more. Anna's picture burned in that inferno and if I had to guess, I'd say it was his last physical connection to her. His lowered eyelids covered the loss that would be swimming there.

"I'm grateful to Trudy and Elias for putting us up," I said quietly. "But I want to go home."

Luke took my hand and ran lazy circles over the top of it with the pad of his thumb. "You're healing, Kristina, and we have nowhere clean or warm for you to sleep out there."

"Where will you sleep?"

"In the barn. It'll have to do until we can get a new cabin up."

"I've been thinking about that," Jeremiah said. "With you two getting married, I think it would be best if we built two separate smaller cabins. Gable will make his way home sooner or later and I aim to find a wife. That old house wasn't meant to hold three grown men and their families."

I bit my lip against the pain of sitting up. Luke pulled the pillow up behind me and held the side of my gown as if it were instinct to protect me from that small pain.

"We haven't talked about whether we're still getting married," I said.

"You wantin' to look for someone new?" Luke asked. "I'd understand if you did."

I shook my head slowly, knowing his next words could hurt me more than any burn.

"If you'll have me, I'm yours," he said softly. "All of me." His eyes lightened from their brilliant moss green to the color of the pale and shining moon.

"You're already my mate, Luke. Just need the circuit preacher to tell me you're my husband."

He kissed the palm of my hand and turned to Jeremiah. "What're we going to do about a place for her to live? My wolf won't stand for her staying in town where I can't easily get to her."

"I can't stomach it either. It'd be a mite lonely up there without her poppin' off at everyone. The problem is, when I change, we don't have anywhere safe to keep her."

The expression on Luke's face looked downright dangerous. "You need to learn to control that part of you better, Jeremiah. Going after a woman? It ain't right."

"I know that. Don't you think I know that? Don't you think I hate myself for goin' after Kristina and not being strong enough to stop it? I don't know how to fix it besides putting some silver shot in my mouth and pullin' the trigger. All I can do is make sure she's safe before I change."

Luke rubbed his face violently and cursed. "There's no help for it, darlin'. We've got to make a safe place for you before you come home."

"What about the barn?" I asked, desperation tingeing my voice.

"It ain't gonna keep him out if he has a mind to get to you. Not as it stands now and we don't need your scent drawing him inside with the horses and milk cows. We'll have to reinforce the walls before you can stay nights out there."

The prospect of taking up space in Trudy and Elias's bedroom was daunting. "How long will it take?"

Jeremiah shrugged. "If we pick up supplies and get out there now, we can have it done in six days if the weather holds. Maybe five. It means you won't be seeing Luke until then though. We'll need to be working from sun up to sun down."

The mention of Luke's absence sent uncomfortable shivers to my stomach. I hadn't planned on being split from him ever again now that I had him back, and to do it so soon? It was a hard bite to swallow. However, if I wanted to get home, he needed space to prepare one for me.

I swallowed hard. "Okay. Five days."

"I don't want to leave you. Not like this."

I put on my bravest face. "Trudy will have me better in no time. Make a place for us and then come fetch me."

The ghost of the smile he gave me was as sad as I felt. He kissed my forehead before he left, and the sound of those Dawson boy's boot prints against the front porch was the loneliest sound in the world.

****

Luke

Nothin' in me wanted to leave Kristina there in Trudy's cabin. I could almost smell her sadness and every animal instinct in my body screamed to stay with her. To protect her, reassure her…claim her.

She'd called me her mate, and until those words left her lips, I hadn't accepted it. Not completely. She was my mate and I was leaving her injured and in pain. The space that widened in between us became a canyon.

"You know you can't see her anymore, right?" my brother asked with a knowing grin.

I turned back around and sat straighter in the saddle. Town had disappeared a mile back and I hadn't even noticed I was still looking for her.

"I missed that woman. It don't feel right leaving her when everything in me is screaming to stay close enough to touch her."

"Yep," he said, the saddle creaking under his shifting weight. "Sounds like you got it bad. Maybe you'll think twice before leaving again. Listen, I have to tell you somethin'." He cleared his throat and looked me dead in the eye. "About a month or so back, I asked Kristina to marry me."

My gut wrenched. "You did what?" I snarled.

Jeremiah held his hand up like he was calming a spooked pony, but it only made me want to cut his fingers off with the buck knife secured at my waist.

"Now listen before you fly off the handle," he barked. "You put us in a bad situation when you left. You put a lady living with an unhitched man all alone in the wilderness and people in town was startin' to talk. I didn't want her like you do, but we got on well enough, and we worked all right at keeping the ranch going together." In a softer tone, he said, "She's a good woman and I didn't know if you were ever coming back or if you were just done, like Gable. She wasn't ever going to stop waiting for you, Luke. She would have stayed on for years and I wanted to give her the option of moving on."

The leather of the reins gave a helpless squeak in my clenched hand. "With you. You gave her the option of moving on with the brother of the man she was engaged to. So you didn't want to kiss her, you didn't want to bed her, but you wanted to marry her?"

"Dammit Luke," he said. "It wasn't like that. There wasn't a physical connection between us. There never has been. I asked her to think about it, and within a few hours she'd turned me down flat. She said she was yours. I just wanted you to hear it from me and early on before it got blown out of proportion."

My rage was infinite. Flashes of imagined trysts between Jeremiah and the woman I loved whirled through my mind. They would've bonded over time and he would've given her all the little baby wolves she asked for. He'd always wanted them. What if he was the better man? What if he was the better option for her? He'd stuck around after I'd run out on her. He'd protected her from the winter and from the darkness within his own self for all those months. He'd fed her and kept her warm and she wasn't even his woman to keep. Jeremiah was two ticks shy of a damned saint and he'd dangled a pretty future right in front of her face.

Everything I saw was red. Red trees and brush, road and horses. Jeremiah was bathed in crimson. My horse started when I jumped from the saddle and tackled my brother from his.

"Do you know what it would've done to me?" I yelled as I pummeled him. "Coming back here and seeing you two all shacked up. It would've cut me in half, Jer!"

"Stop it!" he yelled, flinging me on my back and hitting me hard across the jaw. "She wouldn't be out here if it weren't for my advertisement. She answered it thinking she was marrying me. I saw her first." He gripped my shirt with clenched hands. "I had every right to propose to her!"

I bucked him off and put the back of my hand to my split lip. "Do you love her?"

"Yeah," he said breathlessly. "Like the little sister I never had. I cared about her enough to want to give her a proper name after you ran. It had been months, Luke. You weren't coming back for her and she was already part of our family. If you weren't man enough to take her, I was more than happy to do it." The slice across his cheek was bleeding freely and when he spat, it was red.

"Do you know what I felt last night when that traitor wolf dragged you out of the bushes?" he asked. "Horror, yeah, but underneath it all I was relieved. You'd come back for her and she'd see you that last moment before she left the earth. She deserved for you to be there. You should've been the one teaching her to survive, not me. I was a poor substitute for you, brother. I was relieved because I wouldn't die alone. And I know how selfish that is, but it was going to happen and I couldn't do anything to stop it. If we were dying, I wanted my family together."

I dropped my head in my hands as I was bombarded by the fear I'd felt when I saw the noose around my brother's neck, when I saw Kristina's blood against the white coat of that Hell Hunter's horse, and her beating on the window of the burning house. Her screams of panic and pain would haunt me all my days. I'd spend the rest of my time on this earth making it up to them.

Jeremiah squeezed my shoulder and shook it slowly. "You came back for her. For us. I was relieved that you'd come back."

"You swear she said no to your proposal?"

"I swear on my life. She told me she'd make me a pot roast instead."

I stifled a smile but it was useless. Jeremiah huffed a chuckle, then burst out laughing as he lay back on the side of the road. Blood coated his front teeth and a slow chuckle came to me too.

I didn't like that he'd proposed to Kristina, not one bit, but I understood it. He was a good man and a good husband. I'd seen the way he treated Anna. No one was ever more devoted. But the difference was that he didn't love Kristina. He wasn't the type of man to get over her previous occupation. The number of men she'd been with would sit in his mind, growing year by year like some poisonous weed. He liked quiet, proper women. Always had. They'd bonded over the winter months, but it wasn't love. Jeremiah's wolf wouldn't be trying so hard to kill her if it was. He would've provided her with a safe place to live and babies if she wanted them, but if she'd said yes, she'd never know how it was to be completely loved. She'd likely had some instinct for that when she'd given her answer.

I might be lacking in other ways, but I was going to love that woman until my last breath. She'd grow old knowing what it was to be adored by a man.

Chapter Twenty-Eight
Kristina

"There," Trudy said as she bit the last stitch on the cream and bluebonnet colored floral fabric. "What do you think?"

"It's beautiful," I gushed.

On the inside, however, I was so nervous my knees quaked. I liked to think of myself as a brave person, but five day healed burns being shoved into a dress for the first time sounded about as much fun as jumping back into the fire that caused them.

Trudy spat out the thread. "Stop worrying. I told you I made it looser on that side so it won't rub you as badly, and I'll be gentle putting it on. You need to get back into a dress to lift your spirits and going out today will get your mind off waiting on your man."

As she said that, I was sitting in the rocking chair closest to the window, and every few seconds I would glance out of it with an obnoxious little balloon of hope that deflated as soon as I figured out no one was there. Maybe she was right.

Trudy reached for the bandages on my neck. "You finally ready to look? The faster you look, the faster you'll accept it."

I pouted testily. Avoiding that area of my body at all costs was something I was actually good at. "Fine."

She handed me a mirror and I put it up in front. I winced at the redness. My skin had blistered and smudged together in places, like thick clay I used to sculpt little animals out of during my youth. And on top of it all was a layer of scabbing that was starting to itch.

"You ain't even looking at the good part. Here." Trudy pulled the curtains closed and latched the door before pulling my nightdress over my head. It hurt to lift my arm on that side, but my mobility was improving.

"Why're you smiling?" I asked suspiciously.

Trudy held up the mirror for me to see. "I'm just glad you're finally looking is all. It looks a lot better than I thought it would."

"That makes one of us," I grumbled. The burn on my neck was bad, but the slash of burned skin down my ribcage and on the back of my arm was atrocious. "Good thing I quit whoring."

Trudy's eyebrows knitted together as she pressed on an area with some swelling. "Why do you say that?"

"Because I'd starve to death if I had to support myself by selling this body. Men have lots of fetishes, Trudy. Bedding a hideous burn victim isn't one I've ever heard of."

"Oh, stop your belly achin'. It could've been much, much worse."

I thought about the whip lashes across her back. She was right and I grabbed her hand. "Are you sure you want to eat at Cotton's on your one day off?"

She smiled. "Of course I do. It'll do you good to sit among other people for a while. Now, I think your burns need air more than anything. After these bandages, we need to start letting them out. No more salves except for an ointment I'll give you to help with the scarring, all right?"

"Fine by me. That poultice smells rancid."

She ducked down to check the length of my hem. "It's the possum fat."

Gross. Trudy bandaged me enough to shield my side and arm from rubbing against the fabric, but left my neck exposed. When I asked why she left that one out, she said it was good for the town's people to get used to the way I looked.

My legs were a bit weak under me from disuse over the past week. In an attempt to steer clear of the laudanum, I'd had to stay motionless to limit the pain. The air was crisp against my exposed injury and Trudy and I made matching high button boot prints across the walkway to Cotton's. The eatery was bustling, as always, with nary an open chair to be had.

Trudy made a clucking sound behind her teeth. "I told Elias to get here early and save us a seat."

"Ms. Kristina," a booming voice hailed from the corner. Sheriff Hawkins waved for us to join him. Trudy and I shared a wide-eyed glance.

Trudy recovered from the shock first and pulled me by my good hand through the maze of chairs and tables. A woman in a daffodil yellow dress with light hair and deep blue eyes beamed up at us. While the sheriff scooted down the bench seat to make room for us, the woman offered her delicate, gloved hand.

"I'm Daisy Hawkins. Eugene's my husband and he's told me so much about you."

I gave her fingers a gentle shake, then took the seat beside her with a grateful smile.

Eugene leaned forward and raised his voice over the crowd. "I'm mighty glad to see you healing up. You looked pretty banged up last I saw you." He pointed to my neck. "Looks like it's been a rough week."

I put my hand lightly over the marred skin and tried to stop the heat rising in my cheeks.

"Don't do that," Daisy said quietly, pushing my hand out of the way. "Eugene told me what you did. You're a brave woman who's earned those scars, so don't you cover them up."

I didn't know Daisy from Adam, but I liked her.

Trudy had been right, as she was about lots of things. It was good for me to get out and socialize with other people. My spirits had already lifted with the relief of not obsessing over when Luke would come to take me home, so when he came through the door of Cotton's, I was in the middle of a conversation about the likelihood of the railroad sending a connecting track to Colorado Springs. His presence was so unexpected, surely I was imagining him.

"Luke?" I whispered.

His head snapped right to me and such a delicious smile took over his face, it melted my insides. Hells bells, that man was a beautifully built and masculine creature.

Some of the patrons stopped talking and stared at him, but he seemingly didn't notice. His eyes didn't waver from mine as he made his way through the winding pathway to get to our table. He greeted everyone at our table warmly before straddling the bench beside me. His legs surrounded me and brought the warmth and safety I'd been desperate for since he'd left.

"Hey," he breathed.

"Hey, yourself."

He traced a finger over the marring on my neck and said, "You're a sight for sore eyes, woman."

His legs pressed against my knees and back and I couldn't take my eyes from his lips. I'd never wanted a man more than Luke Dawson. His smile was crooked and knowing and he leaned into my neck and spoke in a velvet stroke against my ear. "I have a surprise."

"What is it?" I whispered.

"Circuit preacher's in town."

I gasped. "Don't you tease me, Luke Dawson, or so help me I won't be a pleasant woman to live out your days with."

The look on his face was pure elation. "I swear it. I've already talked to him and he's willing to do a ceremony today. He's leaving tomorrow for a funeral, but today he's ours."

I squeaked and hugged Luke around the neck. I didn't care about the pain. He was finally going to be mine, and I'd be his. The diners around us went quiet and watched us with curious expressions. Right, I was being inappropriate in front of mixed company. I grinned helplessly at Trudy and Luke cleared his throat.

"It seems that today's our wedding day. Circuit preacher is in town and Kristina will be takin' my last name this evening. Anyone care to witness?"

Luke took my hand under the table as Trudy, Elias, Daisy and Sheriff Hawkins congratulated us. The rest of the diners couldn't care less, but the people who mattered were all smiles.

"What all do we have to do for a wedding?" I asked. One day sure didn't seem a lot of time to plan something.

"I don't know. I never thought I'd be doing one of these," he admitted.

Trudy leaned forward over the swell of her belly. "Food. We need to cook a meal to celebrate. Even if it's just a few people witnessing, you can't have a wedding without some good food."

"Is this all right to wear?" I'd meant the question for Trudy, but I looked at Luke while I said it. I wanted him to think me pretty on our wedding day, because I was sorely convinced he'd be disappointed in the way I looked on our wedding night.

His finger traced the outline of the blue and cream print. "That dress suits you perfect."

"Where're you planning on getting hitched?" Daisy asked.

"I'd always imagined it under that big tree out in front of the cabin," I said.

"It's a hanging tree now," Luke said somberly. He rubbed his healing neck. "Takes the romance out of it."

"It's where we saved each other," I argued. "Let's steal the romance back."

The smile on his face faded slightly but returned when I arched my eyebrow and didn't admit to teasing. I was determined.

"Okay," he said. "Let's do it up at our place. It won't be nothin' fancy, but it'll be memorable."

****

On account of the cold, the ceremony would be short. Wind

swirled lazily, lifting tiny twisters of snow across the clearing, and the lanterns that hung from the hanging tree rocked gently in a tiny celebration of the tradition destined to overpower the blood soaked earth beneath.

The bearskin cloak was warm around my shoulders and the green in Luke's eyes had never been brighter as the preacher, a squat but powerfully voiced man, talked about the importance of our union.

He read scripture and we repeated simple vows. Luke's warm hands were protective over mine, cradling them like he'd never let anything happen to me again, and the seriousness of his voice when he said his own words of devotion were enough to bring steady tears to my eyes. I hadn't come to this land looking for love, only protection, and by some small miracle I'd received both.

There wasn't any pain as I stood here in the frosted January evening, drinking in the power that seemed to cascade from my lover's skin. He was mine, and the rightness of him beside me, touching me, was overwhelming. I couldn't help but smile at Trudy's sweet sniffles from behind.

My heart was breaking in the best of ways, too.

"You may now kiss your bride," the preacher said.

The happiness in Luke's eyes was almost tangible. He brushed my cheek with his thumb. Leaning forward, he pressed his lips to mine. His jaw worked as he caressed my mouth, and when he slipped his tongue against mine, I melted into him.

How could a man be so hardened that he broke his bones every few days, but still kiss in such a gentle way? Ignoring my burns, I threw my arms around him, bearskin cloak and all and nibbled his bottom lip. A contented growl reverberated against his chest, and he plunged his tongue past my lips again, deeper this time. I was going to burn up with the delicious taste of my mate. His hand on my neck pulled me closer, like he couldn't get enough of the taste of me either.

I pulled away, dizzy and laughing at the hootin' and hollerin' carrying on behind us. As the tiny crowd advanced to congratulate us, I knew I'd never had a moment as happy as the one I was standing in right now.

One by one, we untied the lanterns from the tree and made our way as a group to the barn. The crook of Luke's arm was warm and the perfect fit for my hand, like it'd been made with me in mind.

The barn had all new reinforced wood around the bottom half of it, and a small hearth had been built against the back wall. Lanterns were hung every ten feet on old nails that had held dozens of lights before. Trudy and Daisy had helped me set up a table of food near the doorway and benches were hauled in and placed in front of the stalls. The animals chewed their own dinner and watched us curiously.

We descended on the food like a pack of hungry vultures. Trudy, miracle worker that she was, managed to secure the dinner from the kitchen of Cotton's. The stove had already been started there and the recipes were easier to make in the bigger space, so we paid her a dollar and a half and got the best meal in town.

Roasted beef, chicken, mashed potatoes, red beans, creamed corn, and buttered rolls followed by an apple pie to cut the grease. Plates were cleaned until the scraping of forks and spoons could be heard against the metal of the dishes. The barn was warm but it wasn't all due to the hearth. There was something about good conversation and merriment between growing friends that made me forget about the cold creeping in through the cracks.

The preacher left first, followed shortly by Daisy and Sheriff Hawkins, and then Elias and Trudy. In a move that shocked me, Jeremiah shouldered a leather bag and headed for his mounted horse.

"Where will you stay?" I asked.

"I've set up a shelter way back in the woods. A tent of sorts with a wood floor. It'll keep the weather out fine. My wedding gift to you is giving you some space," he said with a wink. He kissed me on the cheek. "Welcome to the family, Mrs. Dawson."

The name gave me chills. I was a Dawson now, and it meant so much more that I even thought it could. Luke's smile was proud and he kissed me on the forehead as Jeremiah patted him roughly on the back.

"You done good," he said before he pulled the barn door open and disappeared into the snowy night.

I wrung my hands together. Everyone was gone and Luke would expect me to perform my wifely duties. I had other plans though. Plans that housed the potential to make him very angry.

And an angry werewolf was a deadly werewolf.

Chapter Twenty-Nine
Kristina

Trembling hands gave away my fear. The dishes clattered against each other like the earth shook under my feet, and Luke slid in behind me and steadied my fingers with his own.

"Hey," he said quietly. There was a worried little frown in his voice. "I'm not going to hurt you."

"I'm scared you'll be mad." Could werewolves hear a lie?

"Talk to me. What's wrong?"

"I don't think I'm well enough to bed you tonight." Did my voice drip enough with self-deprecation?

Slowly, his hands spun me until my cheek was against his chest. "Your heart is racing. It sounds like the wings of some tiny bird. If you don't think you're healed enough, I don't want to push it. We have our whole lives for that. Waiting another week won't kill us." His eyebrows lowered. "Is this about the wolf? I won't be like that when we're together. I won't even talk about that part of me. We'll keep it separate. We'll pretend I have to go tend the cattle for the night when I have to leave."

"Can we pretend tonight?" I asked.

"I...I guess I don't understand."

"If I can't bed you, I don't want to sleep next to you. It'll be a torture for us both. Jeremiah said you haven't changed since that first morning you were back so you're overdue."

"You want me to leave you on our wedding night?"

"You haven't seen the rest of my burns," I pleaded. I'd say anything to get my way. "I want to be alone tonight. That's what I wish for my wedding gift."

The abundant hurt that swam in his eyes made me sick to my stomach. I'd caused it, but the pain was necessary.

His look grew faraway as lantern light flickered in the reflection of his gaze. His mouth was set in a grim, unhappy line, one that clashed with his natural features. "If that's what you really want, I'll do it."

"It is." My voice broke on the words.

The corners of his eyes tightened and he angled his head, like he'd heard something bitter. Without another word, he grabbed his coat and headed for the front.

"Wait."

He turned slowly.

"I know you like your routine. Please stay in here. I'll wait outside and open the door for your escape when you're finished."

"Kristina, I can't ask you to stand out in the cold like that. It'll take me a long time tonight because I wasn't mentally prepared for a change."

"Please," I pleaded. "I'm begging you. It's the least I can do after my request."

His sigh tapered into a growl, and his eyes shone from within like the wolf was already plotting his escape. I grabbed my thick cloak and opened the door.

"Kristina," he said in a gruff voice. "Look up in the loft while I'm gone." He turned without so much as a smile and headed for the back stall.

Outside, I pressed my back against the new wooden wall and stared into the cloudy night sky. Not a single star shone for a companion tonight. He was angry and probably thinking this the worst wedding night ever. Had I gone too far? What if my plan was about to get me killed? No. I didn't believe that. Not for one second. He wouldn't hurt me.

At his first grunt of pain, I slipped back in through the door. My fingers fumbled with the clasp before my cloak fell to the floor. The hearth crackled and threw shadows up ahead. That was where my husband would be.

I trembled less with the laces, and though my heart raced with nervous energy, my dress slid easily to the dusty floor. Only when I was completely unencumbered by clothes did I step into the light of the stone fireplace.

A low growl escaped Luke's lips as he leaned heavily against a wooden rail of an empty stall. His eyes glowed eerily against the warm illumination of the fire, and the white of his teeth cut through the shadows as he snarled, "You need to leave."

"I need to see this, Luke. You need me to see this. You need me to accept all of you and this is the only way I can. Here, let me." I reached for the top button of his shirt and he grabbed my hand in a painful grip so quick, I didn't catch his movement from one position to the next.

I turned slowly and showed him the burns that marred the right side of my figure. "I'm a monster, too."

His crystalline blue eyes raked across every inch of my skin with a hungry look that made me reach for him. His grip on my arm loosened and button after button was undone until his shirt hung open. Only a sliver of his tensed chest and abdomen showed but it was enough to draw a shaky breath from me. I'd never seen a man better made. He grunted as a crunching sound came from his hands and with his eyes closed against the pain, I pressed his hand between my legs.

His voice was agonized. "I'll hurt you. If I bite you, you'll die. Don't you understand that?"

On the tips of my toes, I reached up and brushed his healing neck with my lips. "I trust you," I whispered.

I couldn't tell if his groan was from pleasure or pain but he gripped the railing behind me until it splintered and trapped my body with his. I pushed his shirt back to expose more skin and nibbled gently on the tip of his collarbone. "Do you trust me?"

His face was downcast, and his silky raven hair brushed the tops of my breasts, but in a movement as fast as it was decisive, his mouth crashed down on mine. Pinned against the railing behind me, I opened for my new husband. I wanted more. I wanted everything he had and still, I'd never be close enough to him.

"Please," I begged as a growl ripped through him and his head snapped back. "Don't change until you're finished with me," I rasped as he backed me against the rail. "Turn, run, hunt, and then come back to me. Own this pain, Luke Dawson," I said to the sound of his rasping breath. "The faster you change, the faster you can come back to the warmth of my bed."

Tugging at his trousers, I unsheathed him. His cock jutted between us, thick and long and hard as stone. I caressed the silken skin of it, and his hips bucked forward like he couldn't help himself. A single bead of moisture sat the tip of his cock, and I wanted to taste him. The fiery look in his eyes said we didn't have that kind of time.

He nudged my knees farther apart and pressed the head of his shaft against my wet slit. A low rumble came from his throat as he slid into me and inch. With a look both pain and pleasure, he thrust upward, filling me completely.

Hells bells, he felt so good inside of me.

Jerking his hips, he pulled out of me slowly, then thrust back in even deeper. I moaned and closed my eyes as his fingers dug into my waist. He pulled me so close, it was hard to concentrate on anything but the way his skin felt inside of me. I gasped as he plunged in again and brought a tingling wave of pleasure that just about bowed me over. Clawing at his back, my body filled with pressure I'd never experienced before. His powerful hips pumped against mine with every stroke, and just as I found myself on the verge of an explosion, his cock swelled even bigger within me. His pace was punishing, but still, I wanted more.

"Faster," I cried out, and he obliged until I screamed his name and the first wave of my release crashed through me, clenching around him until his first shot of heat burst into me.

Two more deep strokes and he swelled again and gave me more of his release. Wet heat trickled down my thighs as he growled out my name and emptied himself completely.

He still looked mostly man in the moments after our blinding release, but in a series of cracks, like the rush of gunfire on some faraway battlefield, Luke changed in a moment without even the time to cry out at the pain he surely felt. I fell to my knees without the strength of his arms to hold me upright. There was no point in trying to stand, because my legs had as much substance as jelly.

Luke stood in front of me, appearing about as shocked as I've ever seen an animal look. I supposed he'd probably remember this change for the rest of his life. Head down, tail motionless, he just stared at me like he couldn't figure out what form he was in.

This was the first time he'd been still enough for me to really see him, and what I saw filled me with pride so deep, it was hard to breathe. Gray fur, black tips, a white underbelly and those lupine eyes, softening by the moment as he watched me. My wolf was a looker, and no one on earth could convince me it was wrong for me to be attracted to my husband in both forms.

Spent and exhausted, I curled up beside my wolf and ran my hands languidly through his course fur. He sat there, watching me for a long time with those inhuman eyes. Maybe I was supposed to be scared with his warning about a werewolf bite, but something deep down in my gut told me that, man or beast, Luke would never hurt me. Nestled in the warmth between the hearth fire that crackled away and Luke against my skin, my eyes soon became a burden to keep open.

A low rumble came from deep within him. I needed to open the barn door. Slowly, I made my way to the bearskin cloak piled onto the wooden floor and wrapped it tightly around my bare shoulders. The door rattled as I slid it open, and fat snowflakes floated lazily in, only to melt as soon as they touched the hay scattered floor. A winter wonderland called to my wolf but he turned once more before he disappeared into the night.

"I love you," I whispered with a smile.

He bounded toward the tree line in a flurry of fur and snow and as I waited inside the barn, his voice rose in a haunting lullaby. It was for me.

Sleep my wife, it sang on the wind, *for when you wake, I'll be man once again and by your side.*

I didn't bother with my dress other than to lay it across a rail so the mice didn't shred it for their nests. Instead, I nestled closer into the warmth of my cloak and climbed the stairs to the loft. When I lifted my gaze to the loft before me, I gasped.

The hay had been cleared of half of the space, and a makeshift fence held it back from the bedroom. A simple wooden bed beckoned me from the corner over the fireplace and under the window, and the mattress was covered with thick furs and blankets. A long curtain of thick, red fabric was attached to a rail that ran the length of the loft to give us privacy.

It was perfect.

I set the lantern on the small table beside the bed and closed my eyes. This kind of happiness shouldn't exist for a girl like me.

We'd struggled along the way, and it had taken both of our near deaths to fully accept our destinies in each other's lives, but I'd made the right decision when I chose Luke over Jeremiah.

He was my best friend, my husband, my wolf, my protector, my lover.

He was everything.

****

Luke

Kristina looked so damned pretty in the early morning light, I couldn't look away from her. Dusty rose colored rays of it drifted through the paned window and brushed her cheeks. Her curly hair looked as if it had spun gold weaved through it, and it lay in a soft wave across the pillow. The furs covered her body but still, I could see the outline of her hips.

The vision of her body had stayed with me, even as a wolf. She was flawless, from her creamy skin and hourglass body, to the warrior's scars she called monstrosities. I hadn't seen the burns in their entirety until last night, and the wolf inside of me crowed that I'd be the only one who ever would. I'd never found one feature more attractive on a woman than the scars my mate got fighting to save me.

Did she even know what she'd done for me? That change had been an easier transition than I even thought existed in my world. Holding back the wolf to satisfy her needs had heightened my senses, and where the pain had been staggering, the pleasure had been a blinding pinpoint of light that cast the ache away. And then I was wolf. There hadn't been a drawn out transition. It had been an instantaneous mutation from one form to the next, as if it were actually the magic of legend everyone thought it to be.

Lifting the furs just enough to climb into bed beside her, I took a long draw of the air around her. She smelled of woman, and lavender wash, and both sides of me—the man and the animal. I'd claimed her as my mate and wife, and in turn, she'd accepted me right down to the darkest and grittiest places within my soul.

"Luke?" she said in a sleepy voice as her legs stretched against mine.

I kissed the back of her hair and pulled her tightly against me. "Go back to sleep, wife. I'm home."

Epilogue
Jeremiah

D^{*earest Mr. Dawson,*}
I write to inform you of my interest in an advertisement you placed in a paper some months ago. For reasons I can't quite sort through right now, I have a mind to consider your offer. You have written of your want for a proper wife, and I assure you my high bred pedigree stretches for generations. As I've fallen on misfortune, I don't have any dowry to offer or material possessions to give if that is what you are looking for, but I'll be easily companionable and diligent in my wifely duties. I have to admit, as I would feel terrible for pursuing you under false pretense, that I have been a victim of a serious scandal here in Boston recently and won't bring any prestige to your lineage. However, if you are willing to overlook all of that and still would consider me a candidate for your arrangement, please contact me in Boston.
Yours,
Lorelei McGregor

I had the letter memorized, but I still liked to read over the elegant handwriting. The fire flickered behind the piece of cream linen paper and illuminated the emblem of her initials at the top of the fine stationary. Whatever scandal she was involved in peaked my interest for sure, but I hadn't received any other responses, so my options were limited. It was Lorelei McGregor or no wife at all. And from the way I'd been tearin' at those barn walls at night to get to Kristina, I was damned near desperate to try anything to give my wolf his mind back.

I knew Boston because Da and Ma lived within the city limits. They lived by modest means, but even upon visiting them, I'd heard the name McGregor. She'd been telling the truth about her pedigree, but what could make her fall so far that she wanted to seek refuge in the wilderness?

Kristina giggled as she and Luke emerged from the woods behind me. I'd built the fire near the charred remains of our house and the only surviving piece of our cabin was the rocking chair from the front porch. One of the Hell Hunters likely flung it to the side while they were busy trying to murder us. I rocked lazily in it and rubbed my thumb across the smooth paper.

"You'd better write her back before she changes her mind," Kristina sang over the *pop, pop* of the burning logs of the fire. "She won't wait forever you know."

She was right of course, but I didn't feel good about bringing a lady out to this kind of danger. We'd just been hunted, almost hanged and burned alive, and I was living in a rough camp in the woods. The timing couldn't be worse.

Kristina had it only slightly better because she and Luke lived in the barn, but still—she lived in a barn. And she was a different sort of woman. One easily adapted to the changes of the wilderness we called home. A proper city lady wasn't going to be so patient with our lack of housing.

"I need to change tonight, Jeremiah," Luke said as they passed by the firelight. "Might want to stay out of the barn for a bit."

He didn't sound too torn up about the prospect of a painful turning. Usually he moped about all day if he knew the change was coming, but since he'd married Kristina, he couldn't seem to change enough.

Luke draped his arm around her shoulders and whispered something in her ear. I couldn't hear what from this far a distance, but from the way she giggled and pushed him away, I wasn't going too far out on a limb to guess it was something inappropriate, as per usual. He grabbed her hand and pulled her in close before kissing her soundly. Never once in all of their touching and whispering did they stop their ascent to the barn.

Yep, whatever the change in Luke, it was Kristina who'd caused it. Good for her. My brother had never accepted his wolf like he needed to. It kept him unhappy, and now he'd found somethin' worthwhile and reassuring in the woman he'd married.

I shook my head at the mysteries of their relationship and dropped my eyes to the letter again. Was Lorelei the one who'd fix my wolf like Kristina had done for Luke?

I had no right to drag her out here to live in a tent, to marry a monster, and to bare sons who'd grow up to be wolves. But the most selfish parts of me didn't care about all of that. I needed a woman to hold at night and to soothe the snarling beast inside.

Lorelei McGregor was about to get much, much more than she'd bargained for.

Want more Wolf Brides?

Read on for a sneak peek of the next book in the Wolf Brides series.

Red Snow Bride

(Wolf Brides Series, Book 2)

By T. S. Joyce

RED SNOW BRIDE
(Wolf Brides, Book 2)

Chapter One
Lorelei

"Are you all right, my love?" I asked Daniel. He'd been quiet all evening which was very uncharacteristic of my usually boisterous spouse.

His blond hair threw threads of golden color under the extravagant crystal chandelier, and his blue eyes were like ice frozen into his pale skin. A fine sheen of sweat dusted his brow, and I frowned as his gaze settled on me without really seeing me. Maybe he was ill or perhaps he was having a vision of his time in the war again. Those came frequently in recent months. Or maybe it was just more of the same, ignoring me because he found me useless in some way or another.

The Countess Delecroix d'Maine sat next to me and touched me lightly on the arm with her gloved hand. "And so I said, 'Well get them to the ships then. Get them all to the ships!'"

The dining room exploded with delighted laughter and some small applause, but I still couldn't manage to take my eyes away from Daniel. Something cold moved within my center, like some long buried instinct that told me to run.

The clamor quieted down as my husband rose with a toasting glass and spoon in his hand. "I have an announcement to make to you, all of our dearest friends."

Twelve sets of dancing eyes settled on him as he made a tinkling sound against his crystal glass. The delicate noise was quite beautiful.

Richard Pratter, who sat at the end of the table with his fiancé, lifted his glass. "After a year of marriage, have you finally an announcement of the next heir to the Delaney fortune?"

The crowd burst into a happy murmur and I wrenched my hands under the table. Giving Daniel a son would be wonderful, but he hadn't visited my bed in months, and even when he'd done so before that, I was quite convinced we were doing everything wrong. No, there was no child growing in my belly to announce.

Daniel laughed but it sounded forced with an edge of cruelty. "No, something much better is happening."

Richard's deep set eyebrows turned down. "Well, tell us, Delaney. What could be better than an heir?"

He looked down at me and smiled vacantly. "Right now, at this very moment, I have a team of lawyers working on a divorce between my wife and I."

A few of the ladies at the table laughed. "Oh, Daniel's just putting us all on again," one of them mumbled behind a gloved hand.

The Count said, "Here, what's this about divorce, Delaney? It's hardly a joking matter to utter that word in mixed company."

Something had grown cold and dark within me at the shame he'd brought by joking about it in front of me. In front of anybody, really. Divorce wasn't talked about in society. It just wasn't done.

"The law clearly states a divorce can be granted in the presence of impotence in the marriage. And if a man can be divorced for impotence, then Lorelei can be divorced for leaving my bed cold and wanting. She'll never grant me an heir as is her wifely duty, and so the proceedings have begun long before now."

Different flavors of horror sat upon everyone's face. The only sound was the kitchen door opening, but the servant holding a tray of food froze when she laid eyes upon the table of silent high-born. Heat, burning and telling, crept up my neck and landed in the very tips of my ears until I had to stifle the urge to cover them with my cold, clammy hands for comfort.

"What is this?" The Countess whispered. Under the table she clasped my hand in a steely grip. "The disrespect you've shown your good wife in this joke is insurmountable. I've never witnessed anything so crass in my life. Give us the punch line and be done with this conversation, sir."

Daniel's mouth set in a grim and somber line. "No punch line, I'm afraid. I deserve better than the person I married."

The Whitten's and Ash's stood as one, throwing their embroidered napkins onto their dinner plates with fire in their eyes. Without a word they left the room, quickly followed by Richard and his betrothed.

I couldn't move. Every angry glare was a lance across my heart. My friends stood and left one by one until only a few endured to witness the remainder of my plummet from society. The Count waited by the door for his wife, and the Countess stood over me with a poisonous glare for Daniel.

Her delicate nostrils flared as she said, "You've ruined her with what you said in here tonight. News of her cold bed will reach even the darkest crevices of Boston by morning."

"That was the plan. It's the only way my lawyers will be able to win my case. It has to be common knowledge that she is an undeserving wife," he said dryly before he downed his champagne.

"She's a McGregor," the Countess fumed. "You've just spat on generations of good breeding for the chance to elope with one of your whores." She turned and with a whoosh of deep, red silk skirts, she disappeared through the door after her husband.

"Why?" I asked in a small, trembling voice.

"I've already told you. You don't please me in bed. You bore me, like the flavor vanilla or the sight of yet another brown horse."

The tears that built in my eyes made dual rivers of warm water down my burning cheeks. "I want my dowry back."

He sat heavily in the chair beside me and poured more champagne until his glass was filled to the brim. "Your dowry was spent in the first few months of our marriage, I'm afraid. You'll have nothing and no one from society will call on you after this scandal. Your best bet is to borrow money from your family and move away. The farther the better."

White hot anger boiled inside of me until surely I'd explode into a million broken pieces. "I hadn't any idea you hated me so much, Daniel."

He made a clucking sound with his mouth. "Poor naive Lorelei. Your problem has always been that you're too sweet for your own good. I don't hate you. I just never loved you. We married because my family line benefited by being tied to the McGregors, but now, I don't care about all of that so much. I'll remarry and this scandal will be old news by next season. At least for me it will be." His eyes were cool and emotionless, like some slithering serpent. "I've arranged for a carriage to take you to an inn. You may gather your most personal possessions, but I'm afraid I'll have to ask you to leave the valuables here in my care. Go now. I'd like to eat my dinner in peace."

The palm of my hand itched to slap him across his smirking face, and if I were lower born and able to get away with such behavior, I would've. Instead, I covered my mouth to hide my treacherous sobs and ran from the room. He didn't deserve to see how much he'd hurt me.

Divorce! That was the foulest word you could dare to utter, and he'd thrown me under a carriage in front of the most prominent members of society with it. The Countess was right. I was ruined—utterly, unerringly, and devastatingly ruined.

No man would ever touch me after such a scandal. I'd die cold in my bed, alone and without the comfort of a husband, or of children. He'd cursed me to an existence beneath everything I knew.

Mariel Loche flitted across my mind and my heart sank in terror. I didn't know anyone else in the living world who'd weathered divorce except for Mariel Loche. Her husband divorced her and left her nothing but a meager living to eat on. When that had been spent, she'd fallen further and further and last I'd heard, she was working in a brothel in the worst part of town. Whoring and making coins by selling her body to survive. That would be my fate.

No. I was still a McGregor. I could borrow money, surely, and eventually some man would overlook my scandal and marry me. I shook my head in devastation. What man would ever want a woman who'd been so cold in bed, she'd pushed her husband into *divorce*?

Shame filled my veins until I was filled to bursting. I hadn't known how to fix that part of my relationship, so I just let it go. How could every other woman manage to please their man but me? I'd bare this humiliation like a heavy metal chain around my neck for the rest of my life. My fists clenched until my nails dug into the skin and the smell of moist iron hung faintly in the air. I'd never marry a man for anything but necessity ever again. I'd loved Daniel and look where that got me. Men were harsh and unfeeling creatures, incapable of receiving love, incapable of giving love.

As long as I breathed, I vowed my heart would never be touched by another again.

About the Author

T.S. Joyce is devoted to bringing hot shifter romances to readers. Hungry alpha males are her calling card, and the wilder the men, the more she'll make them pour their hearts out. She werebear swears there'll be no swooning heroines in her books. It takes tough-as-nails women to handle her shifters.

Experienced at handling an alpha male of her own, she lives in a tiny town, outside of a tiny city, and devotes her life to writing big stories. Foodie, wolf whisperer, ninja, thief of tiny bottles of awesome smelling hotel shampoo, nap connoisseur, movie fanatic, and zombie slayer, and most of this bio is true.

Bear Shifters? Check
Smoldering Alpha Hotness? Double Check
Sexy Scenes? Fasten up your girdles, ladies and gents, it's gonna to be a wild ride.

For more information on T. S. Joyce's work, visit her website at
www.tsjoycewrites.wordpress.com

Made in the USA
Columbia, SC
04 August 2019